This wasn't the usual ward-inspection scene Udo sometimes indulged in, this was sheer anger. Maria Fitz, looking embarrassed, sidled away as Udo, red-faced, shouted at Christa.

'I'm asking you, Nurse Christa, whether you do not feel it necessary to carry out my instructions? I'm asking you what happened to the bandages. Furthermore, I would like to know –'

Whatever the 'furthermore' was that Udo had been going to blame her for Christa never found out. He was staring, transfixed, past her left shoulder into the corridor. Christa turned.

The Chief was standing there.

Professor Klaus Brinkmann seemed very calm. Even his voice was calm, calm and precise . . .

BLACK FOREST CLINIC

Novel by Peter Heim

Translated by Frederick Nolan
Based on the script by Herbert
Lichtenfeld
made for ZDF, Mainz

Sphere Books Limited

ONE

It was more like gliding than driving. Comfortably leaning into the seat, his fingers lightly holding the steering wheel, over hills and mountains, up and down, around corners – the next one so tight that Brinkmann had to brake slightly.

How well he knew this part of the world! The morning spreading the sun's rays like a fan, bathing the stems of the pines in a glow. The trees stock-still, bravely defying pollution. He remembered the smell of the pine needles and the rivers, fishing for trout, yellow buttercups on the meadows, a buzzard or a crow starting to soar, broken-down bicycles and grazed knees.

'Do you have to whistle non-stop?'

'As a matter of fact, I do. Any objections?' Brinkmann turned to look at the old lady, her profile changing with the light and shadows, the lace collar up to her chin because her vanity would not permit her to show any wrinkles. He had known this face for as long as he could remember. And for as long as he could remember, liked it.

Dear Kate! Much, much more than a housekeeper: a treasure.

Friend, confidante, keeper of secrets. Discreet, witty, alert, and wise: the perfect woman, he thought. The reason she sat so rigidly upright was the back support which she went to so much trouble to fix to the leather seats of the Mercedes for long journeys. Brinkmann considered it unnecessary. He even proved to her with X-rays how well her back had stood up to her seventy years, but – needless to say – to no avail.

'You're whistling pop songs!'

'Better than the rubbish on the radio.' He tried to oblige with the 'Postillion' and 'Mill on the Brook' but couldn't do it. He lifted his arm, pointing.

'Look at the maize field over there. You remember old Scheufele? His tractor toppled over and he wound up with a stiff knee.'

'What do you mean, a stiff knee? His knee was fine. Your father fixed it.'

'Really?'

'Don't you remember? He sent Scheufele to the University Clinic in Freiburg. They made a right mess of it, so your father fetched him and put a pin in the leg. He worked on it till he sweated blood. That's the kind of man he was. Hard on himself, the way he was hard on everyone around him.'

'You and your memory, Kate. Do you know, right behind that hut on the hillside over there . . .'

'Yes,' she answered.

'Yes, what?'

The Mercedes rolled along slowly past the road warden's hut. Bushes. The water ditch. Salamanders, Brinkmann remembered. God, there used to be salamanders here . . . and then the path to the pond.

'The pond,' said Kate, 'is right after the next bend. That's where you always played that game. What did you call it?'

'Ping-pang-peng,' he laughed.

She put her hand on Brinkmann's shoulder. 'And you pinched the beer bottles from the kitchen of the clinic.'

'But the carbide wasn't mine . . . no, it was Scheufele's son's.'

They swung round the bend. True enough, there was the path that fizzled out into the soft green reeds bordering the pond. Ping-pang-peng. Brinkmann was immersed in memories . . .

He recognised the old platform giving a panoramic view and turned into the car park. Sand and gravel spattered on the mudguards.

'Out you get.'

'With you.'

'All right, give me a hand.'

It was not far. Behind the bushes the flat ground sloped away. Flanked by the mountains, the valley formed a hollow like an open hand pointing westwards. Inside it, nestled the town.

He had forgotten how small it was. The old roofs, the town centre with the two churches. The ring road, the last traces of the walls which had once encircled the town. Over there, the red facade of the bed factory. Next to it, built in tiers, the new bungalow estate. From above, everything was toy size. Streets and paths looked like a spider's web. The old part looked tiny, idyllic and unreal, moving and romantic – like something taken from a toy box.

'Well, what do you say?'

What should he say? In spite of his sober mood, he felt a smile on his face.

The clinic was situated on the southern slope, right above the road leading to the plain and on to the Rhine. He could see the house in which he had grown up: an old dark-tiled roof with two towers. The garden. Next to it, the flat-roofed laundry building. And set apart from the main house the patients' wards, administration and the operating theatre. His father had built it all: the house, the clinic. They could see the windows glistening in the sunlight.

Kate put her hand on his arm. He turned and looked at her.

'Kate . . . ?'

A tear ran down her cheek; another.

Kate Marek from Pforzheim. She had been eighteen when she presented herself at the house with the towers and said to his mother: 'I am very versatile, Frau Doctor. I can cook, too. Schnitzel, Streuselkuchen.'

She had told him about that day; but no matter how hard he tried to visualise it he couldn't. He groped in his pockets for a tissue.

'Tell me honestly, Klaus, how do you feel?'

'Don't know.'

'You should know.'

True, but he still didn't know how he felt. The last time he had been in Offingen he had buried his father. It had been March, and

3

the valley had been shrouded in fog. When they arrived at the cemetery it had started to rain. And how it had rained! A wild thunderstorm which turned umbrellas inside out and drove away the mourners.

He had been soaked to the skin when he finally reached Feldlberg Street. Rittmaier, who was in charge of the clinic at the time, had arranged a meal.

'As sad as the occasion may be, Professor Brinkmann, I think your father would approve of our sitting down and discussing the situation.'

He was apologetic; what for? It all seemed like a farce.

And now he was standing here. And down there, behind one of those windows, was another Brinkmann.

His son.

TWO

He let the car roll slowly around the sharp bends. Only five minutes to go. Until this moment, the memories had been kept at bay. But now . . .

On the left was the riflemen's clubhouse, and the name *Waldesruh* in iron lettering. Why did he feel so uneasy? Father and son: it was an age-old conflict that went back to Greek myth, to the Bible. Freud had evolved a theory on it.

A man marries a woman. They produce a son. The man is left alone with his son. Who is responsible for that? God – by any chance? Who is to blame when death takes the cards out of one's hands? Tell me, who? The youngster didn't have an easy time. He didn't give himself an easy time. Perhaps he decided to show you – by becoming a doctor! *Numerus clausus*. The odds: a thousand to one against. The thorn in the flesh. Show the old man! Show your grandfather as well! All of them!

'What's the matter?' he heard Kate say. 'First you drive like a madman, and now you're creeping along as if you're afraid of getting there.'

'I am, a bit.'

Kate Marek smiled. But the look in her forget-me-not blue eyes was alert.

'You're thinking of Udo, aren't you?'

'Correct.'

'You never really liked it that he applied for the clinic, did you?'

'Come on, don't exaggerate. You know our problems. He really hasn't made it easy for me . . .'

'He hasn't made it easy! You haven't made it easy for him, either. In fact, of the two you're the Aries. Who is the obstinate one? It's your fault!'

'Oh, stop it!'

Fault? Aries? Astrology? Cosmic influences on top of everything else! What about Udo's unprincipled behaviour? His playboy racket? His damned egotism . . . A widower, and on top of that a doctor, trying to bring up a young son. How could that work out? Still . . .

He would have liked to reply, he has to grow up, but instead he swore: two trucks were coming around the corner, like some yellow and red colossus, blocking the road completely. Behind Brinkmann, headlights flashed. He couldn't believe it: did the idiot want to overtake?

'Bloody idiot!' he swore. 'Really, look at that irresponsible fool!'

'Just stay over on the right and don't let it get you angry.'

'Me? No way!'

Brinkmann maintained a steady fifty kilometres an hour into the next curve and into the straight that followed. He'd show that imbecile in his stupid sports car. A chain of cars was following the trucks now.

'Look at that! I told you: mad!'

The red sports car behind Brinkmann weaved in and out like a bull terrier preparing to charge. Three times the driver thought he had seen a gap, but three times he had to pull in. He bombarded Brinkmann with flashing headlights, blinding him. Aries or not, Brinkmann was going to stop and have a go at that roadhog.

But the driver of the red Alfa never gave him the opportunity. He pulled out, accelerated, roared past Brinkmann and shot into a space between two cars. In the split second of sudden movement,

Brinkmann saw the driver's profile: thick neck, chin jutting forward, hair blowing in the wind. Then he heard the screech of tyres, saw white smoke coming from the tyres of an old Opel approaching from the opposite direction as its driver braked frantically.

The red Alfa had vanished ahead.

'Drunk,' said Kate with conviction. 'They should take his driving licence away.' She shook her head indignantly. 'We're nearly home.'

Brinkmann felt his pulse throbbing.

Home. Yes, home. And what a start . . .

The lacquered legs of the piano were damaged, and there were dents in the case. The keys were stained yellow-brown like the teeth of a heavy smoker. The old Bechstein had seen better days.

'Perhaps one of you gentlemen has a solution?' Udo Brinkmann, thumbs stuck into his jeans pockets, was hopping mad.

'How were we to know we wouldn't be able to get the thing in?'

'How? You could have measured the width of the doors, damn it! You're supposed to be transportation specialists, aren't you?'

'Specialists, Doctor? What do you mean, specialists?'

'Specialists means knowing what you're tackling. That's what it means. It applies to you just as much as me,' said Udo Brinkmann, angrily brushing back a lock of hair which kept falling over his eyes.

The packers looked helplessly at one another. Not only this monstrosity of a grand piano, but also this ancient building without a single normal door! And on top of that, just before the lunch break!

'We'll go and get the china. Come back later.'

'Later? Are you planning to leave the piano on the lawn? My father is due any moment.'

A shadow fell over the lawn and the grand piano, and a hand was placed on Udo Brinkmann's shoulder. He turned and saw the familiar, worn, brown leather jacket. The grey-blue eyes. The grey-streaked hair. And his smile.

'Well, what's all the shouting about?'

Udo Brinkmann dropped his arms to his sides. Man, oh man! Did he have to arrive so early . . . ?

'We nearly didn't make it. Some idiot, determined to overtake us . . .' continued Brinkmann.

Udo's handsome, thin face wore a bewildered look. His mouth was dry. It was all he could do to nod.

'Is that . . . ?'

'Yes, Father. Your grand piano. Now do you understand why I'm shouting?'

'Well, give it a rest.'

They shook hands. Udo kissed Kate first on both cheeks, then on the lips, then they embraced and held each other for a while. Watching them, Brinkmann was touched. The packers had vanished. He smiled. Quite embarrassed, his son was, but so was he. Aren't inhibitions supposed to be a sign of uncertainty? Of course, but how long is it since we've seen each other? A long time. Such a miserably long time.

Udo had difficulty meeting his eyes. 'You'll be surprised at the clinic . . .'

'Later. The main thing is that we're together.'

He made it light, almost as if it didn't matter. His son's face flushed. He noticed it and turned away, going across to the grand piano and opening the black lid. He depressed a few keys: two, three notes, then a short scale.

'Terribly out of key, no?'

Udo nodded.

'If they can't get it in, it will have to go in the shed. It could rain, and it would be a shame if such a nice instrument got wet.'

Kate coughed. Brinkmann looked at her suspiciously.

'What's the matter?'

'Nothing's the matter. What's wrong with you two? You're standing around as if this was a school reunion. You look well, Udo, really well.'

It was as if the words removed an obstacle. Young Brinkmann's expression became soft, even tender.

'Oh, Kate, what a good thing you're here. The house is a mess.'

'Knowing you, I didn't expect anything else.'

'Oh, come on, it's not that bad!'

He gnawed his lower lip with his teeth, smiling, his manner hesitant, like a man who has something to get off his chest but doesn't know whether the moment is right. Finally, he took the plunge.

8

'I have to go to the clinic. Don't be cross. I should have gone a while ago.'

Kate noted uneasily that his father merely nodded. Then they were left alone. Alone with the grand piano, the house, the sounds from the garden, the bees in the lilac trees, a distant bell, dogs barking, cars tooting, and a flock of twittering sparrows flying up to the roof.

Brinkmann found the piano stool. He lifted it up with the enthusiasm of a small boy who has rediscovered an old toy, sat in front of the Bechstein, and tried a few chords. The first melody was carried by the wind across the old building; sounds like pictures drifted lightly past him.

'Brigitte loved it so. Do you remember how well she played?'

'Of course, Professor, but perhaps it would have been better if you hadn't brought it here.'

'You know what? You're impossible.'

'Not impossible. Realistic.'

She went over to him, gently took his hands from the keys and pulled him away.

'Come, Klaus. Let's go and see what it's like inside.'

The clocks in both cars had stopped, showing the exact time of the accident: ten to one. Police stood on the slight curve of the slip road to the motorway. Broken glass was strewn across the road like hail. Oil spills, pieces of metal, a bent seat, blood.

The heavy grey Ford Cortina lay in a rape-seed field. Its rear was sheared off. Its sides and roof were dented. The front of the red Alfa was squashed, as if it had hit a wall. Dull groans of pain came from the tangle of metal and torn upholstery. There was no sound from the Ford.

'Leave the Alfa! I've already had a look, he's not too bad. But over there . . .'

Inspector Albert Ott, who was in charge of this patrol, took hold of his driver's arm. 'Don't bother, there's nothing you can do. We have to wait.'

Young Riedl had turned pale. There were two people, a man and a woman, in the Ford. Their mouths were wide open, their eyes shut. Their faces were covered with a dreadful, dark pattern of blood.

9

'Here they come.'

Ott nodded with relief. He, too, had heard the whoop of the approaching sirens. Blue lights flickered as the two ambulances sped out of the woods.

'Where will they take them?'

'Where the hell do you think, man? Every accident up to the motorway is taken to Offingen.'

'The Black Forest Clinic?'

'Where else?'

'I hope they pull through.'

Albert Ott looked at the young man but said nothing. He was well past worrying over things like that. He had been doing this job for nine years. Your compassion wore a bit thin.

The white ambulances roared up and stopped. Men jumped out, shouting, pulling stretchers from the vehicles. They ran to the wrecks.

'Well,' Ott said. 'That's that.'

THREE

Each clinic is a world of its own, having its own timetables, its own hierarchy, its own rules and laws. Life behind its walls is governed by a rhythm which has little or nothing to do with life outside. Its routine is only interrupted when the alarm is sounded, when something happens outside and people's lives are in mortal danger. But when that alarm sounds . . .

The red light in the staff dining room of the Black Forest clinic lit up: an outmoded system long since superseded by the bleepers which each member of the emergency team carried in their pockets. Nevertheless, the red light had a dramatic effect: all talk ceased immediately.

Dr Walter Renz, sitting at the corner table behind the counter, pushed his plate away and rolled his eyes in resignation.

'Oh, well, I wasn't too keen on the food, anyway. It's yesterday's leftovers.'

The chief physician, Dr Schaefer, had already got up from his seat by the window. Tall and gaunt, his face expressionless – as always – he waved across at Dr Renz.

'I'm just coming.'

Dr Renz was not the only one needed. Another doctor, two nurses and an auxiliary nurse ran for the exit.

'I hope it's not a bad one,' someone said. Bad or not so bad, it made no difference: either way you still go through the standard, well-established routine. Because you know that it is precisely this experience which can mean the difference between life and death for someone else.

Renz felt exhausted. The day before, he had visited his parents in the Vogesen, then run into an old girlfriend from his schooldays. They had sat eating and drinking for hours, talking of the past and present: of unhappy love affairs, of the peace demonstration in which Helga had taken part, the anti-nuclear-war petition Renz had recently signed. The long and exhausting discussions had ended in a short and exhausting session of lovemaking, and it was nearly four in the morning by the time Renz had got to his car.

'Good luck!'

It was Liesel Wieland, a trainee nurse sitting at the next table. Her tone was lighthearted, but there was a great deal of seriousness in the remark.

Good luck, indeed, Renz was thinking when he reached reception. Oh, God, they've really caught it badly! A married couple by the look of it, she getting on for fifty, he somewhat older. They lay on the stretchers like pale wax images, drips in their arms. The immediate diagnosis was rupture of the spleen, internal bleeding, the wife a fractured rib, but most serious, the man's damaged spine.

The trolleys were wheeled through the steel doors of the operating rooms. As Renz turned to follow them Udo Brinkmann motioned to him.

'Hold on, Walter, here comes another one.'

'What's he got?'

Udo glanced at the police notes which one of the sisters had copied on to a memo pad.

'Nothing serious, although they had some difficulty getting him out. A few bones fractured. Ah, well . . .'

The grey-haired police officer sitting on the wooden bench in the waiting room looked up sharply.

'Only a few fractures? It's always the same, isn't it?'

'What do you mean?'

'Experience, Doctor. It's the ones who aren't at fault who always come out the worst. We know what happened. The way that fellow cut the corner, the other driver never had a chance. He should be locked up when he leaves the clinic. Locked up, I'm telling you. For life!'

Renz hardly listened. He'd heard that kind of speech before and he had no time for another. He was concentrating upon the work waiting for him in the operating theatre and nothing else . . .

The old wallpaper was still the same: pale yellow ribbons on grey. Even in the study Professor Rittmaier, the last occupant of the house, had changed little. Brinkmann felt something like gratitude, perhaps even affection. The old wallpaper. The dark-brown, walnut, parquet flooring, which sometimes creaked as though protecting memories. And its familiar strong smell. The view of the two beeches and the willow on the small pond. His father had laid the stone border which encircled it. Times past, frozen motionless into a picture.

'I suppose we could give all this a slightly lighter coat of paint. What do you think, Klaus?'

Paint?, thought Brinkmann. What for? Wallpaper cannot be restored. Perhaps varnish would do it. Or maybe I could find something similar in Freiburg. After all, it is a bit shabby.

He knelt down with the measuring tape. The team of packers had dumped the furniture in the hall like so many cabbages and carrots. Here on the other side of the wall with the fireplace would be an ideal place for the chest from Burgundy, providing it was not too big. He looked in his notebook: three by two metres eighty, and the wall was only two metres sixty. Another disappointment. He had looked forward to having it here.

The sound of heavy breathing made him turn to see Kate, with a large pile of clothes in her arms.

'Where do you want to put those? The chest of drawers is downstairs.'

'Well, I thought I'd put them somewhere safe.' She put the clothes down and had a look around. 'It looks as if the Saracens were here.'

'They've died out. And I've made another wrong calculation.'

'Surprise, surprise,' she said. 'The chest of drawers is outside.

It's not all that heavy, you know. We could carry it into your nursery.'

'Okay,' he said, without too much enthusiasm.

'I can do it on my own.'

'What – are you crazy? My old room, you said?'

He got up and walked to the chest of drawers, taking hold of it beneath the polished top. He tried to lift it and gave a hiss of pain as he pulled back his hand, staring at a deep gash cutting across the top of his thumb.

Kate ran to him. 'That's what happens when a surgeon plays at being a removal man,' she said. 'Let me see it.'

He held his thumb high to stem the bleeding. It didn't help much. 'I should have insured this damned hand for a million dollars. That would have given us some peace.'

She did not say a word. She didn't have to. Both knew what this meant.

'Get a bandage.'

'Bandage? We're going to the clinic. Your clinic!'

'Mine?' Brinkmann pulled a face. 'It's a nice thought. But it's a long way from being mine yet . . .'

As he walked up the ramp holding his bleeding thumb in the air, with Kate, breathing heavily, in tow, Brinkmann noticed that the doors to Emergency were wide open.

Inside there was the typical casualty-ward atmosphere: blood-stained bandages, used needles, discarded infusion bags. There were also two exhausted people, a very young girl, obviously a trainee nurse, behind the desk, and a pale young man, apparently a doctor, rubbing his nose with both index fingers.

Brinkmann went across to him and held up his thumb. 'Good morning. Could you have a look at this? I've torn it open with a rusty nail.'

The pale young man pulled a face and slid off the corner of the desk. He didn't seem to be in a hurry. He took the bandage off.

'Ouch!' Brinkmann said, angrily. 'Do you have to be so rough?'

'You'll survive.'

The young man's face was pulled into a frown, and he gave Brinkmann a stern doctor's look.

'Helga,' he called over his shoulder, 'get a tetanus shot ready.'

14

'Charming,' Brinkmann said.

'What's that supposed to mean?'

'I mean, you could take a little more care, Doctor.'

'Listen, if you could have seen the cases we've just had through here, you wouldn't make so much fuss.'

'So you think you can say whatever you want?'

'I think I can say all we needed right now was someone like you.'

Brinkmann was speechless. During the last few days he had tried to imagine what his arrival at the clinic would be like, but he certainly hadn't reckoned on anything like this.

He's winding you up, he told himself, searching for a reply. Before he could find one, the doctor told him to give the sister his personal details.

'Just as you say.'

At least the injection was properly administered, disinfection and bandaging quickly and expertly done.

'Right, what's your name?' called the young woman behind the desk.

'Brinkmann, Klaus.'

'Occupation?'

'Doctor.'

The girl dropped her pencil. The young man, just about to fix the bandage with a clip, let it fall to the floor. There was silence. They stood staring at Brinkmann. The young man's pale face had turned red. His eyes grew big and round. Finally, he managed to open his mouth.

'Oh, no,' he groaned.

Brinkmann bent down, picked up the clip, and fastened it himself. He raised the bandaged thumb to his forehead in a farewell salute. Walter Renz stood there, devastated. He looked helplessly at Udo, who had opened the door moments before, and at the old lady in the waiting room behind who gave him an ironic wink.

Brinkmann went out, and the door shut.

Renz dropped into a chair, stretched his long legs, and pressed his fists against his forehead.

'Udo! You blockhead! Couldn't you at least have given me a nod – or something to indicate your father . . . ?'

'How could I? By the time I heard you saying "all we needed was someone like you", it was too late anyway.'

Renz nodded, depressed. 'Perhaps you could explain I didn't mean it like that. I mean, that I'm not the sort that . . .'

'Explain?' Udo put a compassionate hand on Renz's shoulder. 'We'd better let it ride, Walter. I don't have any influence with my father, and in situations like this I make things worse rather than better.'

Dr Renz groaned. Udo smiled. And from behind the desk young Elke's voice piped: 'Well, he's really done it this time.'

FOUR

Brinkmann was simultaneously moved and bedevilled by the fact that he had been born in this house; the way it fitted him like a second skin, the way each wall and each object was filled with memories that set off a chain reaction of mental pictures. Now it was time to put an end to it.

It's not your special talents in romantic sentimentality that are needed now, he told himself, but your ability to make decisions.

Taking over the clinic: a well-defined task lay ahead. Was it not the same in all the clinics he had been in charge of? Whether the Black Forest Clinic or anywhere else, the goals did not differ. The first objective was to create trust. That applied to doctors and personnel, but it also included his relationship with Udo. For that he needed patience more than anything else. If your son makes things difficult for you, remember that you yourself aren't totally blameless.

Forbearance, patience! And most of all those 'loving institutions without which human rapport cannot succeed'. He remembered how his former teacher, old Keurer, had hammered that maxim into his students' heads. What Keurer had been referring to was the doctor–patient relationship. But here was a young man who armoured himself with a defence that consisted of a smiling 'I'm not going to let you get anything like close to me.'

Patience needs time. Well, he would work to find time. Why worry yourself sick over it? God knows, there are more important things to tackle, and today was the day to start. The sun was shining. The windows were wide open, the breakfast table ready.

Brinkmann marched over to the table, full of bounce, the bandaged thumb pressed to his nose. Kate pushed a newspaper his way: it was the *Offinger Advertiser*. On page one an article headlined PROFESSOR BRINKMANN NEW HEAD OF CLINIC was circled in red.

Coffee was more important. Rolls, too, but most of all, some eggs.

Kate interrupted: 'You can't do that with your thumb!'

'What can't I do? My thumb still works. You watch.'

Just as he peeled off the shell he heard the sound of the piano. Where was it coming from? The piano was still in the garden, wasn't it?

One of a surgeon's most important qualities is his ability to ignore distraction, by anyone or anything. That was now put to the test.

'It's not possible!'

But it was.

What Brinkmann noticed first were the shortest, tightest, blue silk shorts he had ever seen. With legs like hers, the girl at the piano did them justice. Her musical talents were another matter. She was supposed to be playing a popular song, but she was not only straining the instrument but butchering the melody.

'What on earth is that?' muttered Kate, standing next to him at the window.

'Well you may ask,' Brinkmann growled.

'Presumably one of those . . . ?'

'One of what?'

'You know, from Udo's old school.'

Once more she was right. Udo appeared: tall, casual, hands in pockets, his tennis sweater over his shoulder. The blonde received her kisses, first on the neck, then the throat and chin. Casual but accomplished, Brinkmann thought, observing the little scene with a mixture of disbelief and admiration.

Udo looked up and saw them. Embarrassing, very embarrassing! 'Hello,' he said, waving.

'Come up,' Brinkmann called. 'Bring the young lady with you. We're having breakfast.'

Udo demurred. Beaming, as always, he came into the room, gave Kate a kiss, shook hands with his father. Breakfast? He had already eaten. He would go and sit in the sun for a while with Yvonne. Life is for living, and the job takes it out of you. Where family meals and family ties were concerned it was better not to get too close for comfort.

'What do you mean by too close?' Kate asked, angrily. 'Are we a family, or aren't we?'

'Of course we are,' Udo said, disarmingly. 'And how is the thumb?'

'I'll survive,' said Brinkmann.

'Walter Renz is not too sure *he* will. You know, the young assistant who . . .'

'I know.'

Down below the noise went on. One chord in C major. Always the same one.

'Oh, go and get some sun,' Brinkmann said.

The yellow forsythia dancing on the hill, sun-drenched grass, light filtering through the leaves, making him blink. Sun on the skin. Skin: ah, yes, skin. The two mounds of her breasts were silky-smooth and warm. Yvonne! Yvonnchen, so sweet!

Udo felt the blood pulsing in his fingertips. They drew little circles, smaller and smaller, felt the buds as they filled, lifted and became firm . . .

'Cut it out, what d'you think you're doing?'

'I thought you wanted me to . . .'

'Not here.'

'Not here?' Birch trees on the hill; over the crowns of the beech trees the little towers of the paternal home. 'Paternal home': wasn't that the right description?

Maybe she's right. But to lie here, with a girl wearing little more than a slip which is so transparent that you can see the dark mound

19

under the nylon lace, shining brown legs, shiny hair, and such breasts . . . Impulsively, he pulled himself up and turned to put his arms around Yvonne. But that was as far as he got. His eyes widened. Over there, on the steps, something light-coloured – a dress? Was it? Yes!

In his haste to reach the knob of the portable radio Udo pushed it the wrong way, and the radio fell over, blasting out at full power.

Christa! How could he have forgotten that she wanted to come today? There she was, standing on the steps, looking as if she'd been struck by lightning.

Yvonne sat up. 'What is it?'

'Lie down, damn it!'

Too late, much too late. Christa had seen him. And Yvonne. She turned and began to run down the steps, across the flagstones and back to the house. Udo jumped to his feet and chased after her.

'Stop, Christa, for God's sake, stop and listen to me!'

She did nothing of the sort.

'Christa, please be sensible.'

He was by the steps now, panting. 'Sensible', he thought, what a stupid word to use. He saw Christa reaching the courtyard, then the doorway into the house. And there, above, by the sandstone balustrade, was his father!

Christa did not see him either, her eyes downcast as she rushed past him to the garden gate.

God damn it!, Udo thought as the iron doors slammed shut. When he got back Yvonne had put on her blouse. A bit late. Much too late! She straightened her hair. 'Who was that?'

'A nurse from the clinic. Yesterday I happened to say to her, "Why don't you come and see me?" She just came.'

'And now she's run away. With you bellowing like a bull.'

'Oh, come on, don't let's make a big thing of it. What do you mean, bellowing like a bull? You forget, I'm a spontaneous person. No, the worst thing is that my father was down there . . .'

'Why? What's he like?'

'My father? Like everybody else's. Knows everything, can do everything, makes you feel like a nothing. He also has the wonderful ability to pass off all his failures as triumphs. In other words, an incredible personality.'

'And he's going to be your boss?'

'Yes,' Udo nodded grimly. 'Something to look forward to, don't you think?'

Brinkmann stood beside the Bechstein. It was still not in the right place, but they had at least managed to get it into the house with a hoist. The photo placed on it made it look at home.

The face in the silver frame was that of Udo's mother. Brinkmann knew it as well as his own. He had looked at it a thousand times, often feeling she was watching him. He had never before noticed the suggestion of irony in Brigitte's smile. Perhaps you're just imagining it, he thought. Perhaps it was his tight collar and waistband that gave him this oppressive feeling.

An inauguration! Wonderful. And, as if that wasn't enough, the shirt was tight. He loved all this: cotton, pinstripes, waistcoat and grey tie. Like poison.

'Are you ready?' Kate asked.

'I think so,' Brinkmann nodded.

When Brinkmann arrived, he was greeted by Professor Schiermann, the departing head of the clinic. Schiermann gave him a melancholy smile. 'It will soon be over for both of us,' he said, morosely. Mühlmann, the director of administration, also shook Brinkmann's hand. Then the ceremony went ahead as planned. Brinkmann took his place on a dais alongside the county councillor and a large number of guests sporting horn-rims and ties. It promised to be a resounding display of German officialese.

'I think it is fair to say that the clinic has met the standards which in past years it has set itself. For this reason, Professor Schiermann, I would like to express the gratitude of the council and the local community, and furthermore I would like to add . . .'

Even had the councillor tried to increase the volume of his pastoral-political tone, whatever it was he wanted to add could no longer be heard above the whirring drone of an engine that pervaded the room. The councillor's irritation showed on his face. Schaefer, the specialist who was Professor Schiermann's deputy, was already on his feet, shrugging his shoulders as he headed for the entrance.

A helicopter? It looked as if Schaefer knew all about it. Now Brinkmann saw the flutter of the rotor blades. The councillor on the dais had recovered his composure.

'This farewell, ladies and gentlemen, would be the sadder were it not for the fact that we have as his successor someone with the stature of Professor Brinkmann, whom we welcome most warmly.'

Applause. What else? Brinkmann pulled himself to his feet and smiled an attentive, friendly, quizzical smile. He smiled throughout the ovation. He smiled towards the three rows of faces along the windows, the personnel of the clinic. They had joined the celebration, a compact white wall of hidden mistrust.

'Professor Brinkmann, whom we may call a son of this city, whose associations with the Black Forest, its people, its friends and its problems go back to his childhood . . .'

Good God, would it never end?

'We cannot leave unmentioned his immense medical experience, an experience which you, Professor, were fortunate to gain in Zürich, Paris, and Karlsruhe . . .'

The loudspeaker crackled, and they heard the calm voice of the operator. 'Dr Schaefer! Dr Schaefer to the operating theatre!'

'Dr Schaefer has already gone over there,' Brinkmann said, determined not to allow the professional orator up on the dais to continue. 'I would like to thank you, Councillor. I thank you all, ladies and gentlemen, for being here. Now I have only one thing to say: I think we have to get to work.'

FIVE

A different world – how one's situation changed! The glistening
bluish light that bathed the perspiring skin. The hurried glance at
the heart monitor, that machine that everyone fears. The thought:
what now, dear God? Why isn't the adrenaline working?

'Pulse still unstable,' the sister reported. She, too, was having
difficulty remaining calm.

Think of something! But what?, thought Dr Schaefer. Both his
hands rested on the patient's chest. Opening him up was out of the
question. If he followed normal procedure for heart massage,
pressing three, four centimetres towards the sternum, the chances
were that with each compression the damaged vertebrae would be
further endangered.

'Acute shortage of oxygen!'

As if he hadn't noticed that himself! Even the tracheal catheter
wouldn't help now. Nothing would. Whatever he tried, in this
particular case, was going to go against him. He looked into the
attentive, alert face of Dr Renz. The operating-theatre sister's light
eyes narrowed. She shook her head.

Damnation, was there nothing one could do?

He took the only chance there was and started to massage the heart. As he lifted himself up, the illuminated dials of the monitor came into his field of vision, flickering. A final, tiny, oscillating pulse. Then the long, terrible, straight line indicating failure.

Exitus!

Hermann Schaefer straightened up. Renz bit his lower lip. Nobody spoke. There was nothing to say.

Sister drew a sheet up over the now-blue face on the table. Schaefer grimaced. 'I'm afraid it was a waste of fuel, my friend. Was it you who ordered the helicopter, Mr Renz?'

'I'm sorry, *Herr Oberarzt!* I thought his only hope was if we could transfer him to the neurology department at Freiburg. I thought he might make it.'

'Make it? The man was in no condition to be moved!'

'Perhaps he might have . . .'

'Might, might? It might have been a lot better if you'd called me or the Chief a bit earlier.'

'But you were at the ceremony.'

Schaefer gave the assistant a tired look. As he reached the door of the operating theatre he stopped.

'Call the police, Mr Renz,' he said. 'They wanted to talk to him. At least he'll be spared that.'

Experience had taught Udo Brinkmann to think up excuses on the spur of the moment. Everything premeditated sounded wooden and insincere.

But this time his talent let him down.

The surgery door was open as he passed. He saw Christa's slender back, saw the light on her dark hair, the bent neck, and her frown of concentration as she tipped pills into porcelain jars. He stopped, feeling the familiar pang in his heart. He took a deep breath: get it over with! This moment is as good as any. Still counting, she did not hear him. He put his hand on her shoulder.

'I'm sorry. Okay?'

A pill fell on the tray. Christa straightened up and looked him right in the eye.

'What should be okay?'

'You know what. I only wanted you to know, what you saw . . .

24

it's nothing serious. An acquaintance. You know, from the past. Just one of those things. And –'

Udo noticed uneasily that her expression was frigid. Damnation. It wasn't going to work this time.

'She's not in the same league as you,' he assured her, hastily. 'Seriously, she just suddenly turned up. Out of the blue.'

'Naked?'

'What do you mean, naked? We were sunbathing. Christa, really it would be silly to fall out over this.'

'Who says so? I'll be happy to talk to you – as long as it's business.'

'Christa, please!'

'It won't help to beg.'

He scratched the back of his neck. Damnation! The sound of footsteps came from the corridor. A white coat – his father's face. The figure passed by. That was all he needed.

'It's better like this, anyway,' Christa said, coldly. 'What's that saying? "Doctors are doctors, nurses are nurses." An old maxim.'

'Yes.' Udo found his smile again. 'A hundred years old.'

She shook her head. 'Self-esteem is ageless, my dear.'

'Christa! All I can do is apologise. What else do you want me to do?'

'Leave me in peace in future.'

Half past one.

Lunch had been over for some time, the plates collected on the serving trolley and taken back to the kitchen. In the wards there was a sleepy, calm silence, mixed with expectation for many of the patients: visiting hours. A face, a voice you could look forward to. The rest listened to time passing by.

The six patio doors of the male ward led to a terrace. Anything that happened there could be seen by everyone: a stage with real-life performers, where nothing was missed, not even a dog barking. Talking of which, a piercing yelp suddenly burst from a white and brown bundle of hair which dashed between the deck chairs.

'My God, it's Mollie! She's on the loose again!'

In Room 26, Armand Echsle tried unsuccessfully to sit up in his bed, one of three patients in the room. Mischa, the young auxiliary nurse, pushed him firmly back.

'Keep still!' It was Mischa's job to get Echsle ready for the operation which should give him back the use of a hip joint damaged by arthropathy. 'Watch what you're doing, damn it! Otherwise I'll be cutting off a lot more than hair!'

'Listen to him! That's all I needed, a smart kid!'

'Being sixty, you can easily –' Mischa swallowed the rest as Nurse Christa came in.

Friedhelm Hensel, lying on the bed nearest the window, put his book aside and turned to face her. He had already complained several times that he didn't like this dump, let alone his roommates, but nobody took any notice.

'Listen, Nurse, has anything been decided about that single room for me?' Once again he got the brush-off: she met the question with a tired shrug.

Armand Echsle was given his pre-med injection. That done, Christa addressed herself to the next problem: the dog. Wasn't it the little mongrel that had belonged to the old gentleman who'd died the preceding week? What was his name? Baerwald, that was it.

Outside, a small boy crawled over the tiles, although his leg was in plaster. He had brown hair, bright green eyes, and freckles everywhere you looked. Little Werner Schick. He grabbed the dog by its collar and the dog started licking his face. Werner was the ward's pet. Everyone loved him. But this was taking things too far!

'Look here, Mrs Schick,' Christa said to the fat lady sitting in a chair on the terrace. 'I've already told you that Werner can't keep that dog here.'

'Nurse, please, listen to me –'

Christa ignored her. She had to finish giving injections, and she was certainly not in the mood to start arguing over the ticklish problem of a dog in a clinic. If the Chief got to hear about it – unthinkable!

Back in Room 26, Friedhelm Hensle insistently pursued young Mischa with his problem. As far as he was concerned, the lad was just another no-good dodging the army by doing community service, and everyone knew what kind of people they were. But he was ready to make a pact with Satan if it meant getting out of this dump.

26

'You know the system, Mischa. Surely it ought to be possible to fix me up with my own room? Can't something be done?'

'It's not possible.'

'Why not?'

'Why not?' The diminutive auxiliary looked down at the patient. Mischa was wearing nickel-rimmed glasses and had a thin, frayed, goat-like beard. It was not a face you'd easily forget, especially when it had a grin as nasty as the one it was wearing now.

'I'll tell you why not. You're the one who broke your bones, right?'

'I don't get it.'

'Then I'll explain. Look, Mr Hensle. You want a room to yourself. Well, I might be able to get you a bathroom, but you can't fit one of these special extension beds into a bathroom. Okay, so maybe we could put you into the bathtub, but bones don't heal easily in a bathtub . . .'

'Listen, are you taking the piss out of me? I've a good mind to –'
Whatever he had a good mind to do he never got the chance to say. The door of Room 26 had opened again. The man who came in filled the frame. He held a police hat under his arm, and was wearing a green uniform. He smiled, a friendly smile with that alert mildness that often seems to go with a police uniform.

'Sorry to interrupt,' he said. 'My name is Stengelmaier. I'm looking for a Mr Hensle.'

Hensle lifted his hand, not speaking. The effort it took to pull himself to a sitting position showed on his pale, doughy face. The policeman pulled across a stool, and smiled at the matron who had just swept in. Sister Hildegard was in full charge of the ward.

'Mischa! You can carry on with your work downstairs. Mr Echsle, have you any objection to being taken to the pre-med room?'

Her manner was curt and precise. In the years she had been running the place Sister Hildegard had learned to give orders in such a way that they made further queries unnecessary. Queries meant more time wasted.

'Mr Hensle, this is Officer Stengelmaier of the police. He has Dr Schaefer's permission to talk to you.'

The door closed. 'I'll get straight to the point, Mr Hensle,' the officer began. 'I'm chiefly here to take away your driving licence.'

Hensle frowned. His smoky grey eyes were guarded as he watched the policeman clumsily unfolding an official-looking document.

'Here, take a look. The court's findings.'

'May I ask what this is all about?'

'You may. The answer is an alcohol level of 1.8, Mr Hensle.'

'Does this mean someone took a sample of my blood while I was unconscious in the car? A blood sample, without my permission?'

'With or without. The law makes no distinction, Mr Hensle.'

'That's what you think! I see it differently. I'm going to appeal against the court's decision. I was driving well within the speed limit. That idiot who came from the opposite direction –'

'Is dead,' Stengelmaier said, bluntly. 'Moreover, Mr Hensle, our reconstruction at the scene of the accident and the testimony of the witnesses are totally at variance with your account.' The mild smile had disappeared. There was no trace of amiability in the hard, dark eyes looking at Hensle. Hensle took a deep breath.

'You . . . you say he's dead?'

'Yes, dead. But forgive me, I interrupted you. You started to say something. Why don't you give me your version of what happened?'

'Me? What do you mean, my version? Let me think. Well, I had to swerve, because of the cyclist. He suddenly turned left, nothing I could do. Why are you looking at me like that? Oh, I get it. Nobody saw the cyclist, is that it?'

Stengelmaier glanced towards the terrace, where the happy barking of the dog could be heard. Then he turned to face Hensle and shook his head.

'No. Nobody saw him.'

SIX

Brinkmann stared glumly at the pile of files on his desk: administration papers, building plans, case histories, reports. On top of the files lay a handwritten note: *Dear Colleague, I am taking the liberty of drawing your attention to the following points . . .* What followed was a ruthless, but more importantly, self-critical analysis of the clinic's weaknesses. It was signed 'Shiermann.'

A fine chap, this Schiermann. Not only a capable doctor, but a thinking man who did not excuse himself. A wise man. Perhaps not the man of action my father was, Brinkmann thought, but wiser, more distanced. Two different types of doctor: one a philosopher, the other someone whose philosophy existed only in practice.

He glanced up. The picture had hung on the opposite wall: Dr Karl Brinkmann, in his white coat. Stethoscope, pince-nez, the then-fashionable trimmed moustache. He had a square East-Elber skull which always reminded him a little of Sauerbrach.

Back to Schiermann. What was it he'd written? A sentence worth memorising. 'You know, my dear Brinkmann, that as a doctor you are only permitted to have a clear conscience after you've hung up your white coat. Only then are you freed from making errors.'

Klaus Brinkmann nodded in agreement and reached for one of the files that bore Schiermann's green felt-tipped cross. Gerda Beck: he had forgotten the name, but not the drama of the case which Schiermann had drawn to his attention. Cervical carcinoma, fourth stage. From the neck of the womb the cancer had attacked the ovaries, colon and bladder. Discovered too late; the doctor consulted too late. Even radiation therapy couldn't help: inoperable.

Gerda Beck and the victim of the accident who had died yesterday on Schaefer's operating table: two hopeless cases. But there was another one . . .

Making no mistakes? Giving up?

To continue walking the tightrope?

There are some who find walking the tightrope easy. Easy because a mis-step doesn't cost them their health or their life, only someone else's.

Schiermann was well out of it. He had bought himself one of those American mobile homes, and in four or five weeks he would realise his lifelong ambition: to follow in Sicily and Apulia the footsteps of the man he had revered all his life: Frederick the Second, thirteenth-century ruler of the Holy Roman Empire.

To have just one chance to be yourself, Brinkmann!, he said to himself as he leafed through the files and case reports. What have you done in the last few years to get to know yourself? Is there a chance you can do it in the time left to you? And will you use that time? Are the others offering you that chance, or are you just pretending? Maybe there's something intangible inside you that drives you on as it does so many doctors? Some indefinable something: a vocation, God, Fate? Oh, nonsense . . .

The lab reports of the last tissue tests fell out of the folder with the name 'Beck' on it: witnesses to the irreversible. Brinkmann put them back gently and got up. He would talk to Gerda Beck. Maybe Schiermann had been too soft. Every life has to end sometime. Such a banal yet holy truth. To open yourself to that truth and accept it is one of the burdens which has to be carried in this profession.

He looked out through the golden-green net of the branches in the garden. He heard a dog barking, and the mundane sound brought a sort of relief. Some timely action instead of taking on the world's suffering. Yes, that was the way. He looked once again at the place on the wall where the picture had hung. In that respect you are a typical Brinkmann.

For the panting, uncontrolled Mollie, the park close by the Rest Centre was an ideal playground which she ran delightedly around in circles that afternoon.

Taken aback by the sight, the head of the Black Forest clinic had some difficulty believing the evidence of his eyes. There was no doubt about it: pushed-in snout, floppy brown ears, brown and white hair. It was a dog, although the way the thing was bouncing about it could have been taken for a football without too much of a stretch of the imagination.

A dog! In the grounds of the clinic!

Brinkmann set off. As he approached, he saw that as well as the dog there was a plump looking woman and a young boy with his leg in a cast ahead of him. The bundle of hair danced around them in a kind of enraptured frenzy, then broke away and ran towards Brinkmann, barking loudly.

'Get down! Down! Damn it, this coat is fresh from the laundry!'

Brinkmann's commands had little impact on Mollie. There were brown paw marks all over the starched white cotton coat already, and as the woman hurried across the dog's teeth tore a triangle out of it.

'Mollie!' Thank God, he thought, the owner. She grabbed the little beast and started to put it into her shopping bag.

'See here, Mrs –'

'Schick. My name is Schick.'

'Mrs Schick, how did you smuggle that animal in here?'

'Well, actually, I brought it in the bag, because . . . you see, my young son, Werner, loves the dog so passionately. And after he died, there was no one to look after it.'

'After who died?'

'Well, that Mr Baerwald. You know, the old pensioner who owned the dog. He shared a room with Werner. That's how Werner came to be looking after him. The dog. I mean.'

'But dogs are not allowed here. This is a clinic. You understand, I'm sure: the danger of infection . . .'

'Shush, Mollie! Be quiet!'

Mollie was quiet, Mollie was good. Mollie peeped out of the shopping bag. Brinkmann had to turn away so that the woman would not see him smile.

'If Mollie is put down it will kill the boy, Doctor. He promised the old man he'd look after her. Try to understand. You see, my husband can't stand the animal. He's allergic to it. He can't catch his breath when it's around.'

'Allergic to dog hair? I've heard of cat's hair causing allergies, but rarely dogs. Is he under treatment?'

'Werner? I told you –'

'Your husband. For his allergy.'

'No, that's the whole point. I don't know what to do. You see, we're moving. To Freiburg. Into a flat. And the lease stipulates "No dogs". I think it's terrible.'

Brinkmann nodded, and the blue eyes showed hope.

'Mollie doesn't like white coats. My husband's a painter and decorator. That's why she attacked you. Did she . . . oh, my God!'

'The coat can be washed.' Brinkmann said, brushing off some of the dirt. 'It's not too bad. Don't upset yourself.'

She turned to the young boy who was standing motionless, watching her.

'Werner so loves Mollie. He told me if the dog is put down he doesn't want to live either.'

'Put down, put down! Why do you keep on talking about putting the dog down?' Brinkmann took off his coat to stop the dog growling. He bent down and stroked the unruly head; her muzzle met his hand. She gazed up adoringly from the shopping bag. It was clear that, apart from men in white coats, Mollie unreservedly loved all humankind.

'Well,' Brinkmann said reassuringly, stroking the soft hair. 'I'll have a word with Werner. See if we can't work something out.'

Hardly a normal scene!

Udo pressed his forehead against the window: the old boy was taking off his coat, now, and even stroking the animal! But then, what did normal mean? His father had always loved dogs; he loved all animals. Every ounce of emotion left over from his work was distributed generously: dogs, Kate, of course – and his women. But he always passed you over. Still, why get upset? It had always been bearable.

Udo was so immersed in this mixture of envy and professed superiority over such childish emotions that he did not hear the knock on the door.

'Good morning!'

He turned away from the window and his face lit up. 'Well, look who's here! The sun has risen. Good morning, good morning!'

Christa Meurer ignored his exaggerated rapture. Her voice was formal, clipped, almost toneless. 'I just wanted to inform you that the patient Melanie Wieck is hoarding her pills in the cupboard.'

'Who?'

'Miss Wieck is in Room 9. She shares it with Mrs Kirsch. It was Mrs Kirsch who noticed what was going on.'

'So?' Udo said, lightly. 'Take the pills away from her.'

'If you want my opinion, there's more to it than that. We're talking about barbiturates.'

'Well, she ought to take the ones that are prescribed for her. By the way, I'm going to the Titisee on Sunday. How about coming with me?'

There was a little ridge over the bridge of Christa's nose – and that look in her eyes. 'I thought we had already discussed that, and all similar propositions,' she said. 'Neither the Titisee nor any-where else. I hope that is perfectly clear?'

Neither the Titisee nor anywhere else, he thought. And she stands in doorway looking at you in a way that ought to be forbidden by law. Oh no, not like that. Udo rushed across the room and grabbed her wrists.

'Stop this . . . stupidity!'

'It's not stupidity.'

'Ouch! Let go of my arm!'

He took no notice, how could he? 'Christa, listen, let's forget this nonsense . . .'

'What's nonsense and what isn't . . .'

'Christa, try to be reasonable.'

She gasped. Her face turned red.

'Christa, listen to me! Changing from one relationship to

another is never easy. Such changes never happen without friction. But all that is only words. What is important, Christa, listen: what's important is only that we get things clear between us –'

'I said, let go of me!'

Udo did not hear, did not let her go. Good God, even if she didn't grasp it, she must feel it. This *must* became of such paramount importance that it blocked out all thought, all control. She pushed her elbow into his chest and tried to push him away, without success. He held on with an iron grip. She had still not succeeded in getting free when the door opened and Dr Schaefer appeared.

For Christa the shock lasted only a second, then she was gone. Udo put his hands in his pockets. He had difficulty catching his breath. His face was bright red, and he could not summon a smile. Dr Schaefer assessed the situation. He walked past Udo as if there was no-one there, as if Udo was invisible. His shoulders slightly raised as always, he crossed the room and sat down at his desk.

Well, at least he might have shown a reaction, of sorts. Under any other circumstances Udo would have felt some kind of admiration, but not right now. His temper boiled up as he glared at the neat crown of his superior's head. The first words that came into his mind burst out.

'Don't bother to think it over, Dr Schaefer. My father is always a willing listener to this kind of scandal!'

Schaefer swung around. His face remained devoid of expression.

'I mean it, Dr Schaefer! If you plan to report this incident, you won't have to worry about whether you're making yourself popular with him or not.'

'Really?' Schaefer said, raising an eyebrow. It wasn't the first time Udo had been exposed to the man's damned sarcasm. Well, then, give it another whirl.

'Go ahead. You really ought to try it.'

Schaefer's amber-coloured eyes regarded him dispassionately.

'Listen,' he said. 'Whether you believe it or not, there are more important things in life than your capacity for courting trouble.'

'I merely wished to point out that you don't need to battle with your conscience, Dr Schaefer. Carry on exactly as if I were not the head of this clinic's son.'

'Private contact between doctors and nurses is permissible, surely. Outside the clinic.'

'Right. But this was inside!'

'Very well. Have you got it all off your chest? Are you in the frame of mind to take things in? I see you are. Good. In that case, I am formally reprimanding you. Now spare me any more of your nonsense, damn it, and go back to work!'

For two, perhaps three, seconds, Udo thought he had not heard correctly. Then it was all over, and he heard himself stammering 'I'm sorry. My apologies, *Herr Oberarzt!* Apologies . . .'

His face was burning as he silently closed the door behind him.

SEVEN

One does not want to believe it. One fights, one prays, closes one's mind, tries to escape – but it happens.

Now it's final. She knew. She juxtaposed this knowledge which grew inside her and became stronger as did her illness, with Gerhard's encouraging expression and his 'Come on, little Gerda! Don't worry so much. It will all blow over.'

But this would not blow over. It would remain until the end. That conviction lay at the core of her knowledge, and strangely enough it made her feel free. At the beginning she would have fought it. Now she could smile.

'Mrs Beck! Until we have positive results there is no reason . . .'

'Mrs Beck! Please don't fret. What do you mean, you'll never leave here . . . ?'

'Mrs Beck! Don't tell me you're crying again! Come on, it's such a nice day.'

The girls who come into the room have round or small or funny or friendly faces. They shake the cover, help her to sit up if she can't manage it, help her to wash – so embarrassing! They touch the swollen body which is becoming a stranger to her. They hold the mirror when she combs her hair. And then she sees a face which is even less hers than her body.

Only one thing remains constant: the pains which eat through her veins and stomach, up her back, down her legs, sometimes even into her skull. Then they are taken away again with injections and pills . . .

'You see, Mrs Beck! Now we'll have a little sleep. Very gently . . .'

Yes, very gently. They use such kind words, smile so sweetly. That's the way they are: kind, helpful, efficient. As helpful and efficient as their lies. Should she disappoint them? Or play the role the way they expected her to play it, smiling bravely. 'Oh yes, Doctor, I feel much better this morning.'

In the end, not disappointing anyone or anything became a kind of duty, the least that she could do. And the last.

It was only when Gerhard came that it was difficult.

It was not just the face she knew so well, not just the voice. 'Well, little Gerda! We will beat this thing. They have everything at this clinic. The most modern equipment . . . What do you mean, they didn't operate?'

He said it as if it was her fault. Just like when they were at home, an echo of the reproaches that had haunted her all her life. 'What, Gerda, you still haven't applied for the rebate?' . . . 'What, Gerda, they won't give you a part-time job?' . . . 'What, Gerda, the children need more money again for school?'

Here is Gerhard, sitting by her bed, unhappy and angry because he thinks everything should go the way he wants it to. There he sits with a shopping bag full of bananas, fruit and chocolate on his lap. She couldn't even eat the stuff. But she could not bear to hear his annoyed 'Why not? You always liked them!'

So she said: 'Oh, bananas! And my favourite chocolate!' She would give them away later. But now she smiled into his face, a face she had never understood, never wanted to understand, but for which she still felt affection because he could look so forlorn if things went wrong.

'I'm sorry, Gerhard. They don't want to operate. They say I'm too weak.'

She knew what he would say before he said it. 'What are doctors

37

for? Why do we have the clinic anyway? They should operate. They should get you back on your feet again. Damn and blast it! I'll have a word with them. There's a new one just come. Brinkmann, his name is.'

'Please, Gerhard, don't shout.'

'What do you mean, please? I'm going to have a word with him.'

'Gerhard!'

He was gone. There was nothing she could do. In a way, that was the nice part of it. In the past she would have been terribly upset, perhaps even afraid. Now she could lie back on the pillow and look out of the window. It didn't concern her any more. Things just happened, they just passed her by. And she just drifted along with them.

She was smiling. The injections were doing what they were supposed to do, gently carrying her into a sleep in which she knew she could lose herself.

Poor man! He'll never understand . . .

Brinkmann was getting up from his chair when the door flew open, and he heard his secretary's agitated voice in the background: 'See here, you can't just barge –'

Brinkmann could not make out the answer, but he recognised the tone from many similar encounters. Experience in clinics, desperation in clinics. The anger of patients and of patients' relatives.

There the man was, then, standing in the doorway: a heavy-set man, tanned, with blond hair and athletic body. His tie was askew. He blinked with helpless embarrassment and anger.

'You're the new Chief, aren't you? I've come about my wife.'

'This is Mr Beck, Professor,' the secretary said, behind him. 'I'm sorry, but I couldn't –'

'It's all right, Miss Meis.' Brinkmann pointed to a chair in front of his desk. 'Please, sit down. You must be Gerda Beck's husband.'

The name had registered, the situation was clear: terrible and irrevocable, like the photographs of the tissues destroyed by the metastasis; metastasis that destroyed life like a hail of bullets. As he thought of this, Schiermann's words came back to him: 'A shame about the woman. Two children. And so brave!'

Two children? This man would have to bring them up. Alone. That thought stirred up a wave of sympathy in him.

Perhaps it was the room with its books and the friendly, sympathetic face of the doctor behind the desk; perhaps it was the abatement of the anger caused by fear and rebellion; whatever it was, Gerhard Beck sat embarrassed in his chair.

'Professor,' he began, his chest heaving as he tried to catch his breath. 'What is all this on-again off-again business? My wife has been here a week and nothing has been done, absolutely nothing. Your predecessor, Mr Schiermann – Professor Schiermann, I mean – told me this week it would be her turn. He said she was going to have the operation. Now you . . .'

'. . . won't operate,' Brinkmann finished the sentence.

Gerhard Beck nodded.

Silence.

Brinkmann rested his arms on his desk and thought for a moment. He could feel the adrenaline pumping through his veins. Stress? No, weakness. Or nerves. Only just started, and already the nerves are going.

'Look, Mr Beck, my colleague Schiermann was right. But I, too, have done the right thing. What I mean is, although it's true Professor Schiermann envisaged an operation, he would never have gone ahead with it until he had seen the results of all the tests. In the interim they have come through. And I can assure you that, as things are, even Professor Schiermann would decline to operate.'

The eyes staring at him from the other side of the desk were blank with incomprehension. 'And why not?'

Why not? Brinkmann leaned back. He said what he had to say as calmly as if he were talking to a child.

'Mr Beck, your wife has cancer.'

'She's not the only one.'

'Yes, but I'm afraid your wife is at a stage where an operation would not help. The metastasis – that is, the spread of the cancer by the primary tumour – has attacked her vital organs.'

Again the pause. How well he knew that! The man is strong-willed. He also has high blood pressure. Men like that don't readily accept it. He isn't built to withstand it. And here it comes:

'What exactly do you mean? I mean, you can't just let Gerda . . . no, no, not that!'

'Mr Beck, listen to me! We can save her a lot of pain. But otherwise –'

'But otherwise! Saving her pain? Imagine that! Gerda is thirty-nine, Professor. And we have two children. All these years she was healthy, like a horse. She worked until she nearly dropped. We would have noticed something.'

'*She* might have noticed something, Mr Beck. Perhaps she was too brave. Perhaps she didn't want to bother you with it. Perhaps you should have looked after her better.'

Was that too harsh? You can never learn enough about such situations, never be sure how to deal with them. My God, how often he had had this conversation, how many of them wanted the truth, and yet how different were their reactions. He knew this type, too. He would go on shouting.

But he was wrong. Gerhard Beck didn't shout. His shoulders slumped and his heavy hands clenched into fists.

'What can I say . . . ?' His voice was barely audible. 'If it's true, nothing means anything any more . . . I can't make it out, Professor. Gerda never saw a doctor, never. Not until two weeks ago.'

'That's exactly what I was talking about, Mr Beck. Perhaps she should have seen one much earlier.'

Again that dull, heavy silence. Why don't I get up, Brinkmann thought, and go over to him? Perhaps because this is a learning process he also has to go through? Two children. Dear God . . .

'Will she . . . is she going to die?'

'Yes. There's nothing we can do. Dying and living, each is part of the other.' He stopped. Neither words nor truths would help. 'Why don't you take her home, Mr Beck?' he asked, softly.

'Home? Oh, yes, of course. Home to our villa, right, with servants all over the place. Oh, God, God, no! Home, with me looking after her when I have to be at the sawmill? I've built a little house. I've got debts. I slave like a madman. Gerda can't die, Professor, she . . . it isn't fair. Neither of us has done anything to deserve this!'

He wiped his face with his sleeve. He spoke through his muffled sobs: 'Does she know?'

'Yes, Mr Beck. She's known for an hour.'

'And how is she taking it?'

'I've already told you: she is very brave. If she is afraid, it's only for you. She's afraid you will be upset, that you won't be able to manage. And she's afraid for the children, too.'

'Oh, God.'

'You've got to take her fear away from her, Mr Beck. You owe her that.'

Gerhard Beck looked up. His eyes were full of tears. Brinkmann tried to hold his gaze. 'Do you think you can manage it?'

'I don't know.'

'You must try,' he said. 'I don't think she deserves to spend what little time she has left with this fear, do you?'

Beck nodded.

'And something else, Mr Beck: visit her as often as possible. She loves you. You told me yourself how much she has done for you. Even if you can't take her home, at least be with her.'

Gerhard Beck nodded again, and got up out of the chair. He held on to the back of it, as if for support. He mumbled something Brinkmann could not make out. Then the words came out loud and clear.

'Thank you. Also for your honesty.'

Brinkmann walked around his desk. He wanted to open the door but Beck beat him to it, and all he could do was stand and watch as Gerhard stumbled past the desks in the outer office, eyes vacant, seeing nothing.

EIGHT

Wednesday. Twenty-four hours ahead of her and no chores to do. Apart from catching up with the washing up, the mending, the ironing, vacuuming, watering the plants and all the rest of it, which Christa had no intention of doing. It was too nice a day. Twenty-four hours off-duty. No corridors, no beds, no problems, no patients . . .

The sky above the mountains was dark blue. Cirrus clouds drew their strands southwards. Joyful screams came from the childrens' section of the swimming pool. The smells of sun oil, perspiration, and coffee from the nearby kiosk hung in the air.

Christa donned her sunglasses. She felt the warm wood of the changing room beneath her bare feet and took a last hesitant look in the mirror. The scrap of emerald-green bikini was very daring: 'Tanga-Form,' the saleswoman had swooned. 'A poem on your body! The perfect thing for a woman like you.'

Perhaps. But the perfect thing for the open-air pool in Offingen? And what had she meant by 'a woman like you?' A slim body, smooth skin, a cascade of hair that turned men's heads.

She walked slowly towards the slide, her head high and her lips pressed together as arrogantly as she could manage. And yet it was all she could do not to run away from the battery of stares that she was attracting. She caught herself fumbling with the elastic on the bikini bottom: it's like running the gauntlet! Her old bathing suit would have done. Sure enough, here comes one of those types with the gold pendants and the eyes of a would-be conqueror.

'And which little star did you fall down from?'

Christa shook her head and walked away. From which star, indeed! Where did they all get the idea they were irresistible? Where did Udo Brinkmann get it? All right, she was back to that old theme, but perhaps it wasn't so much a matter of Udo, or an Adonis with gold chains and a Rolex, as it was of herself, her nerviness, her need to cut herself off from everyone and everything.

No, what had happened with Udo was not important. Not at all. Udo was what he was. She'd had no illusions on that score from the outset. But sometimes loneliness is harder to bear than the knowledge that, from the start, an affair comes with its own, inbuilt ending. And Udo? He was only one last link in a long chain.

She found a secluded spot to sit down in. She took a ballpoint and writing pad out of her bag, then spread out her towel and lay down on her stomach. The sun caressed her back and her eyes followed the progress of a tiny, shimmering beetle battling its way through the grass right under her nose. One minute it keeled over, the next it pulled itself up, tackled a new obstacle, extended its feelers, groped about insecurely and then set off on a new course until it encountered the next obstacle.

That's you!, she thought. That's Christa Meurer in the last few years – Christa on the road! She was not quite sure where these thoughts were leading her. She raised herself up slightly and looked across the light and dark patterns of the lawns, and at the nude bodies scattered on it like brown, or bacon-coloured, or white stripes . . .

She was glad to be sitting so far away, by the fence. There was no point, however, in deluding herself. You have become touchy, impossible in fact, she thought. And now you're in the process of spoiling your wonderful day with small, nasty thoughts. The same thoughts which follow you everywhere and pop up at the slightest excuse: give it up! Stop kidding yourself. It would be better to hand

43

in your notice and pack your bags! Sure, the flat's nice and the rent's low, the air's good, and Basle and Strasbourg aren't far away. But a small village is still a small village, and a clinic is a clinic.

But that wasn't fair: the working conditions were more congenial than in other clinics. And her colleagues, not counting Hildegard and Udo, were all pleasant.

It was her own fault. Christa Meurer running away from herself . . .

Perhaps it only seemed that way because she was constantly aware of where her flight would end: Marburg. The preliminary exam. It had been practically over and done with when the catastrophe happened. Why did Ulli have to insist on taking her home from the pub on his motorbike? Why had she allowed herself to be persuaded when she hated the damned things? And dear God, why hadn't she noticed he was drunk? And why hadn't Ulli seen the black ice?!

'Hi, Christa, what are you doing here?'

She looked up at the small, plumpish girl who had waved at her. You couldn't even get away from the trainee nurses up here.

'Just writing a few letters.'

'We're all over by the pool.'

So what? But why that reaction? Why did she spend evening after evening mulling these questions over and over, instead of accepting the only possible answer: throw your illusions to the wind! The die has been cast. You are twenty-nine. The last few years should have made it abundantly clear you don't have the stamina to combine work and study any more.

And maybe not the courage, either.

Yes, the solution was so near.

It had only one big disadvantage: it was something she had to do alone. Worse still, melancholia was always lurking nearby and she could slide into it completely. What then? Hoarding sleeping tablets like Melanie Wieck? Not that, surely?

The trouble was ivory towers like the Black Forest Clinic had lost their attraction. As pleasant as the work was, the consequences lay heavily on her: you've lost your aspirations. You get uptight. You are gradually losing any sense of fulfilment.

The sun had moved across behind the birches. It was no longer dazzling. Leaves danced before her eyes. God, life could be so wonderful!

Christa got up. 'We're all over by the pool,' Ulrike had said. Fine, that would give her an opportunity to talk about Melanie Wieck. She could not forget the way Melanie had looked the last time she saw her: just sitting there, isolated, cut off from everything, as if she was under a glass dome.

When she reached the pool area, she showered and dried herself, arms see-sawing vigorously. In the glassy green light, she summoned from her memory, crystal-clear and totally objective, what she knew about Melanie Wieck: car accident, both legs fractured. A very slow recovery . . . and then that strange absent-mindedness. The staring into the void, the slow reactions when speaking combined with frantic activity – symptoms of depression.

'Am I a psychiatrist?' Udo had said, dismissing her when she broached the subject. 'We're here to heal her legs.'

Christa dived into the water, shook her head, took a deep breath and then swam along the side of the pool where she pulled herself up.

She had found twenty-four Valium tablets in Wieck's cupboard. Not quite enough to kill her, but what if she continued to hoard them like a squirrel? So, we'd better stop it. There were now twenty-four placebos hidden under the blouses. They looked remarkably like Valium, but they could not harm her.

What was the reason? Was it really depression? Why, dear God . . . ?

'Why? Well, I can guess why she's hoarding the stuff.' Ulrike had a strawberry ice-cream in her hand. She was sitting with three other trainee nurses and Mischa, the conscientious objector who was doing community service at the clinic. 'Do you want some ice-cream, Christa? Honestly, strawberry is t'rific! Try some!'

'Get on with it, Ulrike. Why does she hoard them?'

'When they brought the woman in, she was in shock,' Ulrike said. She had finished her ice-cream. What was left of the cone went flying into the bushes. She wiped her mouth. 'And she kept saying something strange all the time. "There is no point," she said. "What do you want? There is no point." Right away I thought, she's mad. She looks very attractive. When she's made up, she looks t'rific, you know?'

Christa nodded. 'Go on.'

'You're right, there's more. There was something odd. The day Schiermann operated on her, I was on duty. She woke up. You know how when they come round they often say very personal things. It's how you get to know a lot of private stuff. You find out what's bugging them, you know?'

'I know, Ulrike.'

'They taught us that on the course. You have to be specially nice to them when that happens.'

Christa smiled. She liked the kid.

'She was lying there, looking at me, with her eyes wide open, without tears, as if she was mad. But she was trembling.'

'And then?'

'Then she said a name. A man's name. She said it as if I were the man. Perhaps she couldn't really see me, except as a shadow. "You see," she said. "Now you believe me."'

'Was that all: "Now you believe me"? Nothing more?'

'No. It was strange. A bit mysterious, don't you think?'

Christa remained silent. Mysterious? There was a certain logic to it: an unhappy love affair coming to an end. The accident in fact had been a suicide attempt. And when she woke up in the clinic Melanie Wieck was once again seized by the fear that her threat would not be taken seriously. That awful, blackmailing line of reasoning some women have. That terrible ultimatum: if you don't want me, I don't want to live any more . . . How often thought, how often said, how often whispered into a tear-soaked pillow?

Was that it? Tomorrow she would discuss it with the Chief.

Ulrike jumped up. 'How about a game of tennis?'

Christa nodded and got up. Suddenly Ulrike grabbed her arm.

'Look! Over there!'

Over there? Christa turned her head and then quickly turned away. That was all she needed – Udo standing tall with a face like an offended god. What an afternoon!

Ulrike giggled. 'What's going on? Any other time he would have come straight over here.'

'Any other time,' said Christa.

'At least he'd have bought us an ice-cream. You two were the talk of the clinic, you know.'

Christa didn't even blush. Her heart beat no faster. She knew he was looking across at her, standing with legs apart, watching her fixedly from beneath lowered eyelids.

And there he stayed. She didn't find it unpleasant; merely boring. The others turned their backs on him, too.

'We'll cast him in solid gold and give him to Christa as a pendant,' Mischa said cattily. They laughed, and Christa joined in.

'You like ski-ing, do you, Miss Wieck? Well, I'm afraid you won't be able to go this year, but otherwise we should be very happy with your progress. The joint will heal eventually. Then later, after you leave here, you'll have to exercise and exercise. That's the most important thing: exercise all the time!'

Later . . . After you leave here . . .

Melanie Wieck looked across the lawn with its tulip beds and rose bushes towards the clinic. Whenever she could she slipped away here to the waiting bench, hidden between blooming laburnum. Even in the mornings, during visiting hours. Sometimes, just to get away from her roommate's chatter. Of course, Mrs Kirsch meant well, they all meant well – but everything got on her nerves!

You like ski-ing, do you, Miss Wieck? A new Chief but the same old fatherly routine. Why didn't he cut out the chat? What had he meant by 'we should be happy'? Who is 'we'?

Yes, Doctor, I love ski-ing! And this year we're going to Kitzbühel. Well, not exactly Kitzbühel, Professor, actually the Brixental, the Brixen valley. My lover knows a little guest house there. Just the right thing for two or three days of uninterrupted lovemaking, Professor! You can imagine, he'll tell them at home it's 'a conference' – 'My colleagues in Austria have organised it,' he'll say. 'We'll be meeting in Innsbruck.'

But will he?, the professor would have said. A chap has to keep his mistress good-tempered, right? Especially if she's young. Only now the mistress isn't so good-tempered – now she isn't young any more. She feels used, broken, thrown away. Dead . . . There won't be any 'later', Professor. Sad, but that's how it is. Nothing anyone can do.

Melanie stopped her train of thought. She had thought the same thing too often. She knew only too well what came next if she went on. No, there was nothing to think about. She closed her eyes and lifted her face to the sun. She felt its warmth on her forehead, but it did not warm her inside.

'Oh, excuse me . . .' The voice came from somewhere else, another world in which she did not belong.

'Forgive me, I saw you sitting here and I thought I'd come and sit with you, if you don't mind?'

If you don't mind? – Melanie Wieck opened her eyes. She did mind. Why didn't they leave her in peace? In God's name, when was she going to get some peace and quiet?

She recognised the face. Round, friendly, and quite pretty. Only a little puffy from the pregnancy. They had met on the stairs in the television lounge, smiled at each other, even exchanged a few brief words. A nice face, and even the bulging body beneath the green maternity dress looked somehow touching. All the same, why didn't she just keep on walking. She had everything: a child, a husband, a future.

'How are your legs?' the woman asked. 'Any better?' As she spoke she touched Melanie's crutches. 'You'll be able to do without these soon, I expect.'

'Perhaps.'

'What do you mean, perhaps?'

Melanie shrugged. She fixed her gaze on the clinic with its shimmering windows, and the two outlines of the terraces where people were sitting, talking. A thin, white tendril of smoke rose from the chimney of the laundry and lost itself in the trees. Someone laughed. The sound hurt her. A nice clinic, nice people, nice food . . . it was all so tranquil. And yet everyone was so alone.

'I wanted to ask you something. Please, don't be offended, but I've noticed that you're always so – shall we say, alone? Don't you ever have any visitors?'

'Why does it matter?'

'I was only asking.'

'I don't have visitors.'

'And you feel . . . left out? I get the impression you're, well, a bit sad. Am I right?'

'What if you are?'

'I beg your pardon?'

Melanie took the crutches, steadied them in the gravel stones on the path, and pushed herself round to look into the woman's clear, grey, observant eyes.

'Does my being sad bother you?'

'It's none of my business. Perhaps I worry about it too much. And perhaps I get on your nerves.'

'A possibility,' Melanie said, sharply.

The other woman flushed slightly, but did not let the sharp words throw her.

'Look, I only thought . . . if you ever need someone. I think if you chat it can sometimes help.'

'What is it you want to know?'

'Me? – Nothing.'

'That's fine. Because I'd have only had to disappoint you.'

Silence fell.

'Goodbye,' Melanie started to say, 'see you again.'

It wasn't necessary to finish. The woman in the green dress stood up.

'Excuse me, please,' she said. 'My husband is coming.'

My husband! Melanie's gaze followed the swallows as they flew in circles across the sky above the roof of the clinic. Now they dipped low and flew over the laundry into the garden.

She tried to get up. The pain in the shinbone and ankle joint pulled her back on to the bench. Cold spread through her body from the feet upwards, freezing her nerves, blocking her thoughts. Time and again, in her dreams, in her nightmares, she had imagined this situation. But never like this. Never so banal. No, and never so hurtful.

He wore the same black-and-white checked jacket he'd worn the last time they met. The same red roll-necked sweater. And he smiled, his arms open as he drew nearer to the woman.

My husband! . . .

Now he put his arms around the woman's shoulders and pulled the ungainly body towards him.

No!, thought Melanie. Impossible that it should be a co-incidence, that it should be her?

A child? she thought. Yes, he had mentioned it. Then she probably . . . no certainly, knew everything. And now the woman was playing out this little scene for Melanie's benefit.

49

Melanie closed her eyes. The picture imprinted itself on her mind's eye and remained etched into her memory for as long as she remained on the bench.

NINE

The heat collected beneath the steely dome of the sky, the leaves hung limp on the silent trees. The houses looked like cardboard cut-outs.

Klaus Brinkmann stirred his coffee and groaned. How many cups today? He took a sip – lukewarm!

There was going to be a change in the weather. Somewhere a damned Atlantic low was on its way. No, it hadn't been a good day. The operations scheduled for today were done: two gall bladders, an uncomplicated groin hernia, a couple of minor operations, nothing major. Even so, the work took its toll, not only of his team but of himself. More than he cared to admit.

Sudden changes of weather not only affect patients but are also the scourge of many surgeons. They are your cross, too, Brinkmann thought. Didn't you once plan to write a treatise on the subject? But who gave a damn about this climatic biology and its effects, about the mysterious alchemy of electrostatics, ion-charging, the interactions between what happens in the heavens and in the smallest parts of the body? The subject was still virgin territory, unexplored but touching the deepest secrets of human life – a reality which baffles doctors everywhere. And you in particular! Take this headache that throbs like a kettle full of steam, for example.

For God's sake, pull yourself together. Two o'clock already!

Klaus Brinkmann leafed through the folder containing the mail which his secretary had left on his desk. Requisitions and bills, documents and reports. He glanced through the private mail again, picking up a small envelope. The return address looked official: *Dr Elena Bach – Municipal Hospitals, Karlsruhe.* Not so the contents. He turned it over and over between his pointed fingers. Should he reply? Should he call?

No. Why should he? What was there to say?

When the letter had arrived that morning, he had wondered whether to return it unopened. Theoretically speaking it would have been within the rules: hadn't he and Elena agreed to a six-month 'voluntary ban on any contact'? Theoretically, yes. But he knew Elena. Moreover, being a woman she would consider such a gesture not merely as rudeness but as brutality.

He took the letter out and smiled at the first line. 'Dear Rossi,' she wrote. 'I know . . . But don't worry: it's just a small, non-personal matter.' The non-personal matter? Would he appear at the Oncology Congress in Heidelberg? And: 'I hope to see you there, together with all the other members of the old team.'

'The old team'? There is no 'old team' any more. Only one: the clinic, here. And the Oncology Congress? An excuse, what else? They had promised each other half a year of peace, the six months necessary, according to anaesthetist Dr Elena Bach's theory, to develop a 'clearly-defined relationship from an amorphous catastrophe of the soul'.

He pushed the letter aside, and with it the memory of Elena's pained and avid face. But he could not push aside his own feelings, an anguish more bewildered than unpleasant. One thing was certain: Heidelberg was out of the question! If there was anything he feared, it was the sudden upsurge of memories and emotions entailed by their separation.

They had done it. It was over! Nobody blamed anybody; one had to start being consistent. He had even arranged that Elena be put forward for the job of anaesthetist, hadn't he? Through her work and new responsibilities she would build herself a new life, and with it the confidence to face a world without Klaus Brinkmann.

Would she do it? She had to!

He finished his coffee and closed his eyes. What had Kate said? 'You two in that guinea-pig treadmill! You run and run, but you never get anywhere.'

Kate was right. Only he'd jumped off the treadmill.

Brinkmann went across to the window and looked into the court-yard of the clinic. The headache was back already! And the blue BMW? Wouldn't you just know? And its owner. There she was, Angelika Grossmann, a trench coat around her shoulders, a turquoise band in her red hair, hand on hip, watching the patient Hensle being rolled from the ramp to the car park in his wheelchair.

Arrogant cow!

He applied the insult unemotionally; it was the only description which fitted.

Arrogant cow. That had been his first impression when the lady had arrived unannounced at the villa last evening and pushed past Kate.

'Good evening, Professor. I regret the intrusion, I'm really embarrassed at having to see you this way, although perhaps it could have been avoided.'

'I beg your pardon?'

'It could have been avoided, for instance, had you taken better care of my fiancé. I have tried several times to make an appointment to see you, although unfortunately without success.'

He should have shown her the door right then. But her appearance had created an understandable confusion. 'Who is your fiancé?'

'Mr Hensle. Friedhelm Hensle.'

Of course, who else? It was all Brinkmann could do not to smile. However, he was curious about what would come next.

'Dr Schaefer is in charge of that case.'

'Of course. I am aware of that. May I sit down?'

'Please.'

She opened her handbag, took out some cigarettes, selected one. The look, the pause until he gave her a light, the crossed legs, the whole routine! – He still felt angry, remembering how she had blown smoke across the lounge.

'Professor, the . . . matter is rather delicate.'

'Really?'

'You see, my fiancé feels you're treating him rather, how shall I say, brusquely, because . . .'

'No need to beat about the bush, Miss Grossmann. I saw Mr Hensle before the accident. And I saw how he drove. He overtook my car and gave me a rude sign as he did so. The fact that he was driving like a maniac has been borne out by the catastrophe that followed.'

'May I point out, Professor, that the question of responsibility for the accident has yet to be established. And as far as this rude gesture is concerned – perhaps he was merely provoked by your deliberately slow speed. Psychologically speaking, it's quite possible.'

'Of course, with a certain kind of person. But may I ask you to come to the point?'

'Gladly. First of all, Friedhelm wishes to know whether you have taken it upon yourself to press charges or plan to do so. As it is, this deplorable accident is going to make things very difficult as far as the insurance is concerned. And if, on top of that –'

'I understand. And if it will make you feel any better, I have not asked for charges to be brought. Is that all?'

She had smiled, and still smiling she inspected her cigarette. She had nerve, you had to give her that. 'No, that's not all. There's something else.'

'Such as?'

'Friedhelm keeps thinking the people at the clinic are against him. He feels the reason he is so badly treated is because the other victims of the accident died.'

'Badly treated? Can he prove that?'

'Of course he can prove it! He was refused a single room. He doesn't get enough medicine: at times he is in unbearable pain. And then there's this young auxiliary, Mischa, or whatever his name is, who put on the elastic bandage in such a way that . . .

'Yes?'

'Well, in a nutshell, he believes that the existence of a deliberate campaign to make him suffer cannot be ruled out.'

54

Brinkmann felt a burning sensation in his neck. He knew what it meant: it was always a sign that it was time to control himself.

'Well, that's no problem, Miss Grossmann. All Mr Hensle has to do is go to another clinic. Why don't you take him to the Orthopedic Hospital at Freiburg?'

'We have already considered that, of course. But then there was the question of whether you would see such a move as a vote of no confidence in you, and then . . .'

'. . . bring charges after all, is that it?'

Angelika Grossmann merely nodded. There was a long pause. Finally, she broke the silence.

'Does the fact that my father is the head of Grossmann Industries mean anything to you?'

That did it. Brinkmann got up, threw one last look at this unwelcome visitor, walked to the door and opened it.

'Kate!' he called. 'The lady would like to leave. See her out, please.'

Now, she was taking her Friedhelm away.

Standing at the window, Brinkmann swore in response to the pain in his temple, then watched as the blue BMW turned elegantly in the courtyard, paused to make way for an incoming ambulance, and headed for the exit.

He felt no anger, only relief and surprise that he felt no anger. He saw the car disappear behind a row of houses, then turned back to his desk.

TEN

While Brinkmann was watching the BMW take Friedhelm Hensle away, Christa Meurer was in Room 210, changing some hand towels which the room-service maids had forgotten. In the cupboard she found a hairdryer Mrs Kirsch had reported missing weeks ago. She entered a new medicine on Melanie Wieck's chart: a harmless sleeping pill and tranquillizer based on herbs.

As she worked, she kept wondering how best to approach the silent patient on the bed. Melanie Wieck lay with her eyes closed, her lashes like black half-moon shadows painted on the pale face. Ostrich, Christa thought. If I don't exist, then nobody exists. What should she say? Should she try? In the end, her shyness was stronger than the wish to break down the barriers of protection and self-pity that cut Melanie Wieck off from the rest of the world.

There was a knock. When the door opened Christa felt relieved: life had literally come through the door. An expectant mother, the belt of her pink dressing gown tied over the bulge of her pregnancy.

'Mrs Fitz! Come in, please.'

The woman came in. Under her arm she carried a bundle of

newspapers. 'I thought Miss Wieck might like . . . but she's asleep?' She spoke more quietly. 'Am I intruding?'

'I don't think so. I'm sure she'll be very glad to have the newspapers.'

'You are!'

Christa turned around. Melanie Wieck was sitting up on her bed, both arms braced against the mattress, her eyes wide and staring.

'You are,' she repeated. Her voice was clear, slow, and very calm. 'You certainly are intruding. What do you want, anyway? Both of you are disturbing . . . Both . . . Everybody is disturbing me . . .'

Maria Fitz and Christa looked at each other. There was nothing more to be said. Outside, in the empty corridor, Maria shook her head worriedly. 'You see how she is. I'm worried about her.'

Christa nodded. 'Do you know her well?'

'Know her? Who really knows anyone? I've tried to talk to her a few times, to cheer her up a bit, but it's so difficult. I suppose she's in great pain. Maybe that's what causes it?'

'No, not a lot. At least, I don't think so.'

'Depression, then?'

Christa shrugged helplessly. Then she nodded. 'As you said yourself, who really knows anyone else, Mrs Fitz?'

What else could she say? 'Depression': a word used where other explanations fail. 'Depression': dear God, every single sufferer coming here was wounded not only physically but mentally. She sighed and picked up her tray, but she did not get far.

'Nurse Christa! Just a moment!'

Udo Brinkmann! His white coat unbuttoned as usual, the stethoscope dangling from the top of his poloneck shirt, his dark eyebrows raised, sailing towards her across the corridor.

'Hello.' He managed to favour Maria Fitz with a short nod before he turned to Christa. 'What are you doing standing around here, Nurse?'

'I wasn't standing around, Doctor! I'm working. I've just . . .' She felt the blood rush to her cheeks.

'I'm not interested in what you've just done. It's of no interest. A quarter of an hour ago, I asked you to change the bandages in Room 24. And have they been changed? Answer me!'

This wasn't the usual ward-inspection scene Udo sometimes indulged in, this was sheer anger. Maria Fitz, looking embarrassed, sidled away as Udo, red-faced, shouted at Christa.

'I'm asking you, Nurse Christa, whether you do not feel it necessary to carry out my instructions? I'm asking you what happened to the bandages. Furthermore, I would like to know –'

Whatever the 'furthermore' was that Udo Brinkmann had been going to blame her for Christa never found out. He was staring, transfixed, past her left shoulder into the corridor. Christa turned.

The Chief was standing there.

Professor Klaus Brinkmann seemed very calm. Even his voice was calm, calm and precise. 'Just in case the word has not got around yet, I should like to make it clear that in my clinic there are to be no public reprimands to staff – and especially not in a corridor where all our patients can hear. It isn't just a matter of style, Doctor, it is also a matter of the care we owe our patients.'

'You'll forgive me if I say I thought it was my responsibility to decide who does what on the wards.'

'I don't think you quite understood me. It may well be necessary to reprimand someone. But not out here. As far as your instructions are concerned, however, let me point out that bandages can also be changed by trainee nurses. Nurse Christa was doing something for me.'

The look on Udo's face was a study of conflicting emotions. His eyes darted from side to side. 'Oh, well, in that case, don't let me interfere.'

Brinkmann's unruffled composure did not alter. 'I wish to talk to you, Udo. Shall we say in ten minutes, in my office? You come along with me, Nurse.'

Brinkmann sat down and pointed to the visitor's chair in front of his desk. He put his hands flat on the desk and leaned forward, looking into the friendly, smooth face of Nurse Christa, with its rounded forehead, short, straight nose, wide mouth and expectant eyes. Beautifully-formed eyelids, he thought. Those eyes which he'd noticed the very first time he saw her. Perhaps because they were intelligent and observant, or perhaps because they were pretty. In some strange way there was something in those eyes that made him feel uneasy.

'Forgive me for that. Necessity. I had to lie to poor Udo to get you off the hook.'

'Thank you, Professor.' Her voice was barely audible.

'Would you like to tell me what it was all about?'

'You heard, Professor.'

'Yes, I did. And I propose we forget it. You don't need me to tell you every clinic has its aggravations. There are always problems when people have to work closely together. Call them jams, if you like. They occur when misunderstandings, or anger, or superfluous energy are not channelled off. Now, Nurse Christa: I'm most grateful to you for drawing my attention to our patient Miss Wieck. I have tried to talk to her. You're right, she is showing all the signs of deep emotional trauma. Has anything happened since we spoke?'

Christa shook her head.

'What's your opinion?'

'Difficult to say. I don't believe there's any such thing as true depression. Perhaps it could be depressive exhaustion. Or even a very ordinary love affair which ended in a crisis.' She told him what Ulrike had told her at the swimming pool.

Brinkmann was playing with his ballpoint. He put it back on the desk set and looked up. 'You are very efficient, Nurse Christa. Really. How did you become so knowledgeable?'

'I studied medicine for six terms.'

'Is that so? One can always tell. And why did you give up your studies?'

'I'd rather not talk about it, Professor.'

He smiled. 'I'm sorry. I respect your feelings, of course. In any event I shall express my appreciation to Sister Hildegard.'

'Professor, may I ask you not to do that?'

Brinkmann tried hard not to show his surprise. But he did not probe any further. 'Just as you wish,' he murmured. He hesitated, looked for a way to broach what was on his mind, then decided to ask straight out.

'A very personal question, Nurse. I am interested: are you and my son close friends?'

'No.'

He noticed the slight blush, the nervous flicker of her long lashes. He waited.

'No,' she said again. 'We were interested in each other, it's true.

Perhaps more than that. Interest and sympathy. But that's all over.'

Brinkmann leaned across the desk: 'Please believe me, Nurse Christa: God knows, I don't wish to pry into your private life. The only reason I am asking is because I felt that the matter of Miss Wieck should have, or shall we say could have, been discussed in more detail between you and my son. Don't you think so?'

She remained silent.

Ah well, Brinkmann thought. 'What do you think we ought to do about Melanie Wieck? Calling in a psychiatrist without the patient's consent could cause something of a problem. Do you really think she is in danger?'

By this time Christa, too, had regained her composure. Her look was direct and uncompromising. 'I'm sorry, Professor, but the accident, on a straight road, with no oncoming traffic, no slippery road surface, not even a hint of exhaustion – they all point to the inescapable conclusion that Miss Wieck deliberately drove into that tree.'

He nodded. 'How do you know all this? Why isn't any of it mentioned in her notes?'

'I read it in the paper. Perhaps at first I jumped to conclusions, but now the link with the sleeping pills . . .'

'I understand. You're quite right.' He offered her his right hand. 'Many thanks, Nurse Christa. Really, many thanks. We shall see what can be done.'

Brinkmann observed how she held herself erect as she walked, a very confident walk. Six terms of medicine, he thought. But why did she give up her studies?

A remarkable woman. Really quite remarkable.

ELEVEN

Clinics, hospital visits, and everything connected with them gave Klaus Fitz the shivers.

But the room in the maternity ward was a treat! It was an oasis, pretty, with white curtains, amusing wallpaper, flowers everywhere, music. Someone had their radio on full blast, something classical, Tchaikovsky if he wasn't mistaken. And in the middle of it all, there she was: his Maria! She looked prettier than ever, her face glowing rosily, her hair newly done, her hands folded across her pregnant body.

Klaus Fitz put the flowers down with all the others, but took the cake he had brought over to where she was sitting. 'Vitamin cake' – how about that? Getting fit through noshing. Wasn't that something?

He beamed at her, taking her hand. He put his other hand on her blue maternity dress, feeling the tight, throbbing warmth, and remembered fleetingly how his secretary had called after him as he left: 'Now I'm certain it will be a girl, Mr Fitz. Men who wear pink sweaters always have girls!'

He was about to tell Maria what the girl had said, but the expression on her face made him hesitate. 'What's wrong, Maria? What is it?'

She shook her head. He turned down the music – it was Tchaikovsky! Usually Maria listened to Radio Luxembourg, or something like that. But now it was classical music . . .

'What's bothering you? Is it something to do with the baby?'

'No, no, not the baby. It's one of the patients.'

'What's the matter with her?'

She sighed. 'That's what I'd like to know. A nice woman, you know? No. A nice girl. Still quite young. She broke both her legs in some kind of accident. I like her. She seems so lonely. I've tried to help her but she rejects everybody.'

Klaus Fitz nodded sympathetically. Friendship among patients, loneliness, he'd heard about them. Maria opened her present.

'Klaus, did I ever tell you when I was a child I had two budgerigars?' He shook his head. 'One was called Max, the other Moritz. Then we found out Max was a female, so I called her Maxine. Well, poor Moritz got sick and died. After that, Maxine just sat staring through the bars. She refused to eat, not one seed. Then all her feathers started dropping out. She just sat there in the corner, moulting until, in the end, she died too.'

He stroked his wife's hand. 'What a strange mood you're in today,' he said. 'But I understand. Perhaps this lady's problem is connected with the accident she had. What do you think?'

'Hardly.'

He offered her some cake but she only shook her head. He felt a warm flood of affection for her fill his heart as he looked at her sitting there. How marvellous that they had found each other again. She had always been the maternal type – he had probably been too naïve or too stupid to realise it. But this was overdoing it. It wasn't enough to have a child in her womb to care for, she needed some woman with broken legs to worry about as well.

He took her hand and lifted it to his lips, gently kissing her fingertips.

'I'm sure you'll cheer the lady up,' he said. 'I don't doubt it for a second.'

'That was what I thought at first, but now I'm beginning to wonder. She must be quite intelligent. The nurse said she's an assistant technician of some kind. A local girl. Her name is Melanie . . .'

He was still holding her hand, his head bowed. He was still looking at her small, carefully manicured nails. He was trying to think, but inside him was a terrible knot of apprehension that numbed his mind. Melanie! And she had broken her legs in 'some sort of accident'.

Some sort of accident!

It was very quiet in the room. Down below, tyres squealed on the curve of the main road. A jet rumbled across the sky. Melanie Wieck. He mulled over her name, and said it aloud. He felt Maria's gaze.

'Do you know her?'

He released her hand and walked across to the window, looking out into the pleasant garden, the lilac trees, the lawn, the garden benches.

Do you know her?

He had asked himself the same question many times in the past few months. But never at any time had Klaus Fitz felt this kind of fear, a panic which made logical thought impossible and threatened to paralyse his brain. How could it have reached this stage? How could he have forgotten that Melanie would have been brought to the Black Forest Clinic? After all, it was used for emergencies round here: he could have worked it out! The truth of the matter was he hadn't wasted a single thought on Melanie since the accident. He had banished her from his mind, cancelled out all thoughts of her.

As head of the building planning council, Klaus Fitz set a great deal of store by his lifelong clarity of intellect. 'My work,' he always said, when beginning technical discussions at the ministry, 'is to do with logic.' The fact that this clarity of thinking did not extend to his private life – for Melanie was not the only example of his wild illusions and lack of self-restraint – seemed to him merely to complement his otherwise exact and reasoning way of thinking. After all, he told himself, as an architect one was also an artist . . .

'Were you going to say something?'

'Sorry?'

'I asked you if you knew her?'

It was not her voice: it was still that look. He could feel it between his shoulder blades. He felt an onrush of helplessness, of guilt, the fear of more questions, of every impending word, and of any more lies.

No, there was no way out. There was only one solution: grasp the bull by the horns! Tell her the truth! Melanie was in this very building, beneath this very roof. What a predicament! He turned.

'Yes, I know her.'

A tiny frown creased her forehead. Her eyes were not quizzical; there was no astonishment, just a knowing glint. He had difficulty meeting her gaze.

'I know Melanie,' he said, still crouching next to her. 'She was my assistant for a while.'

'Oh . . . you mean . . . ?'

'Yes, Maria. That's what I mean. She was my mistress. Listen, please, let me tell you what happened. Let me try to explain . . .

Ten p.m.

Anna Kirsch had put her radio headset away some time earlier but her reading lamp was still on. She couldn't sleep without something to read, a habit she had acquired a long time ago when a slipped disc had given her so much pain that she spent whole nights reading books and newspapers.

The circle of light illuminated a photograph in the magazine of Queen Beatrix of the Netherlands: a chubby, severe-looking young woman wearing a tiara. The caption informed Anna Kirsch that Beatrix's husband, Claus von Amsberg, was suffering from a deep depression that had its origins in a childhood devoid of warmth and affection. Anna put the magazine down and glanced over at her neighbour's bed. 'Warmth and affection' – perhaps that was it? Perhaps Melanie had been deprived in the same way?

She couldn't even hear Melanie's breathing. Melanie had put out her light long ago and was lying there, immobile and mysterious. Like a mummy, Anna thought. Eventually she also turned out her light. Outside in the corridor she heard light footsteps pass the door: a night nurse. I wonder who it is tonight? Elke? No, Christa.

'Warmth and affection?' she wondered again. Melanie could not complain of the lack of it here: everyone in the clinic was concerned about her. The minutes ticked by, mounting into hours. Anna Kirsch closed her eyes and thought about the way the sea had looked when she was in Majorca two years ago. 'Think of the sea,' the professor had suggested to her. 'Think of its expanse, its calm. Imagine the sea is breathing as it sends its waves towards the shore . . .' She tried. Her body felt heavy. She felt sleep approaching . . . Then all at once the sea disappeared and she woke up, her heart pounding.

She hadn't noticed Melanie get out of bed: she must have moved as silently as a mouse. Now she was opening the cupboard: – Anna heard the door creak. In the faint grey light of dawn stealing through the curtains, Melanie looked like a dark pillar.

Anna Kirsch held her breath. Melanie was getting her pills from the cupboard. She had no idea they were harmless, though Anna had been told about the changed prescription. There – just as she had thought – reaching for death! At least, that must be the way it looked to Melanie.

Anna felt very hot. She had only half-opened her eyes but she was having trouble controlling her breathing. It's like one of those whodunnits, she thought. She watched Melanie take the mineral water from the table: of course, she'd need that to take the pills. And now? Melanie put on her dressing gown, put the bottle in its pocket, and opened the door leading to the terrace.

Anna Kirsch fought to remain calm. Don't move, play dead, let her go!

Melanie Wieck went out of the room.

Anna Kirsch pressed the call button and kept on pushing it.

The door opened. 'What's wrong, Mrs Kirsch? Aren't you feeling well?'

'Please don't put the light on, Nurse Christa!'

'Why not? What's going on?'

'Look! There!'

The empty bed. The sheet on the floor. The cupboard door wide open.

'You see? If you put the light on, Melanie will know you've found her out.'

'Is she in the garden?'

'Yes.'

Christa went to the phone and dialled Udo Brinkmann's number. 'Udo, it's Christa. You must come to the clinic right away! Miss Wieck has gone out into the garden somewhere. She's taken the placebos with her. Bring a torch and phone Johannsen!'

How calmly she said all that, Anna Kirsch thought admiringly. An efficient girl, Christa, everything by the book . . .

An idea struck her. She got up and went to the terrace. The air was still soft and warm. Outside she saw torches, heard muffled voices.

'Christa!' Anna Kirsch did not care who heard her now. 'Christa! The bench! Up there, by the birches!'

Thank God she had remembered! That was where she had often seen Melanie, where she always sat whenever she could.

'Melanie!'

For a few seconds Christa's eyes had been dazzled by the torch-light, but now they had adjusted to the darkness. She knew the way, every wall, every step. She moved faster, heading for the lilac bushes. Then she slowed, stopped, knelt down.

'Melanie!' There was no need to shout any more, so she whispered, 'Melanie, what's wrong? Melanie, please . . .'

Melanie's upper body was covered with branches. Her nightdress was torn and her dressing gown was thrown wide open. A mineral-water bottle lay next to her.

'Udo, hurry!'

He came running, put the torch on the grass, brushed aside the leaves and branches, and shook Melanie Wieck's narrow shoulders.

'Miss Wieck! Come on, wake up!'

'Not so loud, Udo.'

'What? How do you expect –?'

Christa knelt beside him. Melanie Wieck lay on her back, arms close to her sides like a doll. Her eyes were closed and a faint rattle came from her half-open mouth.

'Switch off the torch.'

Christa bent down. A branch pulled off her cap but she hardly noticed as she reached for the girl's wrist. The pulse was fast and thin, like the beating of a bird's heart. The muscles of the arm were stiff and arched, hard as stone.

'Melanie, can you hear me? Melanie, it's Christa! Melanie?'

No reaction.

There was something wrong. Thin pulse, icy skin, blood pressure down: a severe circulatory disturbance, there couldn't be any doubt of it. But the tablets which Melanie had taken were nothing but harmless caster sugar in tablet form. Nevertheless something was very wrong. What was it? Why was the girl in this condition?

'She's in bad shape, Udo,' Christa whispered urgently. 'What do you think?'

'It's impossible, out of the question. Pure hypochondria. Play-acting.'

No, that wasn't it. More likely it was the hell Melanie had been trapped in ever since Christa had known her. It might be that she was in a state of confused consciousness, suffering a psychotic attack so severe that her bodily functions had collapsed. It was a condition often encountered in clinical psychology, frequently seen in hysterical people. Not only hysterics, but with all hypersensitive types.

Nervous prostration brought on by depression! Hadn't she said as much to the Chief? Wasn't it possible that Melanie's flight from a reality which had become unbearable had caused her collapse?

'Touch her, Udo.'

He stretched out his hand, touched shoulders and arms. 'Muscle spasm,' he muttered. 'Almost catatonic. An obvious syndrome of hysteria. Couldn't be anything else. I'll bring her round.'

He raised his hand, but Christa grabbed his wrist to prevent him slapping Melanie's face.

'No!' she said. 'We can get her back inside like this.'

'If you say so,' he sighed. 'Ah, here's Johannsen.'

And here he was, broad-shouldered, silent, and, as always, calm.

'Can you bring the patient to her room, Mr Johannsen?' Christa said.

'Certainly,' Johannsen replied, bending down. As he placed his hands beneath Melanie's shoulders and knees she whimpered faintly, but that was all. There was no protest as they lifted her. Her head fell back, long hair hanging.

'The power of auto-suggestion,' Udo said, brushing back his hair. 'You have to have seen it to believe it. She eats a handful of caster sugar and acts like she's dead. Just like the movies. Incredible, isn't it?'

Christa said nothing. Incredible? Perhaps . . .

TWELVE

Although Kate Marek had already rung twice to remind him that the food was getting cold, Brinkmann had decided to finish his administrative paperwork before the morning ended; and he had almost succeeded. The alterations to the timetable for the nurses' training programme could be made tomorrow, or better still he could take the files home. What else? The last item on his list was Miss Wieck's strange, tragi-comic attempt at suicide.

'You haven't forgotten that Mr Fitz is still waiting to see you,' Miss Meis reminded him over the intercom.

'Give me a minute. Then I'll see him.'

Brinkmann leafed through the memo pad on which Udo had jotted down the salient points: *Patient found in deep shock. Gave her sedatives and something to improve her circulation. Her mental condition seems to have stabilised.*

He did not miss the word dramatically underlined with the felt pen. He nodded. After the incident in the garden he had spent an hour talking to Melanie Wieck. He knew now the reason behind the depressive passivity which had so extended her recovery – the banal love affair, as Christa had suspected from the outset. The old triangle: boss, wife, mistress. Perhaps 'banal' was unfair. What seemed banal to an outsider could be a matter of life and death to those involved. Perhaps that was true of Klaus Fitz, too . . .

Hold on, he thought. That name rings a bell.

There was a knock. He called, 'Come in.' It was not Fitz but Dr Schaefer, a folder containing the reports on the previous day's operations in his hand.

'Could you leave them, and I'll sign them this afternoon?' Brinkmann asked. 'I still have one more interview, and Kate is going to bite off my head if I'm not ready to leave soon.'

Schaefer nodded. Short of an earthquake registering eight on the Richter scale nothing upset him, Brinkmann thought. In the operating theatre he was a model of tranquillity and caution; in other words, panic-proof. A bit on the slow side as surgeons went, but his cool calmness more than made up for that.

'There's someone outside who I think is a mutual friend of ours.' The slight movement at the corners of his mouth was meant to be a little smile.

'Klaus Fitz. Chief of the building planning council. I've been trying for some time to think where we met. I think he may have been at school with us.'

Brinkmann leaned back in his chair, toying with the letter-opener.

'It makes you think, Schaefer. Here is this woman, thirty-nine years old, the mother of two children, needed by her entire family, who wants to live and has to die. And here's this twenty-six-year-old, single, pretty, no problems worth mentioning, who can live but wants to die. And why? Because of some married man who's old enough to be her father and whose wife is expecting a baby.'

'Spare me!' Schaefer raised both hands as if to say, I've been operating all morning, leave me alone. Brinkmann nodded his understanding.

'I'll see you later,' he said, and pressed the intercom button. 'Send Mr Fitz in now, please.' As Brinkmann said the words, it came back to him: Fitz! Of course, he had been the son of an architect. A tall, dark boy one class below him, always a bit loud, a bit too cocky. Chief of the building planning council, was he? So he'd stayed in the area and climbed up the ladder.

Brinkmann stood up when he heard the knock. The man came in. His hair was still dark, but thinner, carefully brushed to conceal a shiny bald patch. He wasn't slim any more. The white trousers and the smart summer sweater were meant to compensate for that. So this was the man for whom a young woman wished to throw away her life? Seemed impossible. But, Brinkmann thought, a lot of things happened in small towns that didn't make sense.

'Hello, Mr Fitz.' He took the big, soft hand which was offered, and looked into a pair of half-pleading, half-embarrassed, light-brown eyes.

'Klaus!'

'I beg your pardon?'

'Oh, come on, come on, my name is Klaus. The two Klauses. Surely you remember?'

'Oh, you mean at school. I see. Yes, of course, I'm sorry.'

Brinkmann waved at the chair. 'Take a seat, Klaus. And let me start by making something perfectly clear: I've only asked you in here because we have to work out a therapy for one of our patients, not because I have the slightest interest in your personal affairs.'

Klaus Fitz fiddled with a ring on his right hand bearing his family crest. He did not reply.

'First of all, we need a few details about Melanie Wieck's past.'

'What do you mean, her "past"? Surely this business can be handled with a little discretion?'

'I'm not sure I understand what you mean by "this business",' Brinkmann said. 'I'm a doctor, not a judge. I'm interested in only one thing, Klaus: to find out what happened. It's a vital part of the case history, essential to our decision on whether Miss Wieck needs psychiatric treatment.'

'Good God, what's all this about psychiatric treatment? Surely someone unbalanced doesn't have to be labelled mad, do they? She's not mad. I'll tell you what's mad. My wife and my former mistress meeting here as patients, that's what's mad. That's real lunacy!'

'You may be right. But let's face it, you're not entirely blameless yourself, are you?'

Klaus Fitz nodded. His shoulders slumped forward and his right hand massaged his throat as if he was having difficulty breathing. The confident air was gone, replaced by one merely pitiful.

'I don't suppose you're aware of my position in the community? I'm now the director of the city's planning department. You've been away much longer than me, Klaus, but not so long that you've forgotten what it's like here. In a place like this scandals are fatal. Not to mention the political consequences for my job.'

'You needn't have any fears on that score. We have a code of professional conduct in this clinic.'

'Things like this get around. You can't stop them. Still, that's hardly your problem . . .'

'You're absolutely right,' Brinkmann answered coldly.

Fitz's expression was desperate. 'It's a damned shame, you know. Most of all, for my marriage. Oh, we've had our ups and downs but now, with the baby coming, we're really happy. Maria's such a fine wife. And now . . . You know what she said to me this morning? She said, "I'm not angry with the girl. I shall help her." Isn't that incredible?'

Brinkmann said nothing. What was there to say?

'Shall I tell you what I sometimes think?' Klaus Fitz was saying, carried away by remorse and self-pity. 'That women are much stronger than we are. And that there are many men who don't deserve the woman they've got. Don't you agree?'

Brinkmann smiled.

Kate Marek was in a bit of a tizzy. She needed some leather strips for the sewing she was doing, and she had forgotten where they were. In the yellow cardboard box marked *Nexonna – The Effective Eczema Therapy*, or in the little Pfizer carton? Maybe they were in the old chocolate box.

That was her problem: untidiness. Too many bits of velvet, cotton and silk, and not enough cardboard boxes. The result was chaos. She had tried to tidy up the attic but the remnants she had saved to make doll's dresses were getting jumbled up. The dolls lined up along the shelf regarded her with their fixed smiles, but . . . blast it, where was the leather?

She got up, sighing heavily. It was Sunday morning. These past few hours after breakfast had been the most pleasant she could remember. Even the ticking of the clock somehow sounded different. There was the sound of the bells from St Michael's Church, the ticking noise the heating pipes made, then silence. It was so still she

71

could hear Klaus turning the pages of his newspaper on the terrace below.

Kate Marek put away her scissors and went over to the window-sill. And there, in the little straw basket where she kept her glasses, she found the strips of leather she had been looking for: black, yellow, pink. Pink, she thought, of course! Little Anne, in bed with an infected eardrum, would like pink. She could even embroider the child's name on it . . .

Her smile disappeared and she forgot little Anne in the children's ward as she heard the sound of a car. Not Udo's: she knew the sound of his car.

The car was red, with a sun roof. In it sat a lady wearing a hat, gloved hands on the steering wheel. Sunglasses. A smart brown summer outfit. I might have known she would turn up sometime. But not today. Not now. Not on this lovely Sunday morning!

God damn it all to hell!

THIRTEEN

Brinkmann watched her as she got out of the car, looked about uncertainly, picked up her handbag and slammed the door. It was the hat that dissipated his anger. Not anger, annoyance. Had she decided to end the quarantine? Unilaterally?

That wagon wheel on her head with its pink ribbon, the sort of thing gondoliers wear in Venice – where had Elena bought it? Paris, of course, at the Place de l'Opéra . . . They'd drunk Chablis and all had been well with their world. Everything back in order. That had been when he'd noticed the hat: 'Look, it's fantastic! I'll make you a present of it. I'm in a gondolier-ish mood today.'

Today: how many years ago was it?

He leaned over the terrace railing and waved. She looked up at him, very slim, erect, her face shadowed by the hat brim.

'The door is open, Elena!'

He heard the short, energetic steps he knew so well, and then there she was! She had taken off her hat. Her dark hair had come loose during the journey.

'Elena, you look fabulous!' What else was he supposed to say?

73

What else could he do but put his hands on her shoulders and kiss her on both cheeks? How was he to know she was going to turn up? No use expecting anything except the unexpected of Elena Bach.

'You're angry, aren't you?' Her eyes were searching. Fine wrinkles at the corners. 'Go on, Klaus, admit it.'

'What would you like me to say? Tell me!'

'Just don't tell me I look great. I look worn out. And so do you.'

'You think so . . . ?' The embarrassment returned. 'Would you like some coffee?'

'I'd rather have some bubbly, thanks. The journey has made me thirsty.'

Going to the kitchen gave Brinkmann a moment's respite. What the hell was coming next? And damn it all, where was Kate? She always knew what to do. Why was there no sign of her?

'You've put on some weight,' Elena Bach said, measuring him with her eyes as he came out on to the terrace with the tray and glasses. 'What a fantastic house you've got here! A bit run down, perhaps, but it's got a lot of style. Just what I like.'

'Are you trying to tell me you've never been here before?'

'Me? Oh, your memory, Rossi! – When?'

Words, words, words – the rungs of a ladder taking them across the abyss of embarrassment. And that smile – how he remembered it.

'It's odd. We always came through here on our way to Zürich.'

'And to Paris.'

He nodded. 'Yes, and Karlsruhe is not all that far.'

'Strange,' she smiled, 'was it not? Klaus Brinkmann and his homeland-neurosis. Please, I didn't coin the phrase. You seem to have got over it splendidly.'

'Does that bother you?'

'No, why should it?' Her smile faded. 'I'll be honest with you. I've been wondering whether or not to come here for days. First I thought of reasons, then excuses.' She pushed back a wayward strand of hair that had fallen over her left eye. How he remembered that gesture! Her look was clear and challenging. 'I thought of saying I was just passing. In fact, I had a dozen excuses ready. Like asking you why you didn't want to go to Heidelberg, for instance.'

'You know why.'

She nodded. 'Yes.'

'And knowing, you came anyway, right?'

A fine, transparent blush touched her cheeks and vanished. She shrugged her shoulders. There was something touching in the movement, but there was something even more touching in the way she remained silent. And in her look. He tried to make it easier for her.

'How are things with you? How are things at the old place?'

'Just fine. Or does it bother you that we can get along without you at Karlsruhe? After all, I'm not the only one there, Rossi.'

Again that pause. *Rossi* – where had that started? Of course! She had been the young assistant anaesthetist, Dr Bach. He had pushed a note into her pocket: *The great stallion is afraid he has fallen in love with you. Riesenross.* Elena had shortened it to the affectionate 'Rossi'.

'Henninger also thought it was a bit strange that you never called.'

'Believe me, Elena, it was extremely difficult starting here. Rarely a day less than twelve hours. I really had to sweat . . .'

All at once the sound of Mollie's howling emerged from the house. Brinkmann breathed a sigh of relief as a brownish-grey streak of hair shot out of the door, stopped, and turned into a dog, which pushed its nose up against Elena's handbag and spilled the contents all over the floor.

'What on earth is that?'

'Well, if you worked at it, you could call it a dog,' Brinkmann smiled, trying to pull his hand away from Mollie's devoted wet tongue and making sure that the waving tail did not capsize the table which had the glasses on it. In spite of her exuberance he had never been more thankful for the dog's presence. Then Kate finally made her appearance, and he relaxed for the first time since Elena had arrived.

The old lady pushed her glasses up on the bridge of her nose and regarded Elena carefully with pale blue eyes.

'Well, well, look who's here. The *Frau Doktor*!' She used Elena's title like a knife. 'And knowing the *Frau Doktor* I'm sure she will be staying for lunch?'

'I think, perhaps not . . .'

'But I insist,' Kate cooed, sweetly. 'What would you say if I told

75

you I have a leg of lamb in the oven, and zabaglione for dessert, *Frau Doktor?*'

'*Frau Doktor* still wouldn't say yes.' Brinkmann was determined to take control of the situation. It was the only way, as he had learned during his eleven-year relationship with Elena Bach: tell her exactly the way things are going to go, or be left high and dry. 'If we're going to eat, it won't be here. The two of us are going to take a trip. All right, Elena? I've been meaning to go up to the Horningsgrinde for a long time. Want to come with me?'

Elena Bach hesitated. 'And what happens when we get there?'

'We get some oxygen in our lungs. Calm our nerves.'

'Do you need to? While we're on the subject, how's Udo?'

'That,' Brinkmann said with a rueful smile, 'belongs to the story of our teething troubles here.'

She smiled. The years fell away and there she was: the old Elena, confident, purposeful, even enchanting – but not for him.

After they left, Kate Marek turned off the cooker, shaking her head. It wasn't the joint she was concerned about, it was him. And the nagging worry: dear God, is that starting all over again?

Elena Bach had had her doubts before she left Karlsruhe. So many doubts that her journey had almost seemed like running away, forwards. Now she knew she had been right.

It had been right to ignore the agreement and take a chance on the visit. Right that they had taken refuge together on this mountain, like survivors of some catastrophe, which for him had obviously lost its horrors and been consigned to the past, but which still affected Elena's whole life.

She would not conceal that from him; it was important to remind him of it.

All around them was the usual Sunday afternoon scene: observation platform and woodland café, souvenir shop and long picnic tables, courting couples, groups of people eating and drinking, worried mothers, screaming children, ordinary people enjoying their Sunday out.

She sipped a glass of lemonade and watched Brinkmann, who was puffing contentedly on a pipe.

'Klaus, on no account do I want you to misunderstand me. Of course, you can tell me it's none of my business and that I'm stubborn, the way you did in the old days, but I have to say this because, in a way, I still feel responsible for your professional status. For your social standing, if you like.'

'Well,' he said admiringly, taking the pipe from his mouth. 'That was quite a preamble. Whose toes have I trodden on?'

His amused tone annoyed Elena, all the more because she knew she must not show annoyance. She had planned to weigh every word as if on gold scales, and that was what she was going to do. She knew him.

'Whether you like it or not, Rossi, withdrawing so completely would be like professional suicide. At the very least, it would mean the end of your career.'

'Ah, I see. We're back to the congress in Heidelberg, are we? Well, give me your opinion, Elena. What should I do? I can't leave the clinic. Not during the shakedown phase.'

'But it's only for two days! You really must make an appearance once in a while.'

'Make an appearance? I'm not a rock star, Elena. Why do I have to make an appearance?'

He almost felt sorry for her. It was so transparent! Heidelberg . . . the rarefied atmosphere of the Auditorium Maximum, followed by a stroll through the Old Town, the Brunnengasse, the glove museum, lots of good wine in a wood-panelled, smoky *Stube*, a nice conference hotel, perhaps a pension in the Odenwald – it was very easy to see how she had envisaged the weekend. He was almost touched at the way she had set up the snares. But that aside, what benefit could be derived from such a congress? 'Professional status, social standing,' – what nonsense!

What remains when the dust has settled on the rhetoric, when the speeches and the committee meetings are finished? New insights? No. More likely the usual theoretical gobbledygook '. . . and so we hope that when we next meet we shall be able to submit statistically relevant material which will substantiate the importance of our hypotheses . . .' And the next meeting would be in Hamburg or Amsterdam or Lugano or Copenhagen.

Congresses! He kept abreast of the latest findings on cancer by reading all the national and international publications, scanning them avidly for methods he could implement. His own technique could only be improved by practice, by visiting other clinics, attending meetings and lectures in operating theatres everywhere. Observing other people's methods and, where necessary, correcting his own. That was what he called progress. They all did. Elena knew that: he'd said it to her a hundred times. Yet still she tried it on with that 'social standing' routine!

'Come on, Elena, be frank with me, what's this all about? You and I are talking about different things. What you want is to sit with me in some student pub, candle on the table, a good Pfälzer wine in our glasses, and then . . .'

He left it open, but he saw it had hit her harder than he had intended. Her face was blank, devoid of any expression.

'You only ever think about me in one way, don't you? Everything reduced to that level, right?' She was smiling again, but now it was like someone smiling down a gunsight.

'Oh, come on, Elena!'

He took a swipe at one of the wasps buzzing around the table, and Elena felt a stab of sympathetic pain. The same thing is happening to you! You're being waved away like some irksome insect! She closed her eyes. What was there to say? Maybe she should scream. She felt like it. She felt like screaming 'Do you really know what love is? Do you really think it ends, just like that?'

No, time had worn the word 'love' thin. Face the facts, she told herself. If you thought about it, they were all the same: the yearning to reach for the stars, the passion and abandon dwindling into talking shop, bored understanding, evenings spent in hobby classes or at parents' evenings on school committees, flights to Tenerife or discussions with a tax consultant on the subject of joint or separate assessment. Compared to that, Elena thought, we still have more than most: at least there's still some drama.

But today, with people on the benches all around them, was not the right time to do anything about it. Brinkmann sat there, smiling, looking older and more lined. There was no doubt about it, the last few weeks had taken their toll: new wrinkles in his face, the tear ducts slightly swollen – and yet the man was still so damnably contented!

She followed Brinkmann's glance. Two girls stood in the parking lot, both blonde: one was slim, the other shorter and plumper. They looked across and said hello.

'Who are they?'

'Couple of nurses from the clinic.' He leaned forward to take Elena's hand, but she snatched it away.

'Try to understand, Elena,' he said.

She shook her head. 'I don't have to. And I don't think I want to. Come on, take me back to my car. I'd like to get back to Karlsruhe.'

He did not speak. There was nothing to say, and yet so much. He wanted to tell her that she should try to see the world through her own eyes, find her own way to handle life, and trust herself. I suppose you'd call it 'cutting the umbilical cord'. Not the right context, but it was apt enough. But he did not say anything, because to say it would have sounded as if he was mocking a woman who had set so much store by her emancipation and had always talked in terms of personal freedom.

Five minutes later, as Brinkmann drove the Mercedes past the rows of parked cars to the car park exit, the old mixture of uneasiness and remorse swept over him: were you cruel? No, he decided, looking at it from a therapeutic point of view; he had not been. As soon as you get a chance you will talk to her. And you can rest assured Elena will see to it that an opportunity arises very soon.

He hit the brakes rather harder than he had intended. Standing there, legs apart, not ten metres away, the light hair, the long slim legs in jeans! My God, what legs! It could only be . . . He let down the window and leaned out.

'Hello, Christa . . .'

She turned, taking off her sunglasses, and came over, light-footed, as relaxed as a cat. How a nurse's cap can change a face, and a white coat conceal a figure! Even as the thought occurred to him he wondered why of all days he should be so pleased to see her today. Perhaps this meeting had some symbolic value but, if so, what?

'I thought I saw two of you earlier?'

'Yes, Elke just went to spend a penny.'

Brinkmann grinned. 'My friend too. It's nice up here, isn't it?'

'It certainly is!'

An embarrassed expression, awkward banter. Pity.

'Would you like a lift?'

'Oh, yes, but . . . what about Elke?'

'Her, too, of course. Ah, here they both come.'

They got into the car. Elena acknowledged the introductions with distanced friendliness. She sat in the front, next to him. She said not a word all the way down. Every now and then Brinkmann met Christa's eyes in the driving mirror.

FOURTEEN

The vanity case with the red-leather lettering had been bought in the boutique of the Pump Room at Baden-Baden. It looked almost exotic against the white tiles. Melanie Wieck remembered the day it had been given to her as a present. Don't think about it. Or Baden-Baden. And more than anything, not about him.

She pushed the pink foamy bar of soap across the water with the tips of her fingers: how lovely it was to sit in the bath, to close your eyes, to smell the perfume, feel the smoothness of your body!

She sat up, examined her nails and decided that today she would paint them. Starting all over again, how simple it sounds. And at the same time, how pathetic . . . There were some things that didn't wash away quite so easily. What had happened couldn't just be stored away like a pair of crutches. Nevertheless, the decision to erase the last few months 'from the book of life' helped, even if those words were not her own.

'Believe me, I got these wrinkles the hard way.' She saw the pensive face, heard the professor's voice. 'In the process of learning what I'm now telling you, child. It only takes a few years for a defeat we think we'll never survive to become something we smile at. That will happen to you, too, Melanie. There are few real tragedies in life, thank God.'

Tragedy? A silly comedy, more like it. Like trying to commit suicide with a handful of candy. And yet: hadn't she had the feeling she had really died? No, it wasn't a comedy. It was a farce. And you the clown.

Forgotten! Erased!

She got up. The room swayed a little, but her legs held. And that was what really mattered. She wouldn't just make herself look nice, she would even read Stefan's letter again. Insolence can sometimes be salutary. *Listen, Puschy,* he had written. *Didn't I always tell you that every cloud has a silver lining, but that it was smart to stay away from old men? And now, where has it got you? Never mind, I'll get you out of there. Next week I'm going to take a couple of days off. If you're still locked up in that clinic, I'll come and cut a hole in the wall . . .*

Typical! Stefan was always a bit arrogant. Even in his letters. But it made her feel good.

She fastened the belt of her dressing gown and took a last look in the mirror. There were days when she would not have recognised herself, but this was not one of them. It was her, Melanie, the girl who couldn't even stage a decent suicide!

She pulled faces at her reflection, went to the door and opened it, nearly colliding with another patient, a woman with a pale, round face. She wore a pink coat embroidered with flowers. And two blue eyes which were quizzical only for a second. Then they became very friendly.

'Good Heavens, it's Miss Wieck! How nice to see you!'

The voice was soft, the smile warm. Still, Melanie had the feeling that her heart was going to stop beating. She braced herself against the frame of the door, too confused to say even a single word.

'Here are your crutches. That will make it easier, won't it?'

She's even passing me my crutches!, Melanie thought, not sure what she meant by 'even'.

'I hope I didn't startle you, Melanie. Look, I don't want you to misunderstand my motives, but I'd like to talk to you.'

Melanie managed to nod weakly.

'It's too far to go to my ward. Let's go and sit in the conservatory.

I could do with a glass of wine. I'm sure that nice little Italian girl, Pepina, will get us a bottle.'

They sat in cane seats beneath plastic papyrus and genuine rubber tree plants, glasses of shimmering red Offenburger wine in front of them. Confusion raged on inside Melanie's head. Explanations, words, half-formed sentences raced around in her brain, but . . . she could not say a thing.

Maria Fitz, hands folded across her stomach, watched her benevolently, and her look finally made Melanie angry enough to burst out: 'Do you think we ought to be sitting here together like this? Is this necessary?'

'Necessary? No, of course not. But I think it's right.'

'But . . . you knew nothing about – Klaus and I?'

'No.'

'So what do you want now?'

'What do I want?' Maria Fitz leaned forward. 'I'd like it if we could become friends, or at least something approaching friends. Funny, I tried before to become your friend. It was just a coincidence, Melanie. I wanted to take care of you because I liked you. Now, the way things have turned out, I think we could both do with a little understanding, don't you agree?'

Understanding!, Melanie thought. As if what had happened could be taken apart with words and put together anew. As if one case could be compared to another. So many loves, so many deaths. She had read that somewhere. And it was true: first, the excitement which asked for nothing. Then reality, monotony, worse than death. And the children always in the middle, pushed back and forth like pieces of furniture. It had happened to her when her parents got divorced. What did Maria Fitz expect would happen? Couldn't she draw the right conclusion? Of course, there was Klaus's 'position' to think of. What would his superiors say? And what about the posh house on Heuss Street? No, some people can't afford scandals, so they stick it out together.

'Will this be your first child?' Melanie heard herself asking. Maria Fitz nodded. Her smile softened her slightly bloated face so that she looked almost beautiful. 'Yes, it is the first. It is also the deciding factor. Do you understand what I mean?'

Melanie shook her head.

'We've come a long way together, Klaus and I. You don't have to tell me anything, Melanie. I know how he is. But the child makes all the difference.'

Melanie sipped some wine. 'A long way together . . .' It didn't even hurt any more. 'And if a husband has stuck it out for so long, he needs an occasional fling, something to keep him going. Is that what you're saying?'

'Perhaps. Perhaps you could put it like that. But you mustn't feel hurt by it.'

'I'm not. Not any more.'

'I'm glad, Melanie. I really am. You see, that's the way he is. And there will be . . . other affairs like this.'

'Then why do you stay with him. Is it only the child?'

The smile in Maria Fitz's eyes disappeared. 'Frankly, no. Believe me, Melanie, he can be quite different. You know that as well as anyone. So nice that even a pretty young girl like you can fall in love with him.'

'It's hard even to imagine that now.'

'That's all part of what I'm saying . . .' Maria Fitz was smiling again. 'You see, Melanie, in a long marriage you don't love a man "because" but "in spite of". I have my faults, too, but Klaus puts up with them. So when you add it all up we come out even. Now more than ever before. Now we both have something we can look forward to, something that will last. Our child. That's the way it is.'

Melanie was silent. For a few heartbeats she felt the old desperate despair rising inside her, that feeling she knew so well, that she had so often had to endure, a feeling like a wave, ready to overpower and devour her. *I will get you out . . . even if I have to cut a hole in the wall!* The phrase from Stefan's letter came back to her. Yesterday, his arrogant idiocy had merely amused her. Today, she felt a sense of liberation. She looked at her glass and smiled. This time the smile reached her eyes.

'You know something, Maria?' she said. 'You're a very special person. I admire you. And . . . what you said before . . . about us being friends? I'd like that. I'd be very proud to be your friend.'

FIFTEEN

'Oooohh . . . uunnnhhh . . . aaaaahhh!'

The pinkish fat on the gigantic hams quivered. A pleading, sweating face came up like a moon above the mountain of its belly. Udo dropped the needle into a dish. Three more stitches and it would be done, but even though the man couldn't feel a thing – Udo had pumped him full of painkiller – the great blubbering hippopotamus had to whimper and moan like a baby.

'All right, that's enough moaning and groaning for a while,' he said, briskly. He reached for the syringe and pressed the blunt end against the man's ankle. 'Sharp end or blunt?'

'What? What do you mean?'

'Can you feel anything? This? Tell me what you feel.' He turned the syringe around and pressed the sharp end lightly against the skin. 'Sharp or blunt?'

'I can't feel a thing.'

Dr Renz, fists thrust into the pockets of his white coat, grinned at Udo, but Udo didn't think it was funny. 'Why the hell are you making so much noise, then?'

'It's just, well, I'm very sensitive to pain.'

'Sensitive, is it?' Udo said, with a grimace at the mountain of lard in front of him. He picked up the needle. They were all sensitive. How many did he have today? The holidays had begun, and what the publicans referred to as 'seasonal trade' brought in the victims: they had slipped on a path in the woods, or banged their noses on the edge of the pool, or got the usual cuts and bruises in a brawl at a disco. This morning it had been an old-age pensioner who'd split her own shinbone with a hoe. And now this great crybaby, who'd managed to cut himself on the beer bottle he'd broken while he was drunk. Udo tied off the last stitches, swabbed them with antiseptic, and straightened up. His back was aching.

'Give your personal details to the nurse.' At the doorway he stopped. 'Just in case. I want to be sure I'm off duty when you come back.'

Four o'clock. The sun was still strong. Another two hours and he would be off duty. What he really badly needed was a shower, but there was no time for anything. Renz appeared.

'How about a glass of beer?'

Udo shook his head. 'I don't dare. It would send me to sleep. Thanks all the same.'

They sat down on a bench by the ivy-covered nursery wall. From here he could watch the casualty entrance: he would know if someone had been brought in before the first-aid team called for him. He gave a tired groan, stretched out his legs, crossed his hands behind his head, and closed his eyes.

'Man, you wouldn't believe how pissed off I am.'

'Working too hard,' said Walter Renz sympathetically.

'No, it's not that. Anything but.'

'What, then?'

'Do you need to ask? It's everything, the atmosphere in this place since . . .'

'Since your old man took over?' Walter Renz looked at his neighbour, his expression concerned.

'Right, Walter. Right on the button. It's just too damned heavy. I'm off, Walter. I mean it. I can't cope with this.'

'Oedipus complex. A lot of it about.'

'Call it what you like, my amateur psychologist friend.'

'So you're off. And where are you planning to go, may I ask? Haven't you heard there's a glut of doctors in Germany?'

'I'll find something somewhere.'

'You don't really believe that, do you? Do you know how many hopeful talents like yourself become taxi drivers instead of specialists? Would you like the latest statistics? Twenty-two per cent! Be sensible, man! You've got an excellent job here. The best. Yet you and your father fight like cat and dog. What's wrong with you?'

Udo sighed. Good question. An excellent job? Well, yes, the Black Forest Clinic and its darling occupants were very successful. So what was it? What could he tell kind, appreciative, willing Walter Renz that he would understand?

'Think before you jump, Udo. You could be making a big mistake. For both of you.'

'Both?' Udo snapped. 'There's only one person that counts – him!'

'Well,' Renz said. 'He's the boss, after all.'

Udo was silent for a moment. 'If you'd known my mother, maybe you'd understand it better.'

'Perhaps. But your mother's dead, Udo. She has been for a long time. Which means we're dealing with some childhood hang-up, by the look of it.'

'There could be something in what you say, Walter. You have known Kate for a while. You know how hard she tried to be a replacement mother to me. Without her, I would never have finished medical school. What am I saying, finish? I'd have thrown in the towel and run away.'

'But Kate was there, and you didn't. And in the end, you have to thank your father for that.'

'True. I want to be fair. And speaking objectively, what you say is true. He always had a lot on his plate. And then, surgery, it's not like other jobs. Surgeons . . .'

'Are a race apart,' Renz smiled. 'Look at us.'

Udo went on as if he had not heard him. '. . . Constant stress, operations, further education, university, congresses. And then the appointments in Paris and Zürich . . .'

'But you were already a student yourself by then.'

'Yes, but I'm talking about before that, when I was a little boy. Do you know what it's like when all you see is some well-dressed

87

gentleman popping in and out of your life, someone who's always rushing, who never has time for you? But you want a father like all the other kids, even if only to show him off. Only he never has time. And sometimes the door of your room opens and someone is standing there, but you close your eyes and pretend to be asleep. You get a kiss on the forehead, or some money because he promised to take you to the circus and then couldn't, because of work. That's how it was.'

'You're not the only one, you know. We all have something. My parents quarrelled all the time. Which is worse?'

Udo nodded: we know the disease, Doctor, but what's the cure? 'Anyway, for one reason or another, my father was always too busy to have time for me. And not only in the operating theatre.'

'Women?'

'Of course, women, what did you think I meant? You saw his latest: she was here only last Sunday.'

'The anaesthetist from Karlsruhe?'

'He carried that cross for five years. She could have been lifted from an ad in a medical journal: university graduate without ties seeks happy second marriage. Can satisfy high expectations but also expects high standards.'

'You're pretty hard on her.'

Udo did not reply. He watched the nurses crossing from the main building to the commissary, laughing and joking. One of them was Elke, tossing a tennis ball from hand to hand. He felt tired and run down. Everything, the girls, this attractive, well-run clinic in the Black Forest, seemed to him like some old picture postcard you pick up, look at, and put aside with nostalgic regret.

'By the way,' Renz said, 'you shouldn't jump to the conclusion that the professor's interests are so limited.'

His tone jarred Udo out of his reverie. 'What does that mean?'

Walter Renz shook his head and grinned.

'Come on, fellow, spit it out!'

'Okay. That business with Nurse Christa . . . it's probably nothing.'

'What are you trying to tell me?' Udo said through tight lips.

'Don't look at me like that. As I said, there's probably nothing to it.'

'Nothing to what, damn it? Would you be kind enough to tell me exactly what you're talking about?'

'If you like. I was up on the Horningsgrinde on Sunday. Remember, I asked you to come but you said no.'

'Yes, yes. And?'

'And? And in the parking lot up there was a beautiful, silver-grey Mercedes, and next to the Mercedes was a gentleman with beautiful grey temples deep in conversation with a young lady. Then he opened the door of the car and the young lady got in. I'll give you three guesses who she was.'

Udo's stare was so intense that Walter Renz became uneasy.

'Look, it was probably completely innocent. I'm not even certain they were alone. I saw Elke up there as well.'

But Udo was not listening. The shock that had robbed him of thought was gone, and now his mind was in turmoil. So that was it! That was the reason for the business in the corridor when he'd bumped into Christa! That was why there'd been so much drama over his alleged failure in the Wieck case! And that was why Christa made such a show of refusing to patch things up between them! Doctors are doctors and nurses are nurses, she'd said. What about nurses and heads of clinic, though? A man old enough to be her father, that was different, was it?

Christa! He would have believed it of anyone but her. She had always been so introverted, so wrapped up in her own world, whatever kind of world it was to make her quit her studies. A world full of ambition and secret dreams. And perhaps those dreams were about *him*, the supergod who alone decided what was right and what was wrong, who simply took what he wanted, as if the whole world was a supermarket that belonged to him alone!

SIXTEEN

No matter how hard she tried Waltraut Stamer couldn't get the picture out of her mind. Sitting in the glass cubicle which was her office she saw again the four men in dark suits on the stairs to the basement. Outside, a long, black car waiting, tailgate open. The coffin arriving on a trolley on the ramp, and then sliding in on the car's rails. The door closing as they left to go to the church . . .

She sighed. The name on the printed ward report was Beck, Gerda. Born 22.02.46, died 07.07 at 12.30. She heaved another silent sigh and began processing the data into the computer. Gerda Beck. Her husband worked at the sawmill, didn't he? A thickset blond man, always so agitated and angry.

Another report. Maternity ward this time, thank God.

Fitz, Maria. A child: female, born at 10.22. Name, Ursula Maria. Complications, none.

So it goes, Waltraut Stamer thought. One arrives, another departs. It makes you think. That poor Mrs Beck. 'For whomsoever wisheth to understand death must feel sheltered by the love of

God,' the priest had intoned. Sure, she thought, but sometimes you don't feel so sheltered.

The telephone rang. Surgery: it was Dr Renz.

'Have you seen the professor anywhere?'

'No.'

'But he must have gone through the hall!'

'Have you tried paging him?'

'Of course.'

'And?'

He banged down the phone, but not before she heard him say, 'Shit!' There must be something happening in surgery.

And the professor? Why did they need him? And where was he, anyway?

As Brinkmann got out of the car, Mollie started barking furiously, announcing that she had seen, or thought she'd seen, a cat.

'Shut up! You want people to think you're barmy?' Brinkmann dragged the panting, half-strangled mongrel into the air-conditioned establishment above whose doors was the sign *Schipfel Brothers – Newspapers, Books, Tobacco Specialities and Smoking Accessories.*

And there were the specialities, lined up in rows behind shining glass doors. Pipes in every shade: brown, red, and black, the wood patterned like streaked flame, others of Meerschaum or Bruyère; pipes from every province, and from all over the world.

One of the brothers Schipfel, a small, fat man with the rosebud lips of a baby, came across, smiling.

'You know, I love pipes,' Brinkmann said to him. 'I used to smoke a pipe, but gave up a long time ago. Now I'm back to the damned weeds again!'

'But of course, of course.'

'Perhaps it's because of the workload.' Brinkmann yanked on Mollie's lead. 'Stay put! My work, you see . . . no, how could you. Well, let's have a look at what you've got.'

He had no sooner picked up the first pipe, caressing the smooth wood, when he heard a friendly voice behind him. He turned. Clear, grey-green eyes. A well-formed mouth, smiling. Christa, the girl about whom he spent so much time thinking without ever knowing why.

'Ah, I've been caught,' he smiled.

'How do you mean?'

'Well, Nurse Christa, I'd sort of hoped I could buy this pipe incognito. You see, I've fallen into the tobacco trap again, and a man like me, vain through and through, prefers not to admit defeat in front of witnesses.'

She laughed. 'Don't worry, Professor, your secret is safe with me.' She turned to go, then stopped, touching his breast pocket. 'Excuse me, Professor, but I think you're wanted. Can't you hear the bleeper? They want you at the clinic.'

He heard it now. What could have so distracted him? Mollie? Or this girl: that smile, those eyes?

'You see, Shipfel, it's not just Mollie who's on a leash. Can I use your telephone? I'm afraid I'll have to come back some other time.'

'Over there, Professor.'

Concentration and concern replaced Brinkmann's smile as soon as he was connected to the clinic.

'I'll be right there,' he said, crisply. 'Five minutes at the outside.'

Dr Schaefer stood leaning against the enormous opaque glass wall in Operating Theatre No. 11. He had taken off his mask and was breathing slowly and regularly to calm himself. It wasn't easy: he could still hear the child's screams of pain, still see her grotesquely bloated body, the terrified eyes in the pallid, wasted face.

Brinkmann had said five minutes. Where the hell was he?

Acute abdominal cases were the surgeon's nightmare: the first instinct was to run. By the same token, they sometimes came as a challenge, testing an experienced surgeon to the limit of his ability. For Hermann Schaefer, however . . .

What a trick Fate had played here! Of all the children in the world, it had had to be poor little Monica!

The most important factor in such an operation was always the surgeon's detachment, a calmness only possible when all personal considerations are set aside. For that reason, most surgeons refuse to operate on anyone close to them. Dr Schaefer had always thought this attitude difficult to understand; always felt that no matter who was on the table he would remain dispassionate. But now he understood: the twelve-year-old girl, already anaesthetised and awaiting surgery, was very dear to him.

He flexed his fingers. When the stomach is as hard as a board, the likelihood of internal haemorrhage cannot be discounted. If Brinkmann didn't get here soon, he'd have to begin the laparotomy. He knew the others were thinking the same thing, and wondering whether he could cope . . .

He looked across at Renz, standing with both arms crossed over his stomach, a posture common to waiting surgeons the world over. He was lucky to have Renz assisting: he had strong nerves and, although he only had a few years' experience of general surgery, he was very confident. Schaefer knew he could rely on Wolters, the anaesthetist, too. As for Ella, the instrument sister, little Irmi, the theatre sister, and the nurse . . . He had trained them all himself. They were ready.

Except for one man.

He looked over at Monica again, her face covered by the black, airtight, anaesthetic mask. Her breathing was quiet and regular. A mixture of gases was flowing through the tube inserted into her trachea, but the breathing was natural and spontaneous. The airbag inflated and deflated in time with the movements of her chest, accompanied by the light flashes and metallic ticks of the pulse monitor.

Ten-past six! And still no sign of anyone through the wide inspection window in the door between the operating theatre and the anteroom. Brinkmann had said he was on his way. God in Heaven, how long five minutes could seem!

He looked at his watch. Sister Ella was checking the instruments and dishes for the third time. 6.14!

What was making old Schaefer so edgy?, Walter Renz wondered. The old man *would* come, *had* to come.

Of course, there was always the chance of complications with a case like this: at worst, some blockage in the bowel, or perhaps there was bleeding in the peritoneal cavity. The X-rays did not give a clear-cut picture. For that reason Schaefer would have to begin. What was making him wait? It wasn't his usual style at all. With all his experience in abdominal surgery, why had he called for the old man? He looked up: Schaefer was putting on his mask. So, he was going to get started . . .

Walter Renz was just about to take his place when he saw a movement through the inspection panel and raised a hand.

'Hold it, Dr Schaefer. I think he's here.'

Schaefer turned. Behind the panel, Brinkmann lifted a hand, smiling, his face pale in the glare of the lights. Moments later, the ritual of scrubbing up completed, he came through the door. He already had his gown on. He was still smiling as the sister helped him with the gloves. He radiated authoritarian composure, dissipating all their nervousness and tension. Walter Renz recalled hearing the nickname which the doctors and staff in Basle had given Brinkmann: 'The King'. A bit over the top, but probably justified.

Brinkmann raised a hand. 'Right!'

Schaefer pointed to the X-rays, briefing Brinkmann with a rapidly-spoken summation: diagnosis, acute appendicitis. Despite an appendectomy a year earlier at Landsberg, constant flare-ups. No gynaecological findings. Onset of fever yesterday, rectal temperature 37.8°, severe pains in the abdomen followed by colic, abdominal rigidity and breathing problems. The GP had given her antibiotics. They had no effect on the pain.

Brinkmann pondered. It was the old story: an earlier, botched-up operation resulting in a botched-up patient requiring a further operation for which there was not the slightest guarantee of success. As far as diagnosis was concerned, the facts Schaefer had just rattled off wouldn't help much, except to emphasise the fact that something had to be done, and fast. You had no choice. Even more detailed X-rays would be no help.

'Everything ready?' It was a routine question to the team. It gave Brinkmann a moment more to let his brain sort through his experience like a computer, evaluating what he had learned in similar situations. Meanwhile he probed with gentle fingers the contours of the arched, hard stomach.

Increased sounds in the bowels, Schaefer had said. Some sort of obstruction; the bowels were fighting it. On top of that the spreading infection from the primary focus, hence the temperature. The X-rays showed a darkened abdomen, which meant fluid was collecting. Perhaps an adhesion after the previous appendectomy which was strangling the bowel? Or perhaps, in spite of the fact that the gynaecological tests revealed nothing, an inflammation of the ovaries? Perhaps even a torsion of pedicle . . . The patient was a little young for that. A little. But even so? It was like groping about in the dark. Well, then. A decision.

'Cut,' said Brinkmann.

A surgical scalpel is very, very sharp. The one which Brinkmann used was straight from the freezer: frozen scalpels cut even finer.

Brinkmann began his incision at the right side of the navel. The first drops of blood appeared. He continued vertically downwards, the classical right paramedian incision. In a series of almost subconscious movements he cut the fat down to the stomach muscles, his mind still wrestling with the uncertainty that would not leave him. A tumour, perhaps? Why not? Cancer at the head of the colon: hadn't he seen that in young people?

The first small quantity of blood from the fat. 'Swabs!' The routine movements grew faster. No stopping! The bleeding would be stemmed when the bowel-crushing clamp was inserted.

The diathermy tweezers which would seal the vessels while the stomach muscles were being parted were making a low, hissing sound. He met Schaefer's eyes again. What was the matter with him? Schaefer was not on form today, he'd seen that the moment he took his place across the table on the left-hand side, the place of the principal assistant. He seemed to hesitate like a beginner while they were jointly tackling the stomach muscles. But Renz, on his right, was quick. He was already holding the peritoneum apart with the blunt Roux hooks, revealing a bluish tissue, the last curtain veiling the secret of this illness.

'Lift it carefully,' he said, pulling up the delicate tissue with the surgical tweezer.

'Secure.'

So far, good. Schaefer's tweezers held it now as well. Now make the cut, which must only be large enough to allow two fingers through, ensuring that the bowel would not be damaged. The knife cut between the two fingers. A little fluid emerging from the abdominal cavity, but no pus. Brinkmann enlarged the cut and there it was: the small intestine, dull and sickly, the loops deformed and stuck together.

'Stomach cloth!'

The thirty-by-thirty-centimetre piece of muslin now being secured with clamps along the opening was like a backcloth for a stage, highlighting the 'drama taking place. The prongs of the abdominal retractors were also in place.

'The patient is straining,' he said, reproach in his voice.

'I'm giving her more Succinyl,' the anaesthetist replied. Wolters had measured the muscle relaxant very carefully. It was a derivative of curare, the Indian dart poison which could cause total paralysis. After years of work in the research labs, those alchemists' kitchens of modern pharmaceuticals, it had been transformed into an indispensable tool of modern surgery and a true blessing.

The Succinyl worked at once, and the muscle spasms abated. Dr Wolters reported that blood pressure was normal. Brinkmann worked on. The reports of the anaesthetist were as much a part of the sounds accompanying the operations as the metronomically precise ticker of the pulse control. The heart seemed to be fine.

'Oh, shit!' Renz snapped. Schaefer, too, muttered something but it was inaudible. Brinkmann merely nodded. So that was it: the walls of the small intestine were inflamed and thickened all over. The same in the region of the mesentery: callous and covered with infiltrates. Everywhere adhesions, against which the little body had been fighting for months.

'Look, Schaefer! It goes all the way down to the uterus. We may have to remove the entire ileum.'

Schaefer said nothing.

Brinkmann extended a hand: he did not need to say the word 'scissors'. The sister seemed to read his thoughts, paused with him when he took decisions, but made the right choice simultaneously. A veritable gift from God, such a woman! When he had left Karlsruhe, Brinkmann had considered taking his regular operating sister with him. His symbiosis with Barbara had become so much a part of his own confidence that he could not imagine working without her. But he had decided against it. If he was going to start over again, he was going to do so from scratch.

He gave Sister Ella a grateful wink. Perhaps she didn't have Barbara's ability or speed, but she made up for that by working with even more care.

'Thank you, Sister.'

So, what needed to be done was clear, at least so far: adhesions, infiltrates, thickening – even of the large omentum – caused by a botched appendectomy done by one of those 'it's not half as bad as it looks' merchants. He would have to remove a large part of the small intestine. There was no other solution.

'Ileum resection.'

He got no more than a slight nod from Schaefer. Brinkmann started to loosen the infected intestine. How it happened, which part of the fragile tissue suddenly ruptured, he could not say, even much later. It started undramatically enough: a slight trickle of blood that could have come from an adhesion which had opened unnoticed. But then the trickle became a river out of which suddenly rose a tiny, terrible, pulsating jet that covered the field of operation in blood.

'Swabs!'

His voice was flat, totally under control, as were the hands probing to locate the cause of the haemorrhage. The swabs had no effect.

'Suction, for Christ's sake!' he snapped. You could have spared them the curse, he thought. And what the devil was Schaefer poking about for? I can't see anything, and I have to, everything depends on it.

'Suction!'

He held the clamps holding the blood vessels in an attempt to stanch the bleeding. But where? – Then finally he saw it: a rupture in the intestine, five or six centimetres long, epithelial structures which had crumbled like an old brick wall. The patient was fortunate it had happened here. If it had happened while she was at home . . . well, that didn't bear thinking about.

'Blood pressure dropping!' Walters called. Well, that was no surprise. Now he had the offending part. His hands worked as though of their own volition, as relaxed as if he was sleepwalking. New swabs were handed to him and more, and then finally he did not need them any more.

'Blood pressure stabilising.'

Brinkmann straightened up. He saw Schaefer's mask puff out as he released a sigh of relief. He saw them all looking at him, saw how Schaefer nodded, confident again.

'Well, that takes care of that. Let's proceed, gentlemen!'

SEVENTEEN

Udo closed his eyes, letting Leonard Cohen's guitar carry him away as it took over the theme, transposing it to that bittersweet melancholy that so matched his own mood: *I came a stranger* . . .

Oh, to be able to sing like that, he thought, to be able to create poetry as Cohen did, to set yourself free by means of music, never having to be anyone's assistant, never having to be a slave to someone who tries to put you down every chance he gets yet still expects to be called Father!

The sepia shadows disappeared into the corners of the room. Leonard Cohen sang on. Udo folded his hands behind his head and watched the illuminated dials of the stereo flickering. The lament ended. At the same time a bad-tempered Kate Marek opened the door and glared disapprovingly at Udo.

'Now listen here!' she said, marching into the middle of the room. 'What's all this about, this lying around, music on full blast, refusing to eat?'

Udo got up and turned off the stereo. 'Just what I need,' he said, sourly.

'I certainly am. Just look at this room. It looks like –'

'Me!' he said, defiantly. 'Like Udo!'

'Exactly like you.'

'What do you want in here, anyway?'

'What do I want? The food is on the table. You don't even answer the telephone. I've been yelling my head off.'

'And suppose I don't feel hungry, my dearest?'

'You feel hungry. I know you. And you'll feel hungrier when I tell you we're having trout and salad followed by baked bananas and cream. Am I right?'

He sat silently, rubbing his hands together as she bustled about, picking up the newspapers scattered on the carpet.

'Why do you have to leave everything lying about?' she began, then stopped as her eyes fell on the advertisements Udo had ringed with a red felt tip. 'Two-room apartment, Lärchengasse,' she read. 'Fine views . . . Available now: three bachelor apartments on the Neusteig estate . . .' She looked up. 'What's all this?'

'You really want to know, Kate?'

'Yes, I want to know.'

He sat down on the carpet next to her. 'Kate, has it never entered your head that it could become too claustrophobic for me to live here?'

'Claustrophobic?' She looked around the big room. 'You're really looking for a flat?'

'Yes, I really am. And when I say "claustrophobic" I mean the atmosphere, not the actual space.'

She regarded him levelly. Then she shook her head, crumpling up the newspaper with the ads in it and throwing it into the wastepaper basket.

'I'd say it takes two to create an atmosphere, wouldn't you?'

'Of course. So tell me what I'm doing wrong?'

'You've got the nerve to ask that? Come on, Udo, you don't have to needle all the time. You could occasionally make the first move. He finds it very difficult, you know.'

'But the way things are for me, the way I –' He stopped himself, and her heart went out to him. She knew that look. No matter how he covered it up with a grin, his eyes said something else. Help me! It was written all over him. She'd seen it many times, that look. Like when he had suddenly lost his mother. She knew the way he

99

felt, and she had always tried as hard as she could to understand him and to act accordingly. But his wanting to leave home and live in a flat . . . she couldn't understand that at all.

'I just don't understand you.'

'You've got eyes, Kate. You can see how he barely tolerates me. You must know. And you don't know what goes on at the clinic. What it's like to work with him.'

'I'd rather formed the opinion that professionally speaking he was —'

'Kate, let's leave it. I know what they say: a doctor has to get experience. Anyone who has to learn has to do it the hard way.' He gave a bitter little laugh. 'That's one way of doing it. Shall I tell you something. A nice little story about a girl called Christa . . . ?'

'I don't like the way it begins. And in addition, I know the Christa concerned.'

'Then you know that this Christa was seeing a young man named Udo . . .'

'I told you, I don't want to hear this. Particularly because you're being so imprecise. The fact of the matter is that Christa was *one* of the girls this young man Udo was seeing, isn't that more like it? All right, go on, tell me the rest.'

'Maybe you ought to ask him.'

'I haven't the faintest idea what you're talking about.'

Udo got up, went over to the window, and looked out at the soft contours of the valley, bathed in the red-gold evening light, gold flowing into purple, so beautiful it seemed almost unreal. What should he tell the old lady? That he loved her? That he had always thought she would back him up? No, there was only one answer: move out, leave, cut the knot as with a scalpel.

'Udo, tell me, what's wrong?'

He shrugged. 'I told you, ask him. I know what I'm going to do. I'm going to find an apartment, and with any luck it will be a few hundred miles away from here.'

'Udo!' He heard her come across the room to stand behind him. She put her arm around his shoulders. 'Udo, be sensible.'

Her voice was soft and warm. It was the way she had talked to him when he was small. The little-Udo voice.

'You just tell him what I said,' he repeated, and was unable to prevent himself from blurting out the next sentence. 'Of all people why does it have to be with her?'

'With Christa? That's nonsense!'

'Nonsense? They were seen on the Horningsgrinde. Oh, it could be a coincidence, I suppose. But the way he takes her part, the way he treats me where she's concerned, that's no coincidence.'

'That's nonsense, too, utter nonsense. And you know it. Come on now, Udo . . .'

But he remained where he was.

She had never before felt so helpless.

In Operating Theatre No. 11, Klaus Brinkmann glanced at the white clock dial on the wall: the operation had lasted eighty minutes. Considering all the complications they had encountered that was not too bad. His back ached. After an eighty-minute stretch, the back seized up: he could set his watch by it.

He worked his shoulders up and down to loosen them. The main work was done. The affected parts of the intestine had been removed, the stitches which held the new joint together were in place. The bleeding had stopped. The stomach cavity had been disinfected and a drain inserted to keep the wound clean.

The tension abated. The little one would pull through, no doubt of it. But those infiltrates were as hard as gristle! What on earth had that butcher done to her?

He nodded to Renz. The assistant already had the needle with the Synthofil thread in his hand, ready to close up the peritoneum. They had used two litres of blood. That was within the accepted norm. Brinkmann glanced towards the end of the table. He could see only a few strands of shimmering hair, a slender neck, the mask.

Dr Schaefer was the first to notice the change in the metallic ping of the pulse monitor. Brinkmann looked up sharply, his gaze rivetted to the dials and curves of the circulation monitor.

'Christ, she isn't going to –'

'Cardiac arrest!' Wolters shouted.

For a moment it was as if the world had stopped. Brinkmann could see Sister Ella, her hand holding the needle-holder; Schaefer's wide eyes; Renz bending forward. Fixed, like a freeze-frame image.

'Oxygen!' Brinkmann snapped, although he knew it was

unnecessary: the computer-automat of the anaesthesia unit would have already have switched to 'resuscitation'. God damn it! Just as they were about to congratulate themselves on the successful conclusion of eighty minutes of merciless mental and physical effort, this! He went around the table fast, stared at Renz, pointed with his chin at the wound. Renz immediately closed it with cloth clamps.

Brinkmann leaned over the small body. He put both hands on the chest. Inoperative cardiac arrest! God in Heaven, how many times in the last ten years? Three. And it had to happen to this poor kid.

He began massaging, felt the elastic resistance, continued to press with both hands, strongly, as if to push the chest down to the spine: ninety times a minute. The strength used with each pressure has to be gauged so that no ribs are damaged, that the new sutures are not affected, yet be enough to make the heart begin beating! The effort banished the pallor from Brinkmann's face.

Ninety times! Sweat ran down his back. Now he was glad he did those press-ups in his morning workout. Up, down, up down! He closed his eyes, feeling the lifeless body beneath his hands and trying to transfer his reflex mechanism into it: up, down, up, down, and on each 'down' trying to provide the pressure which drives the bloodstream to the extremities of the body and, most importantly, to the brain.

The first minute gone.

Then the second.

Carry on. Don't give up.

The third . . .

The heart has got to respond! Let it start . . . 'Artherenol!' he panted. The brain had enough oxygen. The heart stimulant would set off the longed-for ignition. From the corner of his eyes he saw Renz sink the cannula between the ribs. Again a glance at the monitor, another of so many! Waiting, waiting, for the first signal, the first gentle tick.

Nothing!

Carry on. Once again he put the palms of his hands on the twelve-year-old's chest, pressed, sending curses and prayers after each other to Heaven. Help me, damn you, help me. It's a child. Twelve. Come on, you bastard, help me!

102

Through the hammering pounding of his own heartbeats and the roaring in his ears he heard it: the first tick-tick. Never had it been louder, clearer, or more beautiful. Tick-tick-tick.

'Pulse one hundred. Blood pressure one hundred and ten over ninety!' Wolters reported. Then 'Pulse one hundred and ten. Blood pressure one hundred and twenty over ninety.'

That was it. The heart was beating again of its own accord, strong and regular. Brinkmann reeled away from the table. His arms fell to his sides, muscles spasming. Now he was aware of the sweat running down his body inside the operating gown.

They looked at each other. It was all he could do to smile, but he did it.

EIGHTEEN

Perhaps he was being unfair to the man, or perhaps it was just a conditioned reflex. Whatever it was, Brinkmann always felt a slight uneasiness when he was with the administration director of a clinic. Even with someone like Mühlmann, who was not at all bad. Compared to some he'd known, like that nitpicker in Karlsruhe, Mühlmann, with his winning smile and quick mind, was okay.

He watched as Mühlmann lifted the cigar box, sniffed it appreciately, and put it down again.

'Thanks, Professor, but I don't smoke.'

'Neither do I,' Brinkmann said, feeling guilty. 'Or rather, I didn't up to a few days ago, but now I'm using a pipe. Well. What can I do for you?'

'First of all, you can accept my congratulations.'

'For what?'

'You need to ask? That operation on little Monica Grossmann was brilliant, really brilliant.'

'That was luck, Mühlmann. And the Almighty. The Almighty played a very big part in it.'

'And how is the child?'

'She's still in intensive care, but she's making good progress. Her condition is stable; there's no danger of complications. Now you tell me something: why all the congratulations? Anyone would think I sit around doing nothing all day. You're talking as if we had royalty in the house.'

'Your analogy isn't all that wide of the mark.'

'You think that? Because her name is Monica Grossmann?' Brinkmann said, more harshly than he intended. 'Let me tell you something, Mühlmann. When I was a kid, nobody in this town had ever even heard the name Grossmann. There was no Grossmann factory, no Grossmann corporation, no Grossmann anything else. There was just old Wirtz who manufactured watches. The fact that Grossmann bought him out makes no difference to me, personally. Am I making myself clear?'

'You are,' Mühlmann sighed.

'Fine. Then understand me when I say we would have done no less and no more to pull Monica through if her name had been Maier or Müller. And that reminds me . . . a woman named Grossmann came to see me at my home a little while ago. I had her thrown out.'

'You did what?'

'You heard me. Why are you pulling such a face?'

'Angelika Grossmann?' Mühlmann whispered. 'You threw her out of your home?'

'If she's the fiancée of that traffic gangster with two dead people on his conscience, yes I did. You should have seen the way she acted, Mühlmann: arrogant, rude, efficient, in reverse order. Don't talk to me about the Grossmanns!'

Mühlmann shook his head reproachfully. 'Now it all makes sense,' he said, his expression serious.

'What makes sense?'

'All this hassle over the computer-tomograph.'

'What hassle? I thought we'd been definitely promised the tomograph?'

'It was only a promise, Professor. It was to be a gift from Grossmanns. But they suddenly cancelled it.'

'Are you serious? I didn't know anything about this.'

Mühlmann stood up and took five nervous paces forward and then five back, rubbing his hands nervously.

'I find it less than reassuring to hear you say so, Professor,' he said, tightly. 'Perhaps you should take more interest in such vitally important matters.'

'I thought that was why I had an administration director,' Brinkmann said. His grin was usually infectious but not this time. Mühlmann's face was set and dour. 'Well, don't hold back – say what's on your mind.'

'You know, of course, that the Grossmanns help a great many hospitals with donations.'

'I'd heard that. But, look, the district authority told us we'd be getting that equipment. We need it badly. Now you tell me they're going to cancel it . . .'

'Look, Professor, that tomograph was put into the budget as a rescindable voluntary donation. The director of the district authority has already been on to me. Half the city depends on Grossmann. What am I supposed to do? Man the barricades and tell the world they're crooks?' He laid his hands flat on the upholstered visitor's chair, shaking his head. 'Oh, well, maybe things will change as a result of the operation . . .'

So that was how things were going, Brinkmann thought. 'Let me get this straight, my dear Mühlmann. Are you telling me that the Grossmanns' quarrel with me changed their attitude towards the clinic, and that you're hoping the operation on little Monica will change it back again?'

'I am,' Mühlmann nodded. 'But there's another aspect to it, Professor. Everyone here knows that Grossmann wanted Dr Schaefer to be the new Chief.'

'What?' Brinkmann spun around in his chair, reached for a bottle of cognac and two glasses, and slowly filled the first glass. He stared at the amber-coloured liquid in the brandy glass but did not pick it up. 'Will you join me?'

'No, thank you.'

'You don't smoke, you don't drink. Well, you're only the director of administration and not a surgeon. I need one.' He took a sip, savouring the golden bite of the cognac on his tongue. Then he looked up. 'All right, let's hear it.'

'Grossmann supported Dr Schaefer in the election. He took no trouble to conceal his partiality. We had great difficulty in getting you appointed.'

'Strange that Schaefer never mentioned it. He's usually so efficient.'

'You know Dr Schaefer. He isn't the talkative type.'

'Know him? Who knows anyone, my dear Mühlmann?' Brinkmann thought back to the scene in the operating theatre four days earlier, facing Schaefer across the body of Monica Grossmann. And once again he saw the frightened eyes, the slow reactions he had never observed before. Schaefer's clumsiness had been nothing but fear!

'Did Grossmann have any special reason for supporting Schaefer?'

'You might say that.' The eyes behind the tinted lenses of the steel-rimmed glasses flickered with sly malice. 'Monica Grossmann is Schaefer's niece. He's married to Grossmann's sister.'

Time and again Brinkmann found himself wondering what was going through Schaefer's mind. Nothing had changed, neither during the daily conferences, nor in the operating theatre, nor when visiting the patients; Schaefer carried on as usual, matter-of-fact, taciturn and efficient, his manner so glacially perfect that it made any contact on a personal level impossible. Which was not good where colleagues and staff were concerned, and even worse for patients.

What was it?, Brinkmann wondered. Rivalry? Rivalry was an integral part of their strange profession anyway, a profession that demanded not only scientific knowledge and precise craftsmanship but also an imponderable mixture of intuition, daring, and artistic brilliance not far removed from vanity and humbug. But competition was the driving force of performance, as old Professor Keurer had always said: 'Everything can be learned, but without the vigilant envy of colleagues it does not mature.'

That was one part of it, to be sure, and it was second nature to him. But there was another side to the job, one that Brinkmann thought equally important but which seemed utterly foreign to Schaefer's nature: that was to see oneself in one's patients, and to treat everyone, even the poorest, as though he was a friend or relation.

Maybe he was doing the man an injustice, Brinkmann thought.

What if Schaefer was more than the typical social climber you think he is? What do you know about him? That plodding zeal might be nothing more than a mask, concealing a completely different personality. Face it: his cool efficiency may get on your nerves, but in a day when computer-controlled robots are taking over in the medical field those are the qualities top doctors are made of. Give Schaefer your job, your responsibilities, and perhaps a totally different personality and a completely different surgeon would emerge.

He kept telling himself to stop thinking about it, but it was still going around in his brain the day Monica Grossmann was discharged from the clinic. It was a Wednesday, and it had been raining all morning. Now the sun had broken through, and the leaves on the trees shone as though they had been lacquered.

Schaefer and Brinkmann were coming out of the theatre, exhausted after operating since eight-thirty that morning. A stint like that took a heavy toll.

'How about a hot shower,' Brinkmann said. 'What do you say, Schaefer?'

'I want to finish the lab consignment first.'

'You do that.' Brinkmann held open the swing door. Ahead of him in the corridor he saw a group of people. He recognised Angelika Grossmann right away. The man standing next to her, big, broad-shouldered and confident, in a light summer suit, had to be little Monica's father, Albert Grossmann, captain of industry and philanthropist – when he felt like it.

Brinkmann fought the impulse to flee. He saw the flowers, the smiles, little Monica in the centre of this pretentious delegation, and shrugged: get it over with quickly, he thought.

'Your family, I gather, Schaefer?'

Schaefer nodded, plainly embarrassed. The Grossmanns stopped chattering and turned, their smiles turning to uneasy glances. Then Albert Grossmann's meaningful cough. It was like a scene from some absurd play, Brinkmann thought. The little girl looked at him, and then at Schaefer; then detached herself from the group and ran forward, a huge bouquet of flowers in her arms. She ignored Brinkmann, thrusting the flowers at Schaefer.

'These are for you, Uncle Hermann! To thank you for saving my life!'

Schaefer looked as if he was in shock. His Adam's apple moved up and down as though he was choking. He did not utter a word. Well, well, Brinkmann thought, amused. The kid had made Schaefer lose his cool. Well, perhaps not just the kid: the whole clan.

He turned to leave, neither angry nor disappointed, merely irritated by the whole performance.

'Professor, wait!' Schaefer called. 'I . . . I'm sorry.' Then, presumably to his relations. 'You can't do this.'

Brinkmann turned round. 'There you are, Schaefer, to err is to be human after all!' True enough, he thought, only who knows what is going on inside this lot's heads?

He took grateful deep breaths of the clean, fresh air as he walked to the car park. He saw Mollie bouncing about excitedly inside the car. The show of affection was welcome and he did nothing to rebuff it.

'Come on, old girl, let's go for a walk,' he said. He clipped the lead to the dog's collar. 'I tell you Mollie, the more I see of people, the more I'm glad there are such things as dogs.' Mollie licked his face.

As he straightened up, he saw a shadow. Long legs in jeans, a sun-tanned face.

'Hello, Father.'

'Udo! I'm just going for a walk. Want to come along?'

'Love to.'

They walked a little way in silence, each busy with his own thoughts. Then Udo said: 'Isn't little Monica Grossmann due for discharge about now?'

'She has just left, actually.'

'Oh, has she? You know, I've been meaning to tell you what a fantastic job you did. I'd love to be able to work like that some day. I made Renz tell me about it a dozen times. How you battled . . .'

'Battled? Don't exaggerate.'

'I'm not exaggerating. I just wanted to congratulate you, even if it is a bit late.'

'You don't have to congratulate me, Udo,' Brinkmann said, putting his arm around his son's shoulder. 'A professional is expected to do his job properly. When problems crop up, all he has to fall back on are luck and experience. You've got the talent, and you'll acquire experience. It's a long and painful road, and not only for you. You know I'm basically opposed to the kind of general surgery we do here: having to cover every contingency, the way we do, can sometimes be dangerous. Just think of that cardiac arrest during the Grossmann operation. That's why I say the sooner you specialise, the better it will be for your patients.'

Udo nodded: this was his father's favourite topic, and he was right. 'I'm still glad the operation was such a success, Father. It has confirmed your standing here at the clinic, put your medical authority beyond doubt.'

'There are always doubts. A doctor who thinks otherwise is a bad doctor. To doubt yourself is to keep yourself on a rein, under control. In our profession you can't do it any other way.'

He smiled and put his arm around his son's shoulder again. He felt good. 'Come on,' he said. 'Let's go home.'

NINETEEN

There was nothing visible of Mollie except two wildly-digging hind legs, a brown-white tail, and a shower of dirt. No matter how many times she did it, Mollie never came any nearer to catching a mole or a field mouse – but this never stopped her digging until she was exhausted.

Brinkmann paused. He enjoyed spending his time this way. He savoured everything around him: the coolness of the pines coming from the woods, the sweep of the hills with their scattering of farms, all of it, even himself. He enjoyed this illusion of freedom, even though he knew – with the bleeper carefully clipped to the pocket of his shirt – that he was just as much on a lead as was Mollie. Whenever he found time, this was what he liked to do: put on his old walking shoes and his windcheater, park the car at the Roteck and strike out for the Hochstand. Up the path, along the edge of the woods and past the benches the tourists hadn't discovered yet, thank God, to walk across the top of the hill, with its log huts for feeding livestock during the winter, and with buzzards repeatedly soaring over his head, larks singing, crows lazily traversing the sky, and time after time new panoramas opening up to make the heart beat faster.

'All right, Mollie, that's enough!' he said.

She trotted towards him wearing a defeated look. She was covered in dust, even her nostrils clogged with earth. He grinned and squatted down beside the footpath for a few minutes while she recovered.

All right, so such bucolic happiness was naïve. What more was there? Simple appreciation rests on solid ground. Think how things were only a year ago . . . in Karlsruhe . . .

'What? You want to go to the Black Forest?'

He could still see Bernard Rieck's astonished face that evening when Brinkmann had told him his decision was irrevocable. They were sitting on the terrace. Smog dimmed the lights of the city below, diffusing and refracting them. 'Karlsruhe is bad enough, God knows! But the Black Forest? A man with your talents? Be sensible, Klaus! If you wanted to do scientific research or something, I could understand it. But a provincial clinic!'

A provincial clinic! A man with your talents!

Provincial!

People used the word as an insult. Mollie's potato field was 'provincial', so were the woods, the soft hills with their farms, the village called Kleineck.

Provincial?

People and their destinies, large and small, their way of talking, their large and small catastrophes, their fears, suffering and death, they were all interwoven here, part of a tapestry. Like the young man with the broken femur he'd had on the operating table yesterday. He was from Kleineck. He felt involvement with the people, their problems. Yes, that was it! Not like the conveyor belt medicine of the cities, the isolated illness which requires treatment but which is faceless. He would go and see Rieck sometime and tell him that.

'Come on, Mollie!'

They walked on as far as the declivity where the path ended. Mollie's ears pricked up, and following her gaze Brinkmann saw a man pushing a bike along the bend of the road leading to Kleineck. The man wore a torn blue vest and something shapeless on his head that might once have been a hat. The much-mended jeans were cut off at the ankles. The man's angular body looked ungainly, awkward and half-starved, but he seemed to have plenty of steam as he marched on, whistling loudly and happily as he went.

Brinkmann shook his head: was he hearing things? Think, this fellow on his bike, this scarecrow, wandering around the country whistling, even in this heat. A happy man. He felt something not too far from envy, and tipped the man a reluctant salute, finger to forehead.

'Well, Guzzi, we'll soon be there . . .'

Whenever it was a hard pull, Arthur Wilkins talked encouragingly to his bike. Well, cowboys talked to their horses, didn't they? And Guzzi was a much nobler steed. A super girl, the best he'd ever ridden. Eight gears. Red and black lacquer. Practically new. Probably worth a fortune. Of course, he hadn't chosen Guzzi: she'd chosen him. Leaning so invitingly, so irresistibly against the wall of the pub!

'Nearly there . . . what's the name of the place, Kleineck? Sounds nice enough, eh?'

Arthur Wilkins loved the Black Forest. He liked the villages best of all. They were so small and friendly. There were farms where they treated you really well, because the people there were so glad when someone from the big wide world outside turned up on their doorstep.

So, here it was. What's this, no pub? Just four houses; and they've built themselves a church, I see. Had to have a church. Over there, orchards. Unfamiliar roofs, balconies with geraniums. So, where was one to get a bite to eat? Arthur Wilkins put his trust in his ability to sway the generous heart of a farmer's wife. The five Deutschmarks he had in his pocket were for use only in extreme emergency.

He leaned Guzzi against the wooden platform on which the milk churns would be placed ready for collection in the morning, and walked up the grass-covered path to the first house. Nobody around. Three hens, not even a rooster, and a cat that regarded him sleepily from a sunny windowsill.

Arthur Wilkins put his fingers in his mouth and produced a real sailor's whistle. That did it. A man came around the corner of the

113

woodshed. Corduroy jacket, corduroy pants, red face, angry eyes. And – was it possible? A gun in his hand. Yes, the man had a rifle!

'What's all the noise about?'

'Wanted to see if anyone was around,' Arthur said, in a friendly way. 'Thought I'd –'

'Thought you'd see what you could steal, that it? Well, you're out of luck. Go on, clear off! We don't want your sort around here. Bloody drunk. Go on, beat it!'

'Look here,' Arthur said. 'There's no need –'

The barrel of the rifle came up. 'Don't give me any of your lip, you drunken layabout! Get off out of it! Go on, go to hell, you shit-eating hippy!'

Under any other circumstances, Arthur might have answered back, but he was not about to argue with some thick-headed yokel carrying a gun. He turned and ran for his bike.

'Thick-headed yokel!' he yelled over his shoulder as he pedalled furiously down the hill, taking the bend in an elegant swoop. The bends were gentle, the descent exhilarating. The wind cooled his face and wiped the anger from his eyes and his soul. He began to laugh: put to inglorious flight by a yokel with a gun, a country bumpkin, a thick-headed ignoramus!

Perhaps it was a shard of gravel, or a fleck of mud under Guzzi's tyre. Maybe he yanked too hard on the handlebars as he looked back. Whatever the reason, Arthur Wilkins found himself flying through the air, and then he knew no more. Untidy head first, he landed in a beech hedge, dirty feet in torn gym shoes sticking up in the air.

'Did you see that?'

Four foresters working at the crossing of the path and the road had seen him go by like a human rocket.

'Jesus, come on!' Paul Kammer, the foreman, led the way. He picked up the bent bicycle, admiringly noting the eight gears. 'And what's that? A piece of brown, sticky bottle glass lay in the road. Gusti Rapp bent down and sniffed.

'Vermouth?'

'Makes no difference. Let's get him out of there.'

'Looks as if he's already crossed the Jordan.'

'No, he's alive.'

Kammer was right. Slowly the lights were coming back on in

114

Arthur Wilkins' brain. He moaned softly. His arm was hurting terribly.

'Guzzi?' he managed.

'What?'

'My bike.'

They lifted him on to the tractor, and put his bicycle behind him. Half an hour later Arthur Wilkins became the first patient ever to enter the Black Forest Clinic on an official vehicle belonging to Forestry Department IV-2, Offingen South.

TWENTY

'Is he unconscious?'

'Skull abrasions.'

'Skull abrasions . . . broken wrist, and maybe a concussion as well.'

Lying comfortably on the trolley, covered in a brown blanket, Arthur felt himself gliding over endless vistas of linoleum. A young girl carrying a plastic bag containing his clothes – a pair of grey-black sneakers with a gaping hole where the sole had torn loose, a vest, pants, and windcheater, all urgently in need of washing – walked alongside him. Arthur thought longingly of his bottle of Ramazzi Bitter, broken and dried out on the road.

'Where is he going?'

'To 208.'

'As if we don't get enough of them.'

'What's the matter with you, Elke? Would you throw the poor fellow out because he's a drunk?'

'You know what, Mischa? Sometimes your wisecracks give me a pain you-know-where.'

Mischa? Elke? He an auxiliary, she a nurse. Arthur Wilkins opened his eyes just enough to see. Look at that little Elke! Lovely sweet behind and plenty on top. A bit on the plump side, maybe, but he liked them like that. Even if she'd been thin, he wouldn't have complained. To complain in a hospital was madness indeed. Hospitals were like paradise. Everything free: food, laundry, warmth. Even the towels.

'I wonder how the others will feel about him?' he heard Elke say. From past experience, Wilkins decided to take no chances. He 'dived under'. It was his psycho-strategy, a tactic he had perfected in all kinds of situations. Pretend you are unconscious or sleeping while gathering information all the while. In official institutions, police stations, welfare homes, convent cells or mission dormitories, 'diving under' required each time further proofs of his ability to act convincingly the drunk, the half-starved, the idiot, the victim of hypothermia, an imbecile with a twitch, or – as today – a man suffering from concussion.

He maintained his 'act' as he was put between rustling, freshly-laundered sheets in a beautifully soft bed. Room 208. Fantastic! Just like the Hilton!

He felt a fingernail rasp against the stubble on his chin. He risked a look and saw the young man with the thin beard and the flea-market glasses. His eyes were kind.

'The charade over, mister, or are you just tired?'

Arthur Wilkins grinned; the clever little bugger had seen through his act. Through his slitted eyes, he also saw something else: the two grandfathers who were his roommates. One was a fat old boy with a boozer's nose, the other as thin as a starved bird. With his white plumes of hair and black, beady eyes, he looked like an old rooster whose hens had all died.

'What's his name, Mischa?' the old boy asked.

Mischa put a finger to his lips. 'Shhh, Mr Bischle. Can't you see Mr Wilkins isn't very well?'

'What happened to him?'

'He was in an accident, Mr Hopf.'

'A car?'

'Bike.'

'Looks like it,' Erwin Hopf nodded. 'What do you think, Jacob?'

Jacob Bischle didn't reply. He was looking out of the window, over the walls and roofs and towers, the river, the yard of the old watch factory the Grossmanns had taken over, up the hill to where he could see a small, shining red roof.

Home.

The telephone shrilled and Brinkmann stifled a curse. Was there no peace? 'Brinkmann.'

'Sorry to bother you, Professor . . .'

'Nice of you to say so, Mühlmann.' The director of administration was the only member of the staff who was put through automatically to Brinkmann's office. I'll have to talk to Miss Meis about that, he thought.

'I'm just on my way out,' he said, impatiently. 'What is it?'

'It's about a new admission, Professor. One Arthur Wilkins.'

'Wilkins? Don't know him. What's the problem?'

'I did say he was a new admission. Broken wrist. He's some kind of tramp. The problem: Mr Wilkins is not insured.'

How delicately put! Some kind of tramp . . . 'So get in touch with the local social security office.'

'That's just the problem, Professor. Anyone with no fixed address doesn't have an appropriate social security office. And you know the rules . . . If a patient clearly cannot meet the cost of his treatment . . .'

'Yes, yes, I know the rules,' Brinkmann snapped, his spirits sinking even lower. 'We'll find a way. We can hardly throw the poor fellow out, can we?'

'I suppose not.' Mühlmann's voice indicated clearly that that was exactly what he would like to do. 'And if I may come back just a moment to the Bischle case, Professor . . . ?'

'Bischle? He stays in second class.'

'I really cannot concur.' Mühlmann's tone was exactly that mixture of kindness, diplomacy and urgency which always put Brinkmann on his guard. 'Professor, I don't want to give the impression –'

'Try to be brief, Mr Mühlmann.'

'Very well. Fifty per cent of our first-class beds are unoccupied. We talked about that yesterday. Mr Bischle's family, that is to say, his son and daughter-in-law, are constantly asking me why we don't put their father into first-class accommodation.'

118

'Simple: he doesn't want to go.'

'But, Professor, you must think of the revenue. Not to mention your fees. That's what I'm here for. We still have to pay the wages.'

'Listen to me, Mühlmann. In this clinic the patients give the orders. Not us, not the relatives. There's nothing to get excited about. The decision is based on respect for a human being, or, one might say, within the realm of psychic care. Mr Bischle has known his roommate since they were boys. He can see his own house from the window of his room. He insists that without that view, he could not bear to remain here. I respect that. Furthermore, it's my belief that a man of that age can best be helped to get back on his feet by giving him the right motivation. I don't propose to interfere with that process, and even less so if he does not want me to.'

'But Professor –'

'No buts! I'm sorry, I must go. I have to do my rounds.'

Brinkmann put down the phone and reached for his pipe. Bloody accountants!

On Jacob Bischle's bedside table lay a Swiss railwayman's watch. He had bought it in Basle half a lifetime ago. The dial was cracked; it had happened in a beerhall fight with the Nazis in 1925. Or was it 1927? Never mind. The old thing was still working, although he had repaired it many times.

Jacob Bischle had loved watches for as long as he had lived. Taking them apart, putting them back together, adjusting the springs, making them go faster or slower. First at the factory, when Wirtz had still owned it, and later working at home. But the 'railwayman' remained his dearest possession; without it next to him or in his pocket, he felt lost. A man needed to be able to measure time at a glance, to know whether things were as they should be, early or late. He looked at the watch now. Nine o'clock. Yesterday the sun had risen at seven minutes past nine. Today it would probably be as early as three minutes past.

He took his old hunting binoculars from the drawer. As he did he heard Hopf's voice.

'Jacob. Shall we play chess today?'

'I can't play chess. How often do I have to tell you that?'

'You can. And what you don't know I can always teach you.'

119

'I don't want you to teach me. Why would I want to learn how to play chess? I'm eighty years old, Erwin.'

'Just the right time to start. All right, forget the chess. What about a game of Halma?'

'No Halma. Draw the curtain, please, Erwin.'

Bischle focussed the binoculars, as he did every day. I was right, exactly three minutes past! He watched as rays of sunshine spread over the tall, proud pines along the ridge over the dark curve of the Schlechter meadow. They looked like elegant ladies wearing golden capes, he thought. And here came the sun, its blinding rays spreading a wide, golden band across the hillside. They followed every contour, creating shadows on the mountain and making the cliffs shine. They lifted the mist from the town, picking out blades of light on church steeples, television aerials, cars, and rows of windows.

All this Jacob Bischle ignored. Pressing the binoculars so hard against his eyes that they hurt, he stared hungrily at the woodshed, the apple trees now visible in the bluish light. The tree affected by fungus seemed to be getting better. He shifted his gaze to the plum trees. Then the terrace, with the dog kennel that had been empty for years. The kitchen steps where Elfriede always sat while she was shelling the peas. And Elfriede's curtains behind the shining windows.

Home.

'Tell me something, Jacob. Don't you ever get tired of staring through those binoculars?'

Bischle did not deign to reply to such a stupid question. Behind him, Erwin Hopf angrily swept in the Halma figures off the board, threw them into the cardboard box, and shut it with a bang, his face a study of resigned anger. So obvious were his feelings that Arthur Wilkins, watching from his bed in the corner, could scarcely keep from smiling. Old goats, he thought, Hopf, seventy, and the old boy with the binoculars, eighty. They had argued half the night about who had been Wine Queen in 1950. And whether it had been Bischle who really hung the white flag from his window when the French marched in, even though the local army commander and the SS had threatened to hang anyone who did.

Bischle straightened up and Hopf pulled a face. Watching someone peering through binoculars every day was hardly amusing.

120

But all the nasturtiums would die!, Jacob Bischle said to himself. What was the use of having children if they couldn't even water the garden while a man was in hospital? First class, that was all they thought about. Put him in one of those single rooms where all you could see was the railway line and the valley. But harvesting rennets? It would never occur to them.

An idea came into Jacob Bischle's tired head.

'Hey, Hopf, you've got a granddaughter. Little Louise. Why don't you send her over to my house. The garden is full of rennets.'

'You said that yesterday.'

'Did I really? I keep forgetting. All the same, send her over.'

'Jacob, Louise has to go to school.'

It was always the same. You sat there worrying, waiting for someone to come and help you. Then when nobody came, you thought of a way. But then that doesn't work, either. You run up against the same grey brick wall every time. Hopeless. And nobody understands.

Now on top of everything else the scarecrow in the corner was sticking his nose in.

'Listen, Mr Bischle,' he said. 'I'll sort it all out for you, soon as I can sit on my bike again. No problem. Rennets, did you say? They make wonderful compote. And fine marmalade. Right?'

What would that fool know about compote or marmalade?, old Bischle asked himself. Now in the old days . . . Elfriede standing in the kitchen stirring the marmalade . . . God! In the old days . . .

Tears blinded him, but he kept the binoculars pressed hard against his eyes.

TWENTY-ONE

Mischa had expected all sorts of problems with Arthur Wilkins but to his surprise this strange beanpole of a man, the top of his head burned red as a lobster by the sun, turned into a water baby the minute he got into the bath. He splashed about like a dolphin, even going so far as to squeak, 'Wouldn't have a little, pink, rubber duck for me, would you? A blue one would do.'

'Did you know I once bathed among piranha fish?' he said, shampoo in his hair.

'Where was this?'

'In the River Amazon.'

'I guessed that.'

'Oh? How?'

'I always thought anyone who took a swim with piranha fish in the Amazon would end up looking like you.'

Wilkins grinned widely through the beard of foam on his face. 'I knew it. A man of learning as well as intuition. Which is more than you can say of my roommates. What's your name, by the way?'

'Mischa.'

'And what are you doing here, Mischa? Learning to be a doctor?'

'My God, do I look as if I am? I'm doing community service. I'm a music student.'

'Then let's form an orchestra. I'll play the mouth organ and you can conduct. What do you think of my duck, by the way?' He lifted the brush and dropped it back into the water. 'See? It can swim!'

'Ask it to stop swimming and do your feet instead.'

'If you like. Wouldn't it be better to soak them a bit more? They've had three weeks to get like that. The dirt gets under the skin, you know. Look, here's an iceberg!' He pushed the brush into the foam again. 'An iceberg on its way to America. Have you ever been to America, Mischa?'

'Nope.'

'I have. And I've slept in the finest hotels. And taken a daily bath.'

'Pull the other one.'

'I'm not joking, Mischa.'

'And how did you get to America?'

'As artists do. You see? That's what I am, first and foremost, an artist. A performer! I was an operatic tenor then. That didn't go so well. Then I became an illusionist: truly, a circus magician. You don't believe me. No matter, it's not important. But I *was* in Los Angeles. And Sydney, too. You know where that is? Oh well, perhaps I've always taken a glass too many while travelling.'

Arthur Wilkins leaned back, closed his eyes, and sang out in F-major: 'Oh, the barley wine, the barley wine, it usually made me feel quite fine . . .'

'Stop that!' Mischa yelled.

'Of course. You're a music student. You mustn't let things get you down.'

Mischa nodded his agreement, reaching for Arthur Wilkins' arm to get on with the sanitation job. Wilkins screeched with pain.

'My hand, man! What are you doing to it? And what about my bicycle? Won't somebody steal it?'

'I took it down to the cellar,' Mischa said, grimly scrubbing on.

'Can you get it repaired? Do you know what my Guzzi is? The Rolls Royce of bicycles. I mean it. I love her the way a cowboy loves his mustang.'

123

'Can you afford the repairs, cowboy?'

'Afford? Who said anything about paying? I haven't earned any money for eight years. How long do you think you can manage on that? Ah, well, you mustn't –'

'– let things get you down?'

'So, a psychologist, on top of everything else. You're a likely lad, aren't you? Only, if I were you I'd shave off that beard, my conscientious objector friend. Take it from someone who's an objector, too. And a musician. First the operetta, then the mouth organ. After that, we'll . . .'

'Never mind after that. First of all, we wash the ears. Have you got a toothbrush?'

'I had one. But there must have been someone at the shelter in Hamburg who was keener on cleaning his teeth than I was.'

They smiled at each other through the clouds of bathroom steam. Mischa's glasses were misted up; cleaning them didn't help much. But he didn't need clear glasses to recognise someone who had found out that playing the clown can keep the pain of life at bay. A nutcase, old Wilkins. But the kind of nutcase he liked.

Brinkmann picked up the clock standing on the table in the antique shop and held it carefully in his hand.

'Very pretty, isn't it, Sir? And genuine, too.'

No, that it was most decidedly not, he thought, not with this garland of chased brass leaves. Even so, with its flamed cherry casing, the roman numerals on the white enamel dial and the turned feet, it was a charming piece. But for whom? And, he asked himself misanthropically, for what? Where would you put it even if you bought it? What is this squirrel-like hoarding mania you have developed recently? Are you turning your house upside down, redecorating it, creating some kind of setting for yourself, a 'framework' as they call it? For what? The evenings spent watching television would be the same with or without the clock. Deep down, if you are really honest with yourself, the only reason for these junkshop excursions and all the other similarly unsuccessful attempts to get rid of your money is the urge to do yourself a favour, to fill up the awful void that sets in every Saturday, when the stress of the clinic winds down. Like today.

'You should hear the chime, Sir, it works perfectly.' The woman

124

in the flared pink trousers who owned the shop oozed determined civility. 'May I offer you a chair, Sir?'

'To sit on, or to buy?'

'Why not both?' she said, coquettishly. It was what was known as 'sour gherkin time', lookers-not-buyers time, in 'Linda's Treasure Trove'. There were plenty of tourists pressing their noses against the shop windows, and the hotels, spas and guest houses were all fully booked, but the visitors were keeping their purses tightly shut.

'Look at that veneer – Viennese, you know. Just look at it. The upholstery is nice, too. And if you wish, the material is available in other colours.'

If you wish? Well, what did he really wish?

Brinkmann sat down, stretched his legs and welcomed the cool breeze coming in through the window from the courtyard of the old timbered building. Mollie growled as the fluttering proprietress came hurrying across with an ashtray for Brinkmann's pipe, but it was much too hot for even Mollie to waste energy.

'Very kind of you. You know, chairs like this . . .'

His voice trailed away. The sun-drenched street was no longer empty. A young woman was crossing the sidewalk and opening the door of a battered old Volkswagen. Her dark blonde hair shone in the sunlight. She appeared not to notice the heat but to be walking on clouds. She was not alone. With one outstretched arm she was literally towing along a young man.

Christa Meurer!

He recognised the young man, too. Christa and Mischa. Well, why not? Mischa was a little young, but he was kind-hearted in spite of his insolent manner. Brinkmann rather liked the cheeky auxiliary.

And young? What did that mean?, Brinkmann asked himself, half angry and half amused at his own reactions and the stupid thumping of his heart. What about you? With an age difference of twenty-two years you could be her father. Yet you're upset and sorry for yourself because she's shattered your little reverie.

'There's also a matching easy chair . . .'

'I beg your pardon?'

'I said there's . . .'

Outside the VW engine coughed and roared, died, let itself be coaxed back to life, and rattled off down the street, leaving behind a thin, blue trail of smoke which drifted slowly towards the window.

'Well, I see you don't bother your head too much about the environment,' Mischa said, glancing back at the blue cloud behind them. 'That's the way to do it: live in the Black Forest and kill it off at the same time.'

'I can't help it, Mischa. I can't afford a new car.'

'Buy a bike,' he grinned. 'Or be a bit nice to Mischa and he might even adjust your valves for you.'

'You still haven't fixed my washing machine.'

'And if I do?'

'Little Mischa, be a darling. I'll give you a beer.'

'Who needs beer?' he said with a shrug.

'What else can I offer you?'

'Ask a silly question,' he said, rolling his eyes lasciviously. 'You're so slow on the uptake, I'll give you four guesses.'

She laughed. 'Stop that nonsense, Mischa. I haven't the faintest intention of playing games with you.'

She pulled over to let a bus go by. Placards on its side proclaimed it to be an outing from the Bosch subsidiary in Linday. Red-faced day-trippers behind the windows waved as it went by.

'As friends, we're just fine, Mischa. But only as friends . . .'

'Friendship,' he said. 'That precious thing.'

'Exactly.' The bus had safely overtaken them. Christa leaned over and planted a fleeting, sisterly kiss on the woolly blond mop that covered Mischa's head.

Mischa groaned.

TWENTY-TWO

'You know, I don't think I've ever used this brown glop with the gold flecks before. I usually use black. But it goes with the blouse, doesn't it?'

Christa nodded. The 'brown glop with the gold flecks' was a little pot of eye shadow. Elke was applying it so generously that even little Ulrike expressed surprise.

'My God, Elke!' she said. 'You look like a Bodensee steamboat on a Sunday!'

Regardless of what a Bodensee steamboat might look like on a Sunday, Elke seemed satisfied. Golden-brown eye shadow, brown transparent blouse, tanned face and brown eyes that looked like big cherries framed by carefully trimmed lashes.

'Well, all we need now is for you-know-who to arrive.'

She leaned out of the window of the ward office, then turned round to give Christa a baffled look.

'You . . . you truly don't mind, Christa?'

'Don't start that again.'

'I just want to be sure. Otherwise I'll feel uneasy all evening. Where the devil is the fellow, anyway?'

'It's as well to allow half an hour's leeway,' Christa said, speaking from long experience: she knew what Udo Brinkmann was like. But tonight she was wrong.

'Here he is! Cheers, have a lovely evening!'

Elke was gone. Ulrike disappeared too. Christa stayed, watching the scene below from her hiding place behind the curtains. The usual performance: the green Alfa, the showy turn, the scream of brakes, and, of course, the jaunty leap from the convertible. As usual, the collar of his leather jacket was turned up. He flashed a toothpaste-ad smile, the original irresistible, wild, wicked fellow he thought he was. But was it what he really was? As she watched Udo posing down there, hands in the pockets of his white jeans, casually leaning against the bonnet of the car, conscious of the gaze of a whole henhouse full of trainee nurses, the old question popped up again. What was it that made Udo put on that 'Aren't-I-wonderful' act? Why does he bother with a girl like Elke, or any of the girls for that matter? Flirting? Sex? Or is it because he still feels himself to be a boy, fighting for recognition, no, not fighting for it, needing it so badly because he felt so hopelessly inferior to his father.

She recalled the few times she had tried to broach the subject with him. He had reacted like a snail, retreating into his shell and refusing to talk about it. Well, it was understandable. Both of them doctors: the old master and his young rival, one accomplished, the other with much to learn. His father's personality made Udo unsure of himself, and so he tried too hard.

Down below the Alfa roared off as if it was starting a rally. Christa turned away from the window, then stopped as a heavy black BMW motorbike shot out of the car park, its rider clad in black leather. He wore no helmet and his goggles were pushed up into his hair. Christa knew at once who it was: Lukas, Elke's ex-boyfriend! Only a week ago, the former striker and golden boy of the local football club had been Elke's *ne plus ultra* of masculinity.

The BMW roared off in pursuit of the Alfa, taking the bends at full speed. So, Udo has Lukas on his tail! Christa felt a twinge of malicious pleasure and was surprised to find that it did not surprise her at all.

•   •   •

Out of the corner of his eye, Udo scrutinised the girl sitting beside him. Snub nose. Golden-brown face. A glittering, red, plastic heart stuck in the clumsily-pierced ear lobe. Where should he take her?

He drove faster. The odd thing was that stupid as it sounded, he wasn't really interested in her. She was a sweet little thing, sure. And he hadn't been about to pass up the chance of angering Christa. But then? In an icy upsurge of self-criticism he wondered whether, in fact, he wasn't simply making a damned fool of himself.

Even as the thought occurred to him he found Elke's head on his shoulder. She looked up at him.

'Oh, Udo, isn't it brilliant!'

'Sorry?'

She sat upright, the familiar lump in her throat, so many things rushing about in her brain she didn't know where to begin.

'Don't you think it's absolutely brilliant, Udo, the two of us together like this?'

The two of us? There was nothing he could say to that one, so he just nodded. If you only knew, my little rabbit!

'Somehow I feel sorry for Christa. After all, she is my friend.'

'Is she?'

'Yes, and a good one. It's a matter of principle with me. I believe in sticking to the old rule: never get between two people, it can only bring unhappiness.'

'Very commendable,' Udo said.

'But you never know with Christa. I mean, whether she still cares for you or not. She's always so uptight.'

Udo nodded again, his eyes moving from the side mirror to the rear-view mirror. 'And tell me, is there anyone who still cares for you?'

'Why?'

'The chap behind us on the black BMW bike. He's been following us ever since we left the clinic.'

Elke twisted around to look over her shoulder. She gave an exasperated shrug. 'Oh, him!'

'You know him?'

'It's only Lukas.'

'Who's Lukas?'

'Someone I used to know. It's been over a long time, Udo.'

'I hope he knows that, too.'

Elke nodded emphatically. 'I've told him and told him. I told him again only yesterday.' She smiled dreamily. 'I think you're sweet to be so jealous.'

'Do you really?'

'And where are you taking me now?'

Good question. They were travelling west on the Black Forest highway. The turnoff he was looking for was on a bend, but the chrome metal of that damned black bike, which kept flashing in the mirror, was distracting him. He touched the brakes lightly, slowing as he turned on to the dirt road which led to the small lake. To his relief the BMW tore past and roared away down the main road.

'Well, I could do with some fresh air after all that tension,' he said, parking the car in the shade of the boathouse. Wavelets lapped against the wooden pilings. The grey wooden walls smelled of sunlight and tar. The pears were ripening on the tree. Dragonflies darted between the reeds bordering the water; everything was very still and quiet. Except for Elke.

'You know what I'm dying to know?' she said, brushing away a horsefly buzzing around her head. 'What everyone is going to say?'

'Everyone?'

'Well, your father, for instance.'

'To what?'

'When he hears about . . . us.'

'What do you expect him to say?'

'Oh, I don't know; but you know how quickly he gets to know about everything. I wonder whether he'll like it. You and me. You know, a doctor and a nurse.'

'Who cares? I like you. That's all that matters.'

He turned to face her. She looked rather sweet standing there against the light in that silly see-through blouse. He rummaged in his pockets for the keys to the boathouse. The lock was jammed. Damnation, he'd been meaning to change it.

'Udo,' the girl whispered behind him. 'Udo, where are you taking me?'

He led her into the green half-light, where gold and darkness made a seductive shadowplay. There was a pleasant smell of tar and water, and the familiar agreeable sound his boat made rubbing against the wooden landing, a quiet, almost erotic, whisper that

130

sounded like a welcome and brought back a whole spectrum of memories. Beautiful, sweet memories . . .

At the edge of the wood Lukas turned the bike around.

When the Alfa had turned off the highway, he had freewheeled past the meadow, down the hill and around, over the dusty, gravelly ground, towards the little lake and the boathouse that stood beside it. He could almost taste the brackish water which had evaporated on the reeds. He saw the pear trees and the lake.

Lukas had been here once before. He had never given a thought to the boathouse until now. Now he knew who it belonged to. That shit! Who the hell did he think he was, anyway? Just because his father ran the clinic, he thought he could strut around like a cockerel among these hens, the young nurses. Like Elke . . .

Well, he wasn't interested in Elke any more. Nothing. Finished. But he was going to take young Brinkmann down a peg or two. Oh, yes. He kicked the wheel of the Alfa as he passed it on his way to the footbridge leading to the wooden boathouse. He crept up to it carefully. Water slapped at the bridge. Somewhere a fish jumped. He stifled a curse as a board creaked beneath his weight.

Neither of them heard a thing. They were too busy. Anger burned through Lukas. It was one thing to sit in a cinema and snigger at a scene like this, but in real life it wasn't a bit funny. The whispers, the groans, the giggles were unendurable.

Hating himself for watching, for not kicking down the door or smashing in a window or setting the place on fire, breathless, writhing with self-loathing, Lukas watched them through a knothole in the boathouse wall. He loathed himself for standing there, breathing shallowly, the victim of a torturing fascination stronger than any feeling of revenge, stronger even than his first impulse which had been to turn away, to run, not wanting to know . . .

So he stood there and watched: he saw the wisp of blouse on the floor, the pair of jeans next to it, jeans he knew all too well, dotted with patchwork hearts, now tossed aside, carelessly crumpled. They obviously couldn't get out of their clothes fast enough!

Two mattresses, one on top of the other. Brown and white skin. A hand with red-varnished nails opening and closing. Brown and white skin moving slowly and languorously in movements he could feel in his own blood, pounding as the tempo grew faster, thundering as he pressed his hands against his ears, not wanting to hear any more, yet utterly unable to go, not before . . . before what? What did he want? Why didn't he do something?

Not yet!

And then . . . and then . . . slowly what might have been called control came back. His mind was empty, without thought. He walked back very slowly and crouched down at the end of the footbridge in the shade of an apple tree. The wind stroked the fields. The lake toyed with the reeds. Lukas tried to keep his mind blank. Everything inside him seemed dead. He lost all track of time.

A door squeaked.

It was Udo! Udo Brinkmann, hair tousled, wearing only shirt and pants. Barefoot. There was no sign of Elke.

Lukas stood up and stepped out of the shade of the tree. Udo did not see him. Lukas took three more steps.

'You – what are you doing here?'

'What do you think I'm doing here, you bastard?' Lukas hooked his thumbs into his belt. Look at how Brinkmann was staring at him. Too scared to even open his mouth!

'Want to know what I'm doing here, lover boy? Maybe I can think of something.' He took three more steps forward. 'Like turning a doctor into a patient. How does that appeal to you? Come on, speak up!'

But Udo Brinkmann was unable to speak up. The corners of his mouth twitched in fear. Lukas read it as arrogance, and that was all he needed.

He hit Udo clumsily on the side of the face. Udo reeled backwards and smashed against the wooden wall of the boathouse. He tried to parry the second blow, but without success. Lukas' fist hit him squarely in the eye. Sucking in his breath, Udo threw a left at his assailant, but Lukas avoided it. The sight of Udo's twisted face and rapidly swelling eye sent icy triumph through his veins. He hit him again, this time at the angle of the jaw.

Udo reeled backwards, and Lukas watched him hit the water, sending up an enormous splash. Udo swam about, then his arms dropped and he began to sink. No need to let him drown, Lukas thought. He bent down on the jetty and grabbed Brinkmann, pulling him towards the jetty. With a huge effort he managed to pull him ashore.

Udo Brinkmann sat bent double, coughing, choking, water cascading off him, a picture of misery. He held his stomach with one hand and did not look at Lukas, who was enjoying every second of Udo's discomfiture. Until he heard steps . . .

'What have you done? What have you done to him, you dirty bugger?'

Elke.

Lukas just looked at her. He shook his head. Enough of that screaming. He gave her a shove and she fell, flailing, backwards into the water. Well, at least she could swim.

He turned round and walked away. His back was straight, his toes turned slightly in as he made his way over to the BMW. The way gunfighters walk . . . after it's all over.

'Oh, you shit, you filthy bugger, you wait, damn you . . . !' Splashes, coughs, curses. 'I don't ever want to see your ugly face again, do you hear me? Never again!'

After three attempts, Elke managed to haul herself out of the water. Gasping for breath, her eyes filled with tears of anger, the blouse pasted to her body, she lay on the jetty.

'Oh, Udo, Udo, my poor darling Udo . . .' She crawled over to Udo, who was still sitting bent over his knees, staring into the water. When he finally lifted his head, Elke was shocked.

'My God, your eye! It's completely closed! And your mouth . . . are you bleeding?'

His answer was to spit some blood into the lake.

'Udo,' she whispered, gently touching his shoulder. 'I think you ought to see a doctor. You look terrible.'

'Terrible?' he said, thickly. 'You really want to know what's terrible? Your behaviour!'

TWENTY-THREE

Johannes Brahms. Opus 90. The Third Symphony in F Major . . .
The soaring scale of a flute dying in bittersweet melancholy . . .
Strings taking up the theme . . .

If there was one electronic blessing Klaus Brinkmann was thankful for, it was the headphones of his music centre. The big cushioned earpieces did more than just cover his ears: they protected his whole being, transporting him away from the defeats of the day, wiping out the memory of operation-theatre foul-ups, personal aggravations, and administrative squabbles. He was in another world, so much so that once in a while he even lifted his arms to conduct his invisible orchestra: 'Da dum, dum-dum, dum.'

By God, wouldn't that be something: to conduct an orchestra, to surrender to one's intuition, to live a life dedicated to the true, the good, the beautiful. Without anger or responsibilities, perhaps with a woman who understood you at your side . . . Well, it might have been different, he thought, life offers so many choices. And who is to say that yours belongs to surgery? No, too late! When one is young one has the options, examines them. But who breaks out?

You discover you've worked yourself to a frazzle at the operating table, that behind that confidence you're so proud of there is still fear, the constant fear that you're doing something wrong. And somewhere in there you miss the second chance to walk away from it, so you carry on because it is too late. It's the same for everyone. The wheel of fortune turns and turns, and you turn with it.

Cool fingers touched his neck. Kate Marek lifted the earphones off his head and smiled at him. 'You've had enough,' she said. 'You've been sitting here in the dark for over an hour.'

'So what? And if you're about to tell me dinner is ready, the answer is: eat it yourself!'

'Well, aren't you the charmer! Is that all you have to say?'

'Not all.' From the earphones around his neck came a tinny jingle: the thunderous storm of Brahms' music muted to an electronic echo. Brinkmann rubbed his eyes.

'The trouble with you, Kate, is you always turn up at the wrong moment.'

'Wrong moments, right moments. There's no such thing.' She picked up the glass of burgundy beside him, held it against the light of the standard lamp, sniffed it, tasted it, and put it back on the table. 'Look, Klaus, enough of this: is she coming or not?'

He gave her an unhappy look. 'She's coming.'

'I knew it. Whatever Elena Bach gets it into her head to do, she does. But I've never seen it affect you like this before. Have you fallen in love?'

'You're crazy!'

'I'm not crazy. I can sense it. Is it the blonde one, Christa?'

'Oh, come on, Kate!'

'Then who?'

'Nobody. Enough of this rubbish, now. Let me alone.'

She nodded again, as if his words had confirmed what she was thinking. She finished his glass of wine, then took his hand and pulled him out of the chair and across the room to the dining room door. But there she abruptly let go, staring into the room.

'Good God!' she breathed.

'What's wrong?'

Udo had entered through the other door. He was standing in the middle of the room, a plaster covering his face from forehead to cheek. He gave a sour grin, anticipating their questions.

135

'What happened? The boyfriend of a nurse I went out with. I'm going to bring charges against that –'

'Charges?'

'Yes, charges. It was an unprovoked, brutal assault!'

'Sure it was.'

'Well, what do you think I . . . ?' Udo was confused by his father's reaction. 'Is that all you're going to say?'

'What do you suggest? Should I say "Do unto others", perhaps, or "Occupational hazard", perhaps?'

'Okay, I've got it. You're pleased about this, is that it? You're enjoying it. Well, I hope it chokes you!'

Kate stepped in quickly. 'You two really are the limit! Now don't start all over again. And anyway, Klaus, Udo's right. He doesn't have to take this lying down.'

'Absolutely not,' Brinkmann said, unsympathetically. 'Why not put an ad in the local paper? Let everyone know?'

'I'll give it some thought,' Udo said, tight-lipped. He turned to leave, his expression dejected.

'Aren't you going to have something to eat?'

'I've lost my appetite.'

'Hm,' Kate said, briskly. 'Seems to be catching today.'

Later, the two of them sat down, immersed in their own thoughts. They ate a delicious marrow and dumpling soup, one of Kate's specialities, followed by a stack of crisp, golden-brown pancakes.

'Now listen, Kate, don't you think that young fellow –'

'I don't think anything. I stopped thinking a long time ago. However, if you would care to tell me that the pancakes are delicious . . . ?'

'They're delicious,' he said, hastily. 'And what's that there?'

'Compote. Early rennets, cooked in syrup. You know who brought them? Christa and one of the patients – that funny-looking bicycle rider. The one who looks as if he escaped from the circus.'

'Arthur Wilkins,' Brinkmann smiled.

'That's the one. But here's the best part: he got them from the garden of the old man whose children have spirited him away to an old people's home in Frankfurt.'

'Oh God, yes, poor old Bischle.' Brinkmann carefully spooned some of the compote on to his plate. The subject of old Bischle was yet another topic guaranteed not to cheer you up. That was the sort of thing he was trying to get away from. Fat chance. He wondered how the old man would feel about one of those awful geriatric care machines in Frankfurt. He put it out of his mind.

'If Arthur is so keen on gardening, I'll put him to work on ours. That way he can pay off his debts. Or at least some of them.'

People live too long and then no one has any use for them. In the old days it was different. In the old days the children didn't feel it necessary to disappear to Florida for two months, and the old folks didn't have to go into a home. In the old days they all lived together and talked to each other and told each other stories. There was always something the old people could do, even if it was only splitting a few logs or looking after the little ones. But today?

I have lived too long, Jacob Bischle thought. I am too old. And anyone who gets too old is put away. No, not even put away: thrown away. I am a disposable person, he thought. He got out of bed, put on his pyjama trousers, and went over to the window.

'Now, Mr Bischle, you know you can't walk around in your pyjamas all the time!'

Of course I can if I want to! It's not as if I want to leave my room, or even get out of bed for that matter. Why should I talk to the other patients? Or eat with them? Jacob Bischle wanted nothing to do with that big room where they all sat together like a flock of sheep, where the women in pale pink dresses and white aprons who called themselves 'assistants' told him what to eat, what to wear and how to behave.

It was like some terrible, never-ending dream. The dreams were bad enough. He didn't have to eat as well.

Jacob Bischle stared out at the city, the buildings of steel and glass that seemed to reach the sky. They looked like boxes someone had forgotten to load on a wagon and take away. Not a tree in sight, much less a mountain. Smoggy, yellow, milky sky: any colour you like, but never blue.

'It's called the "Rose Garden",' his daughter-in-law had said. 'Isn't that lovely?'

Just imagine. An old people's home.

'You'll like it there, Grandpa,' she said. 'The best doctors. Tip

137

top. First class. The staff, too. Once you get used to it, you'll live like the King of France.'

Get used to it. As if that could ever happen . . .

Bischle pressed his forehead against the window pane. Twelve floors down, in the little courtyard, he could see a small pond with a fountain. It looked like a pig's stomach which had turned blue.

How often he'd thought, finish it, pack it in, jump! He might even have done it had the pig's stomach not been there.

A disposable person! Except that the dustcart hadn't taken him away. He felt cold, so cold. Summer seemed to have gone. As he watched, it began to rain again. Soon the raindrops were rattling on what they called the 'panoramic window with its superb view of the city' like bursts from a machine-pistol. Jacob Bischle lay down on the 'special mattress constructed by experts to meet the needs of the elderly' and pulled the covers over his head. If only evening would come!

The bedside telephone rang. He picked it up. A voice he knew spoke to him. It sounded as if it was coming from another planet.

'Jacob, is that you?' it said. It was Erwin Hopf. 'There you are! Never thought it would be me, did you?'

No, he never would have thought it.

Erwin asked how he was. If he spared a thought for his old friend once in a while? Had he learned to play chess yet? What kind of place was he in? And wouldn't he prefer to come back to Offingen to Room 208 in the Black Forest Clinic?

Jacob Bischle couldn't bring himself to say much more than 'yes' and 'no'. Yes, the food was all right. No, he had no friends. Yes, he would love to be back home again. No, there were no nurses here. Only stupid women wearing pink dresses like the hairdressers in Ranecker's in the market square in Offingen. And chess? Who would he play chess with here? Who would teach him?

There was a silence at the other end. Jacob Bischle's hand cupped the mouthpiece as though to trap Hopf's voice in it. Then he heard someone else speak.

'Mr Bischle. This is Arthur.'

'Yes.'

'Remember me, Mr Bischle?'

'Yes.' Of course, he remembered him. The scarecrow in the corner of Room 208. The world traveller on his bike. The layabout

Well, maybe he was and maybe he wasn't. He seemed like a decent, kind-hearted fellow.

'Mr Bischle, there's something I want to tell you . . .'

Jacob Bischle listened, but he had difficulty with Arthur's North German accent and understood only about half of what he said. But then Arthur said something, a word that went through Jacob Bischle's body like an electric shock.

'Mr Bischle, we need you here. Because of the rennets.'

'What about the rennets?'

'We've gathered them. They're all picked and bottled, all of them. Christa and Elke helped me. We've stored them all away. A really professional job: marmalade and compote. You should taste the marmalade! Hey, Mr Bischle, are you still there?'

'Still here.'

'Would you like me to send you a jar?'

'No.'

'No? Why not?'

Why not?, he thought. I know why not. But he did not reply to Arthur in faraway Offingen, carried away by an idea that had begun to grow inside him, so right, so obvious! He did not even notice he had banged the phone down and cut Arthur off.

Three hours later, anyone passing the rear of the 'Rose Garden Home for Senior Citizens' at around nine on that Friday evening in August might have seen a tall, thin, old man carefully opening the gate at the basement of the building. Bischle looked around cautiously, then walked quickly up the concrete ramp, around the open square with its neatly-pruned bushes and swimming pool, and out into the road.

It was still raining. The raindrops glistened in the street lights like crystals. There was not a soul about. The old man gave the 'Rose Garden' building one last glance, then turned away, drawing himself erect. He felt as if he had grown taller. Jacob Bischle was marching home.

After a little while he was directed on to a bus going to the station. Someone told him when they had arrived. He was helped off the bus and a woman in a uniform said something, pointing. He did not understand what she said. Everything seemed mixed up, confused. He felt so very tired it was difficult to think straight. If he

139

asked people something they tried to answer him, but he didn't understand their explanations. Only one thing mattered: he was going home. Nothing was going to stop him. I'm on my way, Elfriede, he thought. I can do it!

'We've picked all the rennets, Mr Bischle.'

Your rennets, Elfriede! He murmured her name as he leaned his tired back against a cement wall somewhere deep in the bowels of the earth. The air was sticky, like in a station.

The shop windows were brightly lit, although all the shops were closed. There were cigarette butts, newspapers, paper cups scattered on the floor. Although the underground city was enormous there were only a few people about: teenage girls with heavily made-up eyes and dyed hair. Hardly more than children, with cigarettes in their mouths and trousers so tight they left nothing to the imagination. The young boys looked across at him without interest. There are such things as elderly drop-outs too, you know, Hopf would have said, and it was true. So the elderly drop-out slept, among the beer cans and the banana skins.

DISPOSABLE PEOPLE!

All at once Jacob Bischle felt something constrict in his chest, and knew he must get some fresh air. But where? He was breathing badly, mouth wide open. The station? He must get a ticket. 'Single to Offingen. Just a single.' He wasn't coming back!

When Jacob Bischle opened his eyes again he found himself staring at a worn, battered pair of cowboy boots, dirty scuffed jeans, and a brass belt-buckle. Looking up, he saw a pimply, pallid boy with a broken nose and eyes that looked as if they had seen everything. Next to him was another youngster, not yet seventeen by the look of him, blond streaky hair, blue eyes, something on a chain round his neck.

Jacob Bischle found he was breathing more easily. The earlier feeling of illness had passed and he could see clearly. He noticed that what the blond boy was wearing round his neck was a medal, an Iron Cross from the last war. At the same time he realised they meant him no good.

'Well, what about a cigarette, old man?'

Jacob Bischle tried to lift himself up and push past them. The tall one with the broken nose pushed him back against the wall. Gently: it didn't take much. 'Filthy night, eh, Grandpa?'

Bischle nodded.

'What are you doing all on your own? Missed the train, have you? Or was it your girlfriend? Eh? And what about our cigarettes, eh?'

The blond one started to laugh, the Iron Cross jiggling up and down. Why didn't someone stop them from wearing it? They ought to be locked up. When you think what an Iron Cross had once meant! What men had done to earn one!

Another one, fat, dirty, stubbled chin, watery eyes. A vacant look on his face.

'Come on, Grandpa. Give us some money.'

'What?'

'Money, old man! Bread, dough, loot.'

Jacob Bischle did not reply. You couldn't talk to people like that. The best thing to do was to keep your mouth shut. But he was afraid. Everyone was afraid of kids like these nowadays. Where are the police? Never around when you need them. He could see a sign: LEVEL B, large black letters on grey concrete. LEVEL B: chemists and boutiques – but no police.

The one with the broken nose prodded Jacob Bischle with a grubby finger. 'What's the matter, Grandpa? Don't you like us?'

Jacob Bischle closed his eyes again. What else could he do?

TWENTY-FOUR

Ten-thirty p.m. on Level B in Frankfurt-on-Main. And also in the operating theatre of the clinic in the Black Forest. The patient they had fought to save had been removed. Evidence of how hard a battle it had been was everywhere: bloody strips of muslin, syringes, exhausted faces.

They had rushed him in with flashing blue lights and sirens wailing. A thirty-eight-year-old truck driver, half conscious. Unbearable pains, blood in the faeces, vomiting more blood . . . a perforated stomach ulcer.

They had worked on him for over two hours, each minute seeming like only seconds. Falling blood pressure, a constantly accelerating heartbeat: no time for a lab report. Schaefer performed the laparotomy, Udo assisted. When the stomach was opened they saw the blood clots, saw the way the stomach was adhering to the liver, and called in Brinkmann.

His arrival immediately brought about a change, a calmness, to the room. Everyone watched how confidently his hands moved to make it easier to identify the problem. Whatever happened, here was someone they could rely on.

It looked bad. The ulcer had made the wall of the stomach brittle. Brinkmann pointed with his tweezers at the pea-sized elevations in the mucous membrane. Benign or malignant? There was no way of knowing, and at this time of day a mad dash to the pathology labs at Freiburg was out of the question. One way or the other, the patient would die.

'Gastrectomy, Billroth Two technique.'

Time and again they had to stop the bleeding, time and again react to another new development. And every time they had to fight to remain calm – panic stabilisation, as it was aptly called.

Schaefer really tried. When the damaged tissue was finally removed, and the remainder of the stomach joined up to the intestines, he stepped back, leaving Udo to sew up the wound and clean up.

A hundred and thirty minutes! Not a good time, perhaps, but in the circumstances . . .

Professor Brinkmann took another look at the medical records the ambulance men had brought with them.

'Unbelievable! The man had been under clinical care for the last three years. Can you imagine it?'

They could imagine it, but they didn't want to. Where did the old man get the energy to lecture them now about what had happened? Udo looked at his hands and was amazed they were not trembling. He looked at the table. The blood had dulled the shining chrome.

Over. Finished. The actors had departed, the stage was empty. Mark, the operating-theatre auxiliary, turned out the lights, plunging the room into darkness. Rubber aprons, gowns and vests had long since been stripped off, but in his mind Udo was still going through the operation. He followed Schaefer into his office.

'How about a beer? Or a coffee?'

'I'd rather have a fruit juice.'

Udo fetched the drinks from a vending machine in the corridor, opened them, and took a sip of his beer, staring at the bottle rather than at Schaefer.

'I've just realised why so many surgeons are alcoholics,' he said.

'It's not the operations, it's not even the stress. It's what happens to you afterwards.'

Schaefer nodded, switching on his desk lamp. He bent over the pad on which he was writing down the minutes of the operation. God, what a cold fish he was!

'I suppose it never occurs to you?'

'What's that?'

'Well, surgeons and alcohol.'

'As a matter of fact, no. But then, neither does the thought of a drunken jumbo-jet pilot.'

Udo said nothing. Might have expected it, he thought. He heard Schaefer's chair squeak as he swivelled round to face him. This time there was no irony in Schaefer's large grey eyes, only a serious pensiveness.

'If one is logical about it, we're all vulnerable. I've known a few who not only drank but smoked pot. Or worse. Truly. And what's the difference between them and some doctor who's called from a cocktail party to perform an emergency operation?'

'I didn't mean that.'

'I know. You were talking about the aftermath. The tension. Then having to go home, flirt with the girlfriend, playing with the darling children, right? Listening to the wife talking about the prices in the supermarket . . . It's not easy for us, is it? In the old days I used to take a half hour's walk after something like tonight. Just walking around, anywhere. When I was an assistant in Dortmund I even thought of installing a punchbag in my room, something to take it out on, you know?'

A thin grin. Udo was speechless. Schaefer had never talked to him like this before. Never so much, never so personally.

'Do you still have it? I think I could use it right now.'

'I got rid of it. Can't afford it any more.'

Schaefer turned back to his desk. He looked briefly at his hand and then let it fall to his side. There was something about the gesture that alarmed Udo. Something wrong with the hand. Schaefer had looked tired at the operating table today. He didn't want to pry.

'The old man – he can really stand up to it, can't he?'

Schaefer nodded. 'Why don't you ever call him "my father"?'

'Does it bother you?'

144

'I merely remarked on it.'

'It's a long story. Well, then . . .' Udo got up from his chair. 'I think maybe I'll go and find myself the equivalent of your punching bag in a pub somewhere.'

Beneath his raised eyebrows Schaefer's glasses shone. The amused sarcasm was back in his voice. 'What, again? You've only just taken off the plaster! That reminds me, I meant to ask you: that Mrs Bach . . . ?'

'An old flame of my father's. You know: whither thou goest . . .'

'I see. An impressive lady.'

'Very impressive.' Udo hesitated, then added, 'Like my old man.'

As he walked to the car, Klaus Brinkmann paused to enjoy the heavy perfume of the roses. Not a leaf moved. Across the plain an electrical storm flashed.

They had done their best. Tomorrow they would know more. It looked as if the cancer had not spread. With any luck the poor fellow would have a chance . . .

Brinkmann felt tired but contented. He had done what needed to be done, and he had done it well. He got in the car and headed home.

On the way out, he heard the hesitant spluttering of a car engine. Then it started: the familiar roar of a Volkswagen. Lights came on. He stopped. Mollie shot out of the car into the night, skidded, then jumped up at the green VW, scratching on the door with her front paws until the driver's window rolled down. It was Christa!

'Well, well,' Brinkmann said. 'So I can be lucky too, sometimes.'

What shining eyes! Why didn't she reply? What the devil was making him so tongue-tied? He fumbled in his pocket and brought out the tickets, two yellow pasteboard squares that had *Summer Concert Villingen* written across them. His heart was bumping.

'You see, I bought them after all.' He smiled proudly, displaying them like a youngster who's just won a prize. 'Well, what do you say now?'

She did not reply. He saw there was a furrow between her brows.

'What is it?'

'Nothing.'

'Aren't you pleased, Christa? You so wanted to hear the Vivaldi.'

'But now I would prefer not to.'

'But it was you who suggested it.'

'I know, and I'm sorry. But I've changed my mind.'

'Why?'

Again she did not answer.

'Christa, I realise I'm in no position to ask for an explanation, but . . .'

'It's . . .' Her voice was barely audible. 'It's just that I . . .'

'Go on.'

'I do appreciate your kindness, believe me. But more would be . . . inappropriate. It would only lead to complications. You know that better than I do.'

More would be inappropriate? What was she thinking? Well, what had he imagined would happen? What had he hoped for? Brinkmann searched for words. Above the roof of her car he could see the hulking shape of the mountains, black and sharp in the diffused light of the distant storm. Complications? I suppose I should have expected this reaction.

'Is that really your only reason, Christa? Or is it something else? Perhaps something I did, or said . . . ?'

'Oh, no!'

'Then what?'

'Nothing. Really. Look, I've got to get home.' She nodded to him and put the car in gear. He stepped backwards as she drove off, caught a glimpse of her profile, and then was left alone, the concert tickets still clutched in his hand.

Mollie ran down the road after the VW, yapping. Then she came back, head down, her tail between her legs. Brinkmann shook his head: she looked exactly the way he felt. He patted her head. The first raindrops hit his face.

TWENTY-FIVE

Perhaps something I did or said, Christa? . . .

She drove slowly, very slowly. The driving rain made streaks on the windscreen: it was all the wipers could do to cope. She saw a motorcyclist coming towards her in the middle of the road, the rider leaning over the handlebars, and whirled the wheel to avoid him.

Something I did or said! Aren't we all interdependent? Isn't everybody doing something to someone else? That wasn't the problem. The problem was coming to terms with it.

She pulled over to the side of the road and leaned against the window. The rain still hammered on the roof.

The Chief and a nurse. The God of Gods and the failed medical student, Christa Meurer, who carried around on her back the ruins of her broken dreams and illusions, and who had become skeptical beyond her years. And what about him? The age difference had never mattered to her. What was it? The hand that took hers and stroked it? The smile as he made his rounds, the glances, his voice, the few times they had taken a walk together . . .

But then the constant nagging doubts: Why? What for?

Don't think about it! It would have been nice, though. Like all those hopes and dreams you're afraid of.

The rain was easing off. Christa released the handbrake but did not start the motor, letting the car freewheel towards the town. The best thing to do was not to think about any of it, not even Elena Bach. What was it Udo had called her: 'My father's shadow'. A shadow that he quite obviously could not shake off.

So: that chapter was over before it had begun. Farewell, she thought, farewell sweet dreams. Perhaps the reason it was so hard to say goodbye to them was because they were so impossible . . .

'He doesn't want to talk, he doesn't want to laugh – what's wrong, Grandpa?'

Jacob Bischle did his best to shake off the rough hand, but the fellow was too strong. He simply twisted Jacob's arm, pulling open his jacket, poking around. He stank of beer.

'Well, well, what have we here? A purse, is it? Want to open it yourself, Grandpa, or shall we take care of it for you?'

Bischle felt the back of his head pressing against the wall. He saw the other faces, this terrible echoing empty hall with its neon lights and advertisements. He could see no one who might help him.

'And here's something. Look at that, eh? What a watch!'

Something that was neither fear nor anger flooded through Bischle's body, lending a strength to his arm that swept aside the dirty hand with its broken fingernails. Outrage, that was what it was. Nobody was going to take his 'railwayman'! Nobody was even going to touch the watchchain, let alone put their dirty fingers on his own, special watch. What would a thief like that know about watches? What the devil was the fellow grinning at?

'Hey, Grandpa, you're pretty fit for an old turkey. Looks as if we'll have to begin again. Listen, tell me, what's the time?'

The fat one giggled. The blond one grinned and the one with the broken nose put on an innocent look. Then the faces started to blur, as though they were made of soft putty, and he put a hand up to his heart. He closed his eyes and took a deep breath but it didn't help. Pain swelled in his chest and rose up into his neck. His heartbeats seemed to falter and then race.

Elfriede! He could think only of her name. He shook his head to dispel the dizziness. As he opened his eyes he witnessed a miracle.

A man's fist, big, strong, seemed to come from nowhere. The thug with the broken nose went reeling a couple of metres away, landing on the floor, his arms and legs asprawl. Bischle saw now that the fist belonged to a big man, wearing moustache and a pale-grey military uniform with belt and cap. He took hold of Bischle's shoulder.

'Are you all right, Grandfather?'

Finally Bischle managed to speak. 'My name is Jacob Bischle. I'm not your grandfather nor anybody else's, either.'

'Sure, sure, fine, Mr Bischle.'

A second one marched over. This one had a beard. 'Did those louts harm you?'

Bischle shook his head.

'What were they after?'

'My railwayman.'

The bearded one looked at his friend. 'What's he talking about, Alois?'

'My watch,' Bischle explained.

'Scum! Are you all right now? Can you walk? Where are you going?'

'I have to go to the station. I can manage. I'm going home.'

'Come on, then.' They held his arm. Their uniforms had large pockets on the trousers. The one with the moustache, Alois, reminded Jacob Bischle of his oldest son. Only, Bernard was gone, killed in the war. He'd never have permitted them to take him to Frankfurt, to this mugger's paradise.

The one called Alois took a small bottle out of one of his pockets. 'Here, have a drop of schnapps. It'll do you good.'

It did help. Alois had a drink, too. Bischle decided it wasn't just the schnapps. The boy had a friendly smile, and that helped as well.

'Well, I suppose we'd better get you to the station. There's a welfare office or something over there.'

Jacob Bischle shook his head. 'No,' he said, fiercely. 'I don't want to go there.'

'Where, then?'

'I want to go home. To Offingen. Will you help me?'

'Of course we will.'

Forty minutes later Jacob Bischle was sitting in a train bound for Basle. He looked out of the window. The station clock said eleven

149

forty-five. He saw the faces of the two soldiers. Alois was a non-commissioned officer, like his Bernard had been. But that was a long time ago, in the final year of the war. Low-flying machine-gunners had shot him to pieces. He shook his head. The way the officers dressed these days: they walked about looking like refuse collectors.

The train started to move. Jacob Bischle waved, and even smiled. His eyes were a bit moist, but he wasn't quite sure why.

Midnight.

Through the noise of the shower, Christa Meurer thought she heard something. The telephone? It couldn't be. Or could it?

She turned off the water, threw a towel around her body and ran across the bathroom and along the hall, leaving a wet trail behind her. She opened the door of the lounge. It was the phone. Albert, perhaps? Her brother often had daft ideas like this.

She lifted the receiver, pushing back a wet, heavy strand of hair.

'Christa?' She could not believe it; it was Brinkmann.

'Can you hear me, Christa?'

Through the window she saw the electric-blue lightning flash; the thunder followed instantaneously, shaking the glass. Outside, the storm thrashed the trees and bushes.

'I'm sorry, Christa. I just had to talk to you again. Hello, Christa, are you there?'

'Yes, I'm here.'

'Is the storm as bad over there?'

'We're not all that far apart.'

'Sorry? Oh, yes, of course.'

She pulled the towel tighter around her shoulders and looked down at the puddle forming between her feet.

'You weren't in bed, by any chance?'

What did he expect her to say? Should she reply, 'No, I'm not in bed, I'm sitting in a chair dripping water everywhere. I'm watching the storm and thinking about the end of the world, about suicide and the Devil alone knows what else.'? What was it he wanted to hear?

'It's late.'

'I know. I'm sorry, Christa. I really wouldn't have called if it

150

hadn't been for the fact that I kept wondering about the concert tickets . . .'

Could it be true? Could he be making such heavy weather of it, with these long-winded explanations and excuses? He was acting like some elderly benefactor.

'You don't have to be sorry. After all, midnight is the hour of truth, right?'

'Truth? What truth, Christa?'

'I was being sarcastic. Just a little . . . "King".'

'Where did you hear that?'

'Isn't that what you were called in Basle?'

'That was a long time ago.'

'Even so, a king is entitled to an explanation. To clear up any misunderstanding. That is his right. So why bother with apologies? You see, we've probably both had our dreams. It's not a crime. But there comes a time when we have to finish with them. You asked for a reason. Well, there is one. It has a name. It even has a title.'

'Elena Bach?'

'Doctor Elena Bach,' she replied.

'Christa, listen . . .'

'Goodnight, Professor.' She put down the receiver. All at once she felt very cold. She listened to the storm raging outside: a fitting accompaniment to the conversation that had just ended. But you are not going to cry, she told herself. That would be altogether too melodramatic. Instead, Christa Meurer threw herself on the bed and pulled the covers over her head.

The world swam in a damp greyness. The time was 07.32. Rain pounded on the station platform as Alfons Hofegger checked the readings on the display unit, pulled up the collar of his rubber overcoat, and left the stationmaster's office at Offingen. Damned early shift. No way he'd be able to switch off the lights along the track today.

He looked along the shimmering steel rails to the west. Two lights, blurred in the fog, grew brighter, larger, looming nearer. The early train. Compressed air brakes hissed, doors flew open. Half a dozen people got out. Not one tourist among them.

Hofegger walked along the train closing the doors. Just as he was about to give the signal for departure he looked back, as regulations required him to do, and saw someone else getting off the train. Right at the back, a long, lean, old man.

Hofegger hurried along the length of the train, helped the old man, closed the door, blew his whistle. Then he turned around.

'Bischle! It's not possible! Where did you come from?'

Jacob Bischle did not answer. He looked ill: his white-stubbled face was as grey as the rain.

'What are you doing on the early train, Jacob?'

Again Bischle made no reply. Instead, he started walking very slowly, like a robot, his arms slightly lifted, step by deliberate step. Alois Hofegger walked alongside him, plucking his sleeve.

'Jacob, sit down. Look, there's a bench over there. Please, Jacob, tell me, where have you come from?'

'Frankfurt.' Bischle stopped, turning his head slowly as if it hurt him to do so. He took a deep breath and half closed his eyes. When he spoke again, however, the words came clearly. 'But now, now I'm back . . .'

'Come, sit down, Jacob.'

Jacob Bischle walked on slowly, taking short hesitant steps, ignoring Hofegger's request. He was so weak that Hofegger had to support him. Every so often he would mutter something inaudible. Then he said, 'I need a taxi.'

'I'll call Rau for you. He's parked outside. Are you going home?'

'No. To the clinic.' The word seemed to please Bischle. He opened his red-rimmed eyes. 'Yes. The clinic. They still have my bed . . .'

It was all so simple: get into the taxi, lean back till you got there, then get out and pay. But when he got out things became complicated again, and all the confidence ran out of him. He stood in front of the entrance to the clinic. He was cold. It was still raining. Inside, the building was brightly lit but there was nobody to be seen. The big glass door was locked. Because of him, perhaps? No, no, they would, they *had* to let him in. He tried to work everything out, but in vain. And his legs weren't working properly, either. It was only the cold raindrops that kept him from passing out. Come on!, he told himself. Try, at least.

He turned right, towards the garden. That was where the terraces were. There was also a small flight of stairs. He wouldn't risk climbing them, but at least he could look up. The distance seemed endless.

At last he reached the terrace. The lights seemed to be on in all the rooms. They would be getting the patients out of bed around now. He saw people in dressing gowns, nurses in white uniforms. They were having breakfast. And . . . there was Room 208!

He called, 'Hopf!' What seemed to Jacob Bischle like a name was in fact no more than a croaking, pitiful hurt sound, the moan of an injured animal washed away by the rain.

'Hopf!' He could see the man, for Heaven's sake! Erwin!

He saw the other one, too, the scarecrow. By now they would be going to clean their teeth, the beds already made. Then there would be coffee or tea and fresh rolls. He saw it all as clearly as if he were in the room. He could even smell the familiar scent of polish and soap. And Hopf's perspiration, and Hopf's cigar.

It was then that Jacob Bischle saw the third person, a fat pale face above a blue dressing gown. The man was laughing.

A third one?, Jacob Bischle thought wearily. But . . . I was the third one . . .

And then it came to him: they have taken my bed away from me!

Jacob Bischle's strength was going. He did not want to carry on, and could not have done so even if he had wanted to. His knees buckled. It seemed to him as if he had no legs, no bones. As if his whole body was a cold, jelly-like mass. He collapsed against the wall. The rain continued to drench his grey hair.

TWENTY-SIX

They found him half an hour later.

It was thanks to Mollie, really. Nothing could change her routine, and that early-morning walk around the house was part of it. This particular morning she had nearly been put off by the rain, but after hesitation she sniffed her way along the wall, turned around the corner to the back of the house, and thereupon began barking like mad.

'That damned animal! What's wrong now?'

Matron was in the basement checking over the breakfast schedules. With a disapproving glance at the trainee nurse, she moved to the window.

'Mollie, be quiet!'

But Mollie had no intention of being quiet. Her barking became a thin howl that sounded like a siren.

'Something's wrong. She's crazy but not usually this crazy.' Sister Hildegard picked up a towel, threw it over her head, and went out into the rain. As she came out, Mischa appeared ten metres away. He looked over the railings and saw the old man in the same moment she did. A bundle of clothes, soaked by the rain, lying amid the tulips.

'Mischa! Can you see who it is?'

'It's Mr Bischle!'

'Mr Bischle? But . . . he's in Frankfurt!'

'Doesn't look like it!' Mischa retorted. He jumped over the garden wall as Sister Hildegard ran to the telephone.

Within minutes the old man was in intensive care. An oxygen mask was placed over his bony skull. Electric blankets warmed the chilled body while skilled hands tried to locate the fragile veins to give injections. The whole technical apparatus known as 'reanimation' was in progress.

Of all this Jacob Bischle knew nothing. He was a prisoner of his own nightmare. He felt as if he was trapped in a coffin in which black jungle creepers reached for his chest, encircling it and forcing out his breath. He could hear the sound of the hammers driving the nails into the wood. Elfriede, he thought. Elfriede, please help me! Tell them I'm not dead. Tell them!

'I'm not dead!' Jacob Bischle screamed and opened his eyes.

A face loomed above him, a kind face. The pale eyes that returned his gaze were so luminous that Jacob Bischle began to tremble. He had seen God! And God's face looked exactly like the professor's. Surely, if God could look at him so kindly, if God was this forgiving, this merciful, this loving, then all would be well with him, and Elfriede would not be far away . . .

Jacob Bischle remained in intensive care at the Black Forest Clinic for eight days, after which it was considered safe to move him. He even coped with a flare-up of pneumonia.

'Amazing! Just look how he's improved. Tough as old boots!'

Dr Brückner could not believe it; the others concurred. Hard as nails, old Mr Bischle was.

'Well, Jacob, so you're back at last!' Hopf beamed when they brought him back. And Arthur had 'borrowed' some flowers from the garden. Yellow daisies.

That was how it came about that Jacob Bischle was back in his bed in Room 208. The man who'd occupied it had been discharged. Bischle allowed Hopf to embrace him, permitted Arthur to pat his back, consented to their filling his glass and let them persuade him

155

to have some smoked ham. They celebrated his return with a bottle of Ruländer.

Then Arthur went over to the cupboard, from which he ceremoniously took out three jars containing golden yellow fruit swimming in syrup. 'Look! Rennets!'

His rennets. Bischle tasted them and nodded politely. He said nothing about his experiences in Frankfurt, nor did he wish to talk about his children. 'I don't know them any more!' And that was that.

On his first day back he demanded that Hopf teach him to play chess. He watched silently and reverently as the pieces were moved. He listened to the instructions without saying a word. For a whole day the two talked to him, then that evening they played their first game, followed by a second next morning after breakfast.

'Jacob, if you're not careful you'll lose your queen!' Hopf warned. Bischle shook his head.

'Why not?'

'The knight,' Bischle pointed out.

Hopf rubbed his nose. Would you believe it, the old boy had hidden his knight so well he'd missed it completely.

'Dropped you right in it,' Arthur tittered. 'Jacob, you're the greatest!'

'Still Mr Bischle to you.'

'Mr Bischle, then.' Unperturbed, Arthur stroked Jacob Bischle's grey head. If the old man minded he gave no sign of it. 'You're the greatest, Mr Bischle!'

Practically everyone was present: personnel from gynaecology, from the orthopaedic unit, the surgical staff, Dr Brückner, and of course Wolters, whose tanned face beamed as Dr Brinkmann gestured towards the slim woman in the brown leather suit who was sitting in the place of honour at the head of the conference table.

'Ladies and gentlemen, our deplorable lack of feminine company is finally at an end. I have great pleasure today in introducing you to our new second anaesthetist, Dr Bach.'

Smiles, applause. Brinkmann stopped them with a gesture.

'I worked for many years with Dr Bach in the hospital at Karlsruhe. Unless she's forgotten everything since then, I can assure you you'll be collaborating with a top specialist in the field of anaesthesia.'

They all applauded; only when Elena Bach stood up did it stop. She smiled charmingly, looked around. 'I'm very pleased to be with you,' she began. The rest of her short speech was spoken lightly and eloquently. It was followed by the usual handshakes, and Elena's assurance that she would soon be starting work. She allowed Wolters to kiss her hand, smiled at Udo who seemed unexpectedly friendly, said goodbye to Brückner, and walked across to the window.

She looked out at the town and the mountains, their slopes disappearing into the wine-coloured evening mist, moved by their beauty. Well, you handled that all right, she thought. Yet there were still a few nagging doubts.

Had she made the right decision? Whichever way she examined the proposition, the question marks remained. It wasn't the job: she had no fears on that score, although they'd warned her often enough in Karlsruhe about the dangers of exchanging the well-oiled machinery of a large hospital with all its technical innovations for a clinic such as this. Working here would mean utilising every aspect of your training, being a medical jack-of-all-trades. On the front line, as they said.

That was one part of it, but there were others. Uneasiness took hold of her: this was Offingen, in the Black Forest. Would fresh air, the beauties of the countryside, the mountain walks, be enough to compensate her for what she was leaving behind? At least Karlsruhe was a city. You could go to Heidelberg . . . and quite apart from cultural pursuits one had an opportunity to meet interesting people all over the place, to make friends, and to have colleagues you could talk things over with when you needed to. Here, her whole life would revolve around the clinic and the man who ran it. Was that what she truly wanted?

Almost as if she had conjured up his presence, he spoke from behind her. 'Well, how do you like our club?'

'A bit early to decide, wouldn't you say?'

'Of course. But you'll find they're okay.'

He laid his hand on her shoulder and Elena felt her body tense. Before the sensation that she both feared and loved grew any stronger, he withdrew his hand.

157

'First impressions are a matter of instinct, as in so many things,' he said. 'But I can usually tell right away, either this is going to go smoothly, or else, there's something wrong in this outfit.'

'There is something wrong.'

He laughed. 'Really?'

'We two.' She took a deep breath then went on, almost plaintively, 'I imagine I'll get on all right with the others, don't you?'

'Of course you will. And with me, too. You'll see: we'll be the perfect team.'

That friendly formality – what a wonder weapon! And work would take care of the rest, his manner told her. He really thought it was as simple as that.

'What's your apartment like?'

'It's quite pretty. You can see as far as the Feldberg from the lounge window.'

'If there's anything you need . . .'

'My God!' she said, almost sarcastically. 'Don't put yourself out. I'll manage on my own.'

'Fighting words,' he said. His look irritated her. Was it indifference, unspoken, or had he really slipped into that famous 'impersonal working relationship' that all the tutorial colleges recommended?

'Come on, Elena, Kate's made coffee. And a cake, to welcome you.'

She nodded. Nothing had changed.

The sky was dark and overcast.

Elke's thoughts were gloomy, too. She couldn't help it: she knew it was over, and yet she kept thinking about Udo. Well, to hell with him. There was no future in racking her brains trying to understand him. Where would that get her? What really hurt was the way he treated her! Just a nod, or at the most a 'hi', or 'good morning, Nurse.' Not so much as a glance if they met each other beside a patient's bed or at a conference. It was as if she was invisible, a piece of hospital furniture, something you take, use, and throw away.

'Thank your lucky stars it turned out this way, Elke! That's how Udo is. Maybe he'll grow up one day, but right now he isn't even born. Can't you see that?'

Even Christa didn't understand. Well, she might have known. Who could possibly understand how she felt? Nobody!

Arriving at this conclusion always made her cry. When that happened, she either hid in the park, the bathroom or the toilet, or wrote yard-long letters in her imagination, or banged her head against an imaginary wall. And eventually had the inevitable run-in with Sister.

'Elke!' Sister Hildegard fumed. 'I try to be a patient person, but I've had enough of you!'

'And I've had enough of you!' Elke snapped. 'And not just you, either!'

Fortunately for her Christa had managed to avert the catastrophe that would otherwise have ensued. But why should she be grateful for that? Everything was going wrong. Take last Wednesday, for instance.

Elke had had a day off. The sun had at last broken through, and she'd spent the day at the open-air pool with some other members of staff. She had been about to go for a swim when Lukas Schneider, Centre-Forward of Offingen Football Club, came up the ladder, his tanned body shiny with water, his eyes bright and hard.

It was too late to run away, too late even to smile. Attack was the best defence. 'Well, why don't you throw me in? You're very good at that sort of thing!'

She didn't even get a response. With a shake of the head Lukas was gone, leaving Elke with only one thought in her mind: to get back home fast.

As if that wasn't bad enough, as she got to the dressing rooms she had had to bump into Bert, another member of the team.

'Hi, where are you off to?'

'Home.'

'In this weather? Why?'

'Ask your friend.'

'Lukas?' Bert grinned and shook his head. 'You two are nuts, you know that? But I'll tell you something. He still fancies you like mad.'

She remembered his words during the lecture, as Dr Brückner explained that love, infatuation, joy and depression were closely linked to hormones in the body. Perhaps she should ask Hildegard for some pills, or maybe get Brückner to give her an injection. Maybe that would help. At any rate . . .

'Good heavens, Elke, what on earth's the matter with you?' Sister hissed. 'There are twenty sheets missing. We're supposed to be replacing the linen this morning.'

Elke shrugged as she bustled off to 'replace the linen', and pushed the trolley towards the lift. The doors opened and, as if she didn't have enough problems on her plate, there was Udo Brinkmann. He gave her a nervous look, waved his hands: it was just a big act. He pretended to be in such a hurry that he hardly had time to give her a nod. Elke's heart felt like a lump of ice. At last the lift began to descend.

At least she was alone in the basement, alone with the humming of the pipes, the familiar clunking of the bath installation, neon lights, warmth, and the faint odour of lemon from the piles of fresh, dry laundry. She pushed down the door handle with her elbow and went into the laundry room. A second surprise awaited her. In the middle of the room with its shelves of sterilised white laundry sat a man on a bike.

'Arthur?' she exclaimed. 'What on earth are you doing here?'

He looked up and she saw there were black oil smears all over his face. 'I get thrown out of everywhere else.'

Elke nodded understandingly. She knew just how he felt.

'I'm supposed to be cutting the professor's hedge and lawn. I'll do it. Arthur will do it. But Guzzi comes first.' He gave the front wheel a spin and smiled dreamily as it whirred around.

'That's a nice bike,' Elke remarked.

'Isn't it. Not beautiful, perhaps, but likeable. Like you, little Elke.' He stood up and stretched out his hand towards her.

'Arthur, watch out!' she protested. 'I'm wearing whites.'

Arthur seemed not to hear her. His eyes were on the chrome rims of the bicycle. 'Lawns, hedges, trees to be cut, wood to be chopped. Oh, Elke, aren't people stupid . . .'

'Not only stupid. Bad.'

'They're bad second because they're stupid first. Which is why people like you and I sit in basements and are sad. That is, you're sad. I'm not sad any more. I'm getting my magic carpet ready, and then – poof! Off I go. Tell me why you're sad, Elke.'

'I don't know.' What could she say to this strange fellow? He wouldn't understand, anyway.

'Your trouble is you have no fantasies, little Elke.'

'How do you know that?'

'All sad people lack fantasies. They don't know what to do with themselves, so they sit around all the time thinking about the same thing, over and over. And they're . . . faint-hearted.'

Elke nodded. Could he be right? She no longer cared about the dirty paw he put on her shoulder. Arthur smiled, still watching the slowly-turning wheel. 'Get me far away from here, that will,' he said. 'Who knows where Guzzi will take me.'

'I'll come with you, Arthur.'

'I'm afraid that wouldn't work. Believe me, child, I'd love to take you with me, but you're not ready to go. However, there's no reason for you to be sad. Everything passes, believe me, it's true. When you get into one of these moods, you just tell yourself this: you don't need a bike, you can travel just as far in your thoughts. Then you'll feel better. You just think of me.'

She looked into the friendly eyes smiling at her and nodded.

'All right, Arthur,' she promised. 'I'll think of you."

TWENTY-SEVEN

Three days later, as Klaus Brinkmann was going to lunch with Elena Bach after a busy morning in the operating theatre, he stopped suddenly and took hold of her arm.

'Just a moment!'

Through the glass they stared at the strange apparition outside: long and bony, with stork-like legs, wearing mended blue shorts, trainers, and a faded gold cap worn back to front.

'I'll be damned!' Brinkmann muttered. 'Arthur is doing a runner.'

It was true enough. By the time Brinkmann reached the door and shouted his name, Arthur had pushed his bike across the ramp. A friendly if somewhat embarrassed smile spread across his thin face.

'Nice day, Professor. I was just about to . . .'

'Just about to say Goodbye? Is that it?'

'Something like that. I mean . . .'

'What?'

'Well . . . I thought perhaps a greeting card might not do just as well, since I'd asked myself whether it would be permissible to disturb the professor at home. However, since the professor is here now . . .'

'The only things you could disturb at my home are the pile of wood that is waiting for you and my neglected garden, not to mention the hedge. But you know all that already, don't you? Isn't that so, Mr Wilkins?'

'Ah yes, well, how shall I put it?' Arthur Wilkins' birdlike eyes had become restless, and his long nose pointed like a beak at the sky. 'You know, Professor, one could perhaps assume a certain, shall we say, mental disturbance in my case. You see, when I'm feeling all right, then I look around me and see the world . . .'

Arthur looked up at the sky, dark slatey clouds edged with sulphur yellow. Watching him, Brinkmann suddenly had a flash of insight. 'Oh, all right, let's forget about the wood and the garden. Just tell me one thing, Arthur: were you ever in Kleineck, that little village over behind the hill here? Ten houses and a church?'

'But of course, Professor! That's where I made my crash landing.'

'So it was you!' Brinkmann smiled. 'Look, it's starting to rain. Better get going, Mr Wilkins. Before you get wet. Or rather, before I change my mind.'

Arthur Wilkins mounted his bicycle, his movements dignified and purposeful. When he was settled in the saddle he sat up, saluted with his hand against his forehead, and rode over the ramp towards the exit. Brinkmann watched, then waved.

'What happened in Kleineck?' Elena Bach asked.

'Sorry? Oh, that? Well, that's where I saw him for the first time. It was stinking hot that day, and there was this fellow pushing his bike up the hill, whistling. Later on they brought him in but I never made the connection, never realised it was one and the same person. Imagine it – pushing your bike through the countryside, whistling as you go . . .'

'You envied him? Is that what you're trying to tell me?'

'I did. And I do now.' Brinkmann smiled sadly. 'Do you think I'd have let him go otherwise, owing me so much money? But I envy him, and that's a fact. He's free. Free as a bird.'

'Come on,' Elena Bach said, pulling his sleeve. 'Get into the house before your hair gets wet, you bourgeois mouse, you.'

•   •   •   •

He must on no account miss the turning: it was easy to do so. The roadside markings had faded; bushes grew down to the road. And still it rained.

Dr Ignaz Marker, country doctor from Kirchstett, changed down to second gear and guided his old Mercedes on to the overgrown verge. The ruts in the road were full of dark mud. Damned rain, would it never stop? Might as well forget all about summer. Well, at least it was good for the forest. Or so the foresters and experts said.

His visit to the farm at the top of the hill would be the last on Ignaz Marker's schedule for the day. His stomach rumbled; he felt the ache of exhaustion in his bones. Thirty visits today. He had criss-crossed the whole county. And now there was Lutz . . .

He felt the car skid. If only someone would fix the road. But, of course, there was nobody to fix it. Old Lutz's son was over in Offingen selling Japanese cars, which was far more important.

Marker slowed down but he was still going too fast for the tight bend. The wheels locked and the Mercedes went into a skid. Neither a touch on the accelerator nor a turn of the wheel against the direction of the skid helped: the car slid gently into the ditch.

Marker turned off the engine. He was too tired even to swear. He took a deep breath and rolled his shoulders to ease the stiffness of his neck. He leaned back and shut his eyes. What else would you expect on a day like this?

He had survived the last thirty years of country practice on a mixture of fatalistic optimism and optimistic equanimity, an attitude compounded of resignation and hope. He also managed to transmit this 'somehow there is a way' conviction to his patients.

Recently, however, it had seemed to him that the stars of hope were disappearing behind the clouds of resignation. More and more Marker found himself saying that the simplest way out would be to think the worst. In the present instance, that meant getting out of the car and walking up to Lutz's farm in the rain. He had to see old Lutz. Lutz needed him.

Five minutes later a resigned Marker took the keys out of the ignition and opened the door. Then something happened that restored his optimism: through the silent, foggy darkness he heard the familiar chug of a tractor engine. Moments later he saw the dark shadow lurching down the track on caterpillar wheels.

164

Dr Ignaz Marker flashed his lights, but the signal was unnecessary. As the angular nose of the old Deutsch-Diesel tractor loomed out of the mist, Marker even knew who would be sitting at the wheel. He got out of the car again.

'Hey, Ranecker, can you pull me out?'

The farmer got down from his seat and slopped towards him in his rubber boots. Rain ran from his soggy felt hat down on to his jacket. 'Where are you going, Doctor?'

'To see old Lutz.'

'Yes, yes, you're needed up there. I'll get you out.'

The look on his face alarmed Marker. 'What's wrong with him?'

'He's in bad shape, Doctor. He's doing badly today.'

Well, the old boy had been in bad shape for a long time. It wasn't just the eighty-three years he had under his belt, and the body that had become tired and brittle. In the many years Marker had lived among these forest people he had come to know them well: he could follow not only their train of thought but gauge their feelings. If one of them decided not to go on there was nothing one could do about it, and never mind the invited speeches at the medical symposia, the long articles in trade journals, the talk about psychosomatic appearances or depression caused by old age or loss of motivation. What did they know? It was the same with the old Indians, Marker thought. They, too, simply said 'that's it', and lay down to die.

'Turn the tractor around, Ranecker. I've got a tow rope.'

The farmer nodded, went back and clambered into the driver's seat. Shortly after half-past six, exhausted and hungry, Ignaz Marker reached old Lutz's farm.

The house stood in darkness. The barn roof had collapsed and, in the cemented hopper which had once held the dungheap, there was a pile of wet garbage. Marker glanced up at the top floor. There was a light in the two windows there, where old Lutz was lying. He opened the door and heard the old wooden stairs creak.

'Doctor? Is that you?'

He took off his coat and hung it on a hook. 'Who else, Mrs Körber?'

The neighbour was tall, tall and bony. She barred the stairs with both arms, her face sullen and accusatory. 'He's not eating again,' she said. 'I've been after him with soup the whole day. I was going to ring you.'

'I'm here now.'

'It can't go on like this, Doctor. Honestly, he's never looked this bad. I don't think he's going to make it.'

'Then let me by.'

'I made him egg soup. That's supposed to help. But no, not him. What can I do?'

'Go home, Mrs Körber.'

'Yes, and what then? He's so poorly . . .'

'I will stay with him. I'll help him. Then I'll give him something to make him sleep.'

All so lightly said. Doctor's sayings. Marker felt uneasy as he opened the door. He heard the old man's short, fast, rattling breathing coming from the bed in the corner. A lamp burned on the pine bureau. A bitter smell, the smell of old age, sweat, decay, sickness, rotting wood, and dead flowers assailed his nostrils. The religious statue in its corner niche. Also the pictures.

Marker was familiar with all of them. Beneath the picture of the Virgin Mary a bunch of heather stood on a shelf. Then there was the brown photograph of a city by the sea with a huge suspension bridge: San Francisco. Lutz's uncle had emigrated to San Francisco because the farm could no longer feed all of them. Another picture showed a soldier in a grey uniform, with a Kaiser-Wilhelm moustache and riding boots, the inscription *Gott Mit Uns* – Sergeant-Major Lutz as an Offenburger dragoon.

'There you are, Doctor.'

'Yes, here I am.' Marker pulled over a chair and sat down beside the bed. The old man turned his head. His skin was grey-white and the stubble looked as if it had been glued on. Marker could hardly see the patient's eyes in the half-darkness.

'You could have saved yourself the trouble.'

'Oh, well,' Marker said, 'everyone has a job to do. Think yourself lucky you're inside where it's dry, Lutz. It's terrible outside.'

Old Lutz mumbled something but Marker could not catch a single word. He went over to the washstand and poured water from the china jug into the basin, watching the spider circling quietly at the bottom. Then he washed his hands, drying them and the rain off his face. He cleaned his glasses and took the stethoscope from

166

his bag. He pushed the earpieces into place and put the stethoscope against his patient's chest, listening to the thin rushing of the blood.

'Hold your breath.'

The old man ignored the instruction: it was all he could do to breathe as it was. Beyond the sounds of the labouring lungs, Marker heard a distant throbbing, irregular, barely audible, the rhythms of the life which was slowly ebbing away, already interrupted by the malfunctions of the heart.

He touched the damp, cool skin. He could hardly feel the old man's pulse. In spite of all this, though, the eyes were not yet ready to surrender: they searched for him and the mouth tried to form words; the brain had not given up trying. But the pupils? There was hardly any pressure, Marker thought.

He had known the old man's condition for some time. There was not much he could do. But this dramatic collapse took him by surprise. He looked around. There was a glass on the windowsill. Milk had been drunk from it, but the whitish substance encrusted at the bottom had nothing in common with milk. He turned around and found what he was looking for: the phial which had contained the pills was lying empty in the pottery tray.

'You won't eat soup,' he said, as calmly as he could, 'but you can take pills.'

'Today nothing hurts, nothing. Finally nothing hurts any more.'

'How many of those pills did you take?'

'There are two left. I should have taken them all, Doctor. That way I'd be at peace. That way I could go quicker.'

'That way you'd get to intensive care quicker.'

The old man's eyelids slowly lowered over his eyes, thin lids like parchment, the colour of faded golden leaves marbled by blue veins. They reminded Marker of the eyes of a lizard which has become winter-torpid. Although the movement of Lutz's chest was hardly visible, his hand twitched spasmodically. Marker tried again to find the dying man's pulse, and again had trouble locating it.

Then old Lutz started to talk. 'Go over to the chest of drawers, Doctor. Then you'll understand . . . there on my bureau . . . a letter.'

Marker got up. The envelope was open. The paper was lined, covered with large, bold, somewhat awkward script.

'This isn't your handwriting, Lutz.'

'No, it isn't . . . I dictated it to Mrs Körber. But that's not important. The signature . . . only the signature matters . . . and that's mine. Do you understand?'

Marker read the three lines again. 'I want to die here. I do not want to be taken to hospital. This is my wish. Otmar Lutz.'

He sat down by the bed. He tried to think of something to say, but it was not that simple. An old Indian chief, he thought. That was how Lutz looked: the nose sticking out of the sunken face, its structures marked by death. Somewhere Marker had read that the Cheyenne chiefs, when they felt that their end was near, made a bed of branches in the trees and lay there, hands folded, looking east to where the Sun-Ship would come to take them to the Great Spirit.

It was an end in harmony with themselves and with Nature. They knew their laws. They even decided the time of their own departure. They willed themselves to die, and they died. What was the phrase for it? Somatic syndrome? Stopping the clock?

Lutz, too, was ready. Only his dying would not renew the law of life, it was a final protest against a life which had lost all meaning. The wife dead, the farm and barn empty, the last cow sold years ago. Marker remembered how proud Lutz had been of his guinea-fowl. He had even had ducks; they had paraded all over the dung heap where now there was only wet rubbish. Even the forest, which Lutz had loved, was dying. He was lying in his bed like an old Cheyenne in his tree. No, it was not really a protest: his time had come. He could feel it and he accepted it. Time had passed over people like Lutz.

'Have you read it, Doctor?'

'Yes, but I have to tell you, it has no legality.'

'What's that? What are you talking about? What do you mean, legality?'

'Ach, what's the use of talking about it,' Marker said. He folded up the stethoscope and put it in his bag. He felt so wretched that he had to lean on the table. 'Lutz, I'm hungry. I've got to get something to eat. I'll stay with you, but I've been on the road since ten and if I don't get something into my stomach I'm going to collapse.'

Lutz nodded, but not in response to Marker's words. It was if that little glow in the bony brain was working still, working on other problems. 'Drips,' the old man muttered. 'Needles. Hospitals . . .' And then: 'I've heard what it's like. You lie there, you're not even human any more. That's how it is. First they don't let you live, then they won't let you die. Two wars, Doctor. I didn't want to die then . . . but I should have. Wars are made for people to die in . . . people are dying all over the world. Women and children . . . but nobody wants to. But now I want to . . . I'm old, I'm sick. I have the right to die.'

'Yes, Lutz, you have.'

'Good, all right then. It wasn't all bad, no. Eighty-three years, some of them good, some of them bad. But now it's all over. The wife gone . . . Did you know her? . . . Anyway, the grandchildren are doing well . . .' Marker was unable to hear the rest, it was no more than a faint whisper, like dry leaves rustling on a tree. Lutz turned his head and looked at him. His eyes opened wide, veiled eyes, filmed over.

'Am I getting on your nerves, Doctor?'

'No, Lutz.'

'If you're hungry, Doctor, you can have the soup. It's still downstairs on the stove. You can warm it up and eat it.'

'All right, Lutz, I'll do just that. And then I'll come back to be with you.'

TWENTY-EIGHT

The room was all white and gold. There were carved rococo borders on the door frames, gay cherubs handing out grapes from golden cornucopia. Even the red upholstered chairs were gilded. Gilded – and very comfortable.

Inside Klaus Brinkmann's head the sound of flute and viola, bass and harpsichord combined into a pleasantly lulling mixture. For the third time in the last ten minutes his head nodded forward.

'Hey, don't go to sleep!'

He did not hear Kate Marek's hissed warning but her dig in his ribs made him sit up sharply. The programme fell off his lap as he dutifully joined in the applause. Chair-legs scraped as people stood up, but Klaus Brinkmann got another jab in the ribs.

'What's the matter now?'

'There!' Kate Marek raised the glasses dangling from the silver chain around her neck. 'By the second door. Can't you see?'

'I can't see anything.'

'You obviously didn't hear anything, either.'

'My God, *mea culpa!* What is one supposed to do when one is bone-weary? All right, just what is over there?'

'Your Christa.' The words hit him like an electric shock.

'What do you mean, "your Christa"?'

'Oh well, your favourite nurse, then.'

They headed for the exit, nodding at acquaintances. Someone said, 'Good evening, Professor. It was wonderful, wasn't it?' Evening dresses, blue suits, dress shirts, scarves . . . all this filtered through the edges of Brinkmann's consciousness, but he was too preoccupied with other thoughts, doubts, the effort of classifying this little tremor of unease. She had also turned around. He saw her freeze, and then smile.

Then he was swept outside with the rest of the audience.

'What's the matter with you? Why are you pulling such a strange face?'

'Me? Am I being strange?'

'Oh, for Heaven's sake . . .'

He saw her again: between people, coats, jokes, greetings. A steel-blue dress, her thick blond hair piled high, pearls around her neck . . . A new, quite different Christa. A vision which made his throat feel tight. She lifted her hand.

'Here, Kate, let me introduce you to Christa, one of our nurses.'

'It's obvious that's what she is. I wasn't born yesterday, you know.'

Christa smiled shyly. 'It was nice, wasn't it?' The kind of thing one says. He could only manage a nod. He couldn't take his eyes off her face, and it annoyed him that she could hardly help but notice it.

'Well, Christa, he didn't hear much of the concert,' Kate taunted. 'He slept through half of it.'

'Guilty. But I love the music. So don't think of me as a philistine. Have you got your coat yet? Ah, here, let me help you.' Which he did, ignoring Kate's surprised stare. Let her stare. Do her good!

What was Christa saying? 'It was unfair of me to turn you down that time, Professor, wasn't it?'

'Oh, I quite understood.'

'And he found a replacement straight away,' Kate chimed in. 'Although I don't hold much with music. I'm the most unmusical person on the face of the earth but at least I sat through it. When I get an invitation I don't shilly-shally.'

Another of those smiles. What should she say, what could she say?

'Well . . . it was very nice to have met you, Mrs Marek. I'd better be on my way . . .'

'Do you have your car?' Brinkmann asked, quickly.

'No, it had to go in for repair. But there'll be a bus in a little while.'

'Bus, bus? You'll come with us,' Kate Marek said. 'And if we're going to travel together we may as well have a snack together. I've made goulash. A whole pot.'

'Don't start that again. You can't force her to eat.'

'Force her?' Kate lifted her glasses and inspected Klaus Brinkmann as though he had just arrived from outer space. 'Me, force my cooking on someone? Now see here . . .'

Christa began laughing, loudly, heartily and without embarrassment. For some reason she felt wonderful.

Yes, wonderful. No matter how unexpected, how unbelievable it seemed to her, she felt really good. Here, at a candle-lit table amid the heavy dark furniture, handling Brinkmann's family silver, sitting under the gaze of the gentleman on the wall about whom Christa knew only that he was *Medizinalrat* Professor Friedrich Karl Brinkmann, founder of the clinic.

Perhaps it was the wine which Kate kept pouring out so generously, perhaps the discovery of how touchingly off-balance Brinkmann became when you smiled at him – and him the Grand Panjandrum, God and Chief, who Kate mothered and criticised like a little boy. Or perhaps it was Kate, this phenomenon of a woman whose motherly manner spread not only warmth but lucidity, and a vitality that was irresistible.

'I'll help you to clear up!'

No, she wouldn't permit that, Kate decided. They had finished the rest of the dessert and drunk their coffee. So Christa sat back with a feeling of having spent not only an unbelievable but a very happy evening.

Brinkmann unfastened the collar of his dress shirt and poked tobacco into his pipe. Christa, sitting in a comfortable easy chair,

172

felt a warmth running through her which made her a little afraid. No matter how often she had devised just such a fantasy as this – and there had been more than a few times during the past weeks when she had done just that – the reality was completely different.

Then all at once the atmosphere changed as the second male occupant of the house came silently and unexpectedly into the room. Udo Brinkmann! Udo flushed but was able to manage a surprisingly casual, 'Well, look who's here! Good evening!'

Brinkmann put down his pipe. 'I went to the concert with Kate. And that's where Nurse Christa . . .'

'Met us in the cloakroom,' Kate added, beaming. 'You might even say we stole her from the cloakroom. I invited her back here – your father is a bit slow in such matters, don't you think? Sit down and I'll get you some coffee.'

Udo shook his head. He remained where he was, standing in the middle of the room on the heavy Tabriz carpet, his hand on his chin as though he was going to rub something off. His father was standing now as well looking a trifle embarrassed, Christa thought.

Udo somehow managed to take everything in his stride and accept things as he found them. 'Well, then,' he said, 'have a nice evening. I really can't stay, Kate. I'm not on my own tonight, so I must go. Good night, everyone.' He stopped as he reached the door. 'Have a nice evening, Christa.'

A nice evening, yes, sure. Red wine, easy chairs, the grand piano – and the question: why didn't I leave when Udo left? Then that passed and she heard herself talking without any clear idea of what she was saying, a victim of the confusion that sets in when words and feelings run on parallel lines.

'My wife,' Brinkmann was saying, as he puffed on his pipe and disappeared into a cloud of smoke. 'She died eleven years ago.'

Christa nodded. When the silence lengthened, she decided to ask a question. 'I suppose I embarrassed you a bit in the cloakroom when I mentioned the invitation.'

'You mean because it made Kate feel like a stand-in? Don't worry, she never does.' He leaned forward and for a moment she thought he was going to take hold of her hand. 'Christa . . .'

'Yes?'

Again his diffident smile. 'It's nice to see you sitting here. It's exactly the way I'd hoped our evening would end.'

Good Lord, isn't he formal, she thought. And now? What now?
She swallowed. 'You know, of course, that I've been out with your
son a few times.'

He nodded, saying nothing.

'That's what made things a bit . . . difficult. I hope you understand. And then there's . . .'

'Yes?'

She looked at the glass in her hand. Her thoughts became
jumbled: why did she have to start on that again?

'You were going to say . . . ?'

'Well . . . we already talked about it once before. It's just
curiosity, really. The new anaesthetist, the one who's been with
you for so many years . . .'

'Did Udo tell you? Was that why you turned down my
invitation?'

She met his eyes. 'Yes.'

'It's true. I mean, it's true that Mrs Bach and I have been friends
for a long time. But for some considerable time our relationship –
perhaps friendship would be a better word – well, it's not what it
once was. It is just business now. And perhaps it's important that I
make this clear to you: she didn't come here because I wanted her
to. You know that we needed a second anaesthetist at the clinic.
Elena took the initiative and . . .'

'Professor!'

'I see. Now I get punished with a title?'

'No, I just thought . . . I mean, it's none of my business.' How
could Christa say what she thought and meant when she was so
mixed up, mixed up and angry with herself. How could she even
broach the subject?

She was still mixed up when Klaus Brinkmann drove her home
half an hour later. He drove slowly, relaxed and smiling. The car
rolled through the night. The lights of the bridge melted in the dark
water as they crossed the river. Coloured neon lights shone on hotel
fronts. Then, behind the big nursery, Brinkmann stopped, the
dreamy smile still on his face.

'Christa . . .'

'Yes?'

'It's all nonsense.'

What nonsense he was talking about Christa never found out.

174

She was conscious only of his hands on her shoulders, hands which were neither restrictive nor possessive, nervous nor rough . . . hands which exuded peace and warmth. The eyes that gazed at her. The lips which came towards hers . . .

Marker sat in the room at the farm in which Lutz was dying and thought about his nice warm bed. The rain had stopped; the damp night was almost tangible. A wall of silence surrounded the two men. Occasionally, if the raucous cry of a night bird woke him, or if the hands folded on the bed moved and the rasping breath came faster, Marker would get up, take five paces and put his hand on the damp, icy forehead, before returning to the creaky old wicker chair and leaning his head against the wall beneath the picture of San Francisco in 1910.

At some time in the morning he would have to take the death certificate out of his pocket. Under the Roman numeral three, beneath the heading 'Manner of Death: natural, unnatural or not certain', he would put a cross in the box for 'natural'. A personal lie for a quiet, courageous, long death. And his part in it: that of helper.

This time it hadn't been so bad. So many other, worse variations occur: the endless prayers of the priest while the cold-blooded impatience showed on the faces of the relatives, the speeches that had to be made, the lies that had to be concocted, the consolations that had to be found. But worse still was when the patient was attached to cables and drips and electrodes in intensive care, and then, when he finally gave up, you watched him become part of the machinery for a few hours. There was always such terrible protest in those eyes, eyes which no longer understood.

It could also be beautiful sometimes, the way it had been a week ago when Ignaz Marker had told a cancer-ridden old lady about the palm trees growing beneath the blue skies of Spain, and how she would be seeing them as soon as her grandchildren came to fetch her. When the end came he held her hand and sang an old folk song.

There was no need to sing for Lutz. There was no priest. Only the waiting, and a harmony which Marker had never felt before: understanding a man who wanted to end his life.

The banging on the door broke the silence like a pistol shot.

Marker sprang up and went across to the bed. The nostrils still moved but the face was that of a corpse. He turned to face the door.

The man who came in was about forty, his fat, heavy body squeezed into a suit which was far too small for him. He even wore a waistcoat and a tie with white dots. Michael Lutz, the old man's son.

'Mrs Körber phoned me,' he said. 'What's wrong with him, Doctor?'

'Quietly, Michael. Don't make so much noise.'

Michael Lutz looked at him then tiptoed across to the bed. He frowned. 'He's not dead?'

'No, he's not dead. Not yet.'

'And you're just sitting here doing nothing? He's got to go to hospital immediately!'

'That wouldn't change anything. And anyway, he doesn't want to go to hospital.'

'What do you mean, he doesn't want to go? How long have you been sitting here, doing nothing?'

Marker rubbed his eyes. 'Since about eight last night,' he replied. Michael Lutz just stared at him.

'You're telling me you've been here since last night? Is that it? A human being – my father – is dying here, and the doctor sits there twiddling his thumbs all night?'

'That's what he wanted. He even put it in writing.'

But Michael Lutz did not hear him. He was already over by the phone on the wall beside the door leading into the sitting room. He put on his glasses, read the emergency number, and dialled.

'Yes, hello, can you hear me? My name is Lutz. I need an ambulance. Yes, it's urgent. Bichenbach. Yes, you take the turning by Oberstwald. Get here as fast as you can. Bring a doctor. Every second counts, do you hear?' He put the receiver back on the cradle. His heavy breathing was the only sound in the room.

'Why didn't you do anything?'

'I've already explained that, Michael.'

'You've explained nothing.'

'And why didn't you get here sooner?'

'I was with a client. I didn't know anything about this. But you – you're supposed to be a doctor! I'm telling you, you're going to pay for this. Do you hear me, Doctor? This is going to cost you dear. I guarantee it!'

TWENTY-NINE

It was a little after four when Brinkmann went into his office. He read the messages Lena had left for him, then reached for the phone to call Christa. He did not complete the spontaneous gesture. It would create more problems for her than for him.

He leaned back and scratched Mollie's ears. The Chief and a nurse? Well, that was what you wanted – now you've got to come to terms with it. Perhaps they could work out some sort of code, some strategy of discretion? No. He would have to talk it over with her. Maybe she had some thoughts on the subject. One way or the other they could hardly behave as though nothing had happened. There were some lies one was just too old to need to tell.

Brinkmann sighed and pushed the button on the intercom. 'Lena, please send Mr Renz in right away.'

'There's another gentleman waiting to see you, a Mr Lutz. He is the son of the patient who died in the ambulance early this morning.'

'That's precisely why I want to talk to Mr Renz. He was in the ambulance, wasn't he?'

He heard a slight, apologetic cough behind him. 'Yes, Professor, I was in the ambulance.'

Brinkmann had not noticed Renz come into the room. He waved the tall, reddish-blond young man to a chair. 'What actually happened?'

'What always happens if you drag a living corpse out of a bed. The man was already two-thirds dead. He was eighty-three years old, Professor. In a coma. A diabetic for the last ten years, and highly sclerotic on top of that. The walls of the heart were completely eroded, kidneys gone. And as if all that weren't enough, there were the barbiturates.'

Brinkmann nodded. 'Then why does his son want to talk to me? You've issued a death certificate, haven't you?'

Walter Renz studied his nails. 'The man has gone mad. Completely off the rails. Ever since last night. He is blaming his father's death on their doctor, who he says delayed the admission.'

'And who is their doctor?'

'A Dr Marker. Young Lutz wants to press charges against him. And there's more: the old man is supposed to have put it in writing that he didn't want to go into hospital. And, as I've already said, he'd taken God knows how many sleeping pills. Whether he meant to commit suicide or not can't be established.'

Brinkmann looked past him at the window. 'Marker, you said?'

'That's right.'

'And it's true that he sat with the patient all night and did nothing?'

'I spoke to him and he admitted it freely. I mean, it's possible that at the time . . .' Renz stopped and studied his nails again.

'What kind of note are we talking about?'

'No idea.'

'Marker?' Brinkmann mused. 'Oh well, let's have the son in.'

Renz got up as if to go, but Brinkmann waved him back.

'Better stay, Walter. After all, you're the only one who knows all the details.'

Michael Lutz wasted no time on small talk. Brinkmann waited patiently until he had let off steam.

'I understand your feelings, Mr Lutz. But if you could just ease off a little on Dr Marker . . .'

'Ease off? On someone who killed my father? What would you do if you were me?'

'I hardly think "killed" is appropriate . . . You understand, I need a more detailed picture . . .'

'What kind of details do you need? He let him die like a sick dog. Watched him peg out . . . and never lifted a finger.'

'Try to control yourself, please, Mr Lutz. Look, my colleague Dr Renz tells me your father was in a coma.'

'I'm talking about earlier. What happened earlier? Dr Marker came at six-thirty, he said so himself. When I arrived at the farm it was three o'clock in the morning. You're not going to try to tell me anyone who calls himself a doctor would sit there for seven and a half hours and watch his patient die, are you?'

'Mr Lutz, calm down, please!'

But Michael Lutz was in no mood to calm down. 'Sure, sure, everyone knows you doctors all stick together. Dog doesn't eat dog, right? Why don't you admit it? And us, the relatives, we're supposed to calm down. Well, thank God, I've got proof. You hear me? I can prove that Dr Marker broke the law. And I'm pressing charges against him. Nobody can stop me. Not even you, Professor!'

Brinkmann leaned back in his chair and folded his hands. He spoke softly and calmly because he knew from experience it was the most effective method of defusing such situations.

'Now you listen to me,' he said. 'I know Dr Marker. We studied medicine together and we were interns at the same hospital. He is a good man, a conscientious doctor. More than that, he has an excellent reputation around here. You know all that as well as I do.'

'I'm not interested in any of that. I saw what I saw. It was his duty to help my father and he didn't do it. I was right, you're just trying to brush the whole thing under the carpet. You doctors are all the same . . .'

Brinkmann sat up. Obviously restraint was not the answer. So be it: Lutz could have it the other way.

'I forbid you to talk such drivel!'

'It was his duty . . .'

'Whether or not Dr Marker neglected his duty will be decided at an inquiry. When we know the result we can talk again. Goodbye, Mr Lutz!'

. . . .

Ignaz Marker quite liked ivy: it looked rather nice in the spring. But when it started to get out of hand, when it crept all over the walls of the surgery annex and made the walls damp, then it was time to do something about it. Even if it was a Sunday.

He had been chopping away at it with the shears for about three hours. The wet summer had made everything shoot up like mad, but he was making progress, steadily clearing the wall. It was hot today. The sun was finally making a contribution on the credit side, but it had taken until September to do it.

Marker jammed the shears into his belt and took hold of the ladder, ready to climb. Then he paused and looked back towards the front of the house. A Mercedes stood in the drive. And what a car! Glittering, fabulous. He watched as a man got out and rang the doorbell. Obviously didn't see me, he thought.

Marker raised his hand. 'Klaus?'

'Yes, me. Hello, Ignaz!'

Marker went across and opened the door, wiping his hands on his trousers. 'Well, Klaus. It's taken you a long time to come and see me.'

'Well, you know how it is, old friend. You have the same problem: no time.'

'But today you have time?'

Brinkmann nodded. He looked around. 'Beautiful garden. Mine produces weeds, mostly, but this! – and look at those lettuces!'

Marker asked himself whether he should invite Brinkmann inside. No, not in such lovely weather. He led the way to a little bench under the rose hedge.

'Can I get you something to drink?'

Brinkmann shook his head. 'It's ages since we saw each other.'

'Does that surprise you? You're in the big time, but I'm still a farmer's doctor.' Marker folded his hands between his knees. He looked across the road, along the row of trees leading to the wood. 'And this isn't a social call, Klaus, so don't pretend it is. Get it off your chest.'

Brinkmann chewed on his pipe. 'The medical board has asked for a report on the death of Otmar Lutz,' he said.

Marker nodded. 'I know. Have you already signed it?'

'No, I wanted to talk to you first. That's why I'm here. I simply cannot imagine why . . .'

'Why what?'

'Why you didn't hospitalise the patient. Why you didn't bring him to the clinic. Someone like you doesn't just sit there, a whole night, watching a patient die who could have been kept alive.'

'Kept alive? What for? Do you know what kind of life the man had? He wanted to die.'

'Wanted to die? Good God, man, I shouldn't have to tell you it's a doctor's job to prolong life not shorten it!'

Marker stood up and hooked his thumbs in the loops of his belt. 'You're right, and you don't have to tell me. But only someone blinkered would talk that way, someone from one of those big clinics where they keep dying people alive for months instead of granting them a quick, peaceful death.'

'Now wait a minute . . .'

'I really didn't expect anything else from you, Klaus. That machinery you have has to be fully utilised, or it doesn't pay for itself, does it?'

This was strong language, indeed: no punches pulled. Yet in spite of his anger, Brinkmann had to admit that from Marker's standpoint the realities of their work must look very different. In his thirty years of practice he had probably seen a great deal that made him bitter and angry.

He followed Marker past a bed of leeks and the rainwater vat to the little shed at the bottom of the garden. As they came to a stop, Brinkmann took the offensive.

'The way you feel won't change the way things are, Ignaz,' he said. 'It wasn't the heart, it wasn't the liver. It was the pills that did it. And he had told you about them, you admitted as much. Not only that, but you seem in some godlike way to have concurred, and done nothing about it.'

'Done nothing? What does that mean? The old man had been in terrible pain. There was nothing that could be fixed: not the pancreas, not the kidneys, not the heart, not the circulation. Lutz wanted to go home, to his Ida!'

'And you, as a doctor, decided you were master of life and death.'

'Not me. You, perhaps.'

Brinkmann knocked his pipe against the wood-plank fence. 'Let's leave me out of this one. Tell me about yourself. Tell me where you draw the line: at eighty-three, at eighty, seventy-five?

Have you got a hot line to God? Does he tell you how long a life is worth living?'

'In this case, the patient told me.'

'Oh, sure. Fear and pain create reactions none of us can control, Ignaz. You know that, I know that: I'm not dismissing my own experience. If you take away the fear you can heal. That's your duty as a doctor. But one thing you most certainly are not, and that is an extension of Almighty God.'

'Neither are you.'

'Ignaz . . .'

Marker took hold of a spade and pushed it into the earth. 'Just do your report and leave me alone!'

'Ignaz, we're talking about your livelihood.'

'And that should impress me? What kind of livelihood is it, anyway? I don't have a six-figure income. Some of my patients pay, some send me a basket full of food. Others forget both. I don't need to tell you there are plenty of areas in Germany where people don't have health insurance. This is one of them. For me, that means I just about break even. And if they take away my licence, I'll just sit on my backside and finally get some peace. Then it'll be you who has to get off his high horse and drive over hedges and ditches to forest farms and villages you've never even seen. And when you get there you can bring babies into this world or rub down old grandfathers with bedsores.'

Brinkmann's anger had evaporated; all that was left was resignation. 'Ignaz, that's not the point. The point is you've practised euthanasia. Active euthanasia, if you contributed to his death by medical means, passive euthanasia if we manage to show the last pill was taken without your knowledge.'

'We? Who is "we"? What's your involvement in this?'

'The case will go to court, Ignaz, and I will have to give evidence.'

'And of course you want to arrive at a just decision, right? You of all people. Someone who attaches half-dead people to machines and is proud of every day that the vegetable stays alive. You'd have to be against me from the start. That's how you make your living. You're concerned with medical achievement, Klaus, the optimum use of your machines. Not with the mercy of a humane, dignified death!'

Enough. Too much, even. Brinkmann shook his head: this was pointless. He turned to go. 'I came here to try and help you, Ignaz, not hurt you.'

'Save your breath!' Marker called after him. 'Do whatever you want to do! To me, the death of someone over eighty is entirely natural. And I'll tell you something else: I'm not coming into your clinic when I'm old and terminally ill!'

Brinkmann paused. 'Anything else?'

Marker shook his head. He'd said all he had to say.

THIRTY

'I think we should treat ourselves to something nice,' Brinkmann said, tugging Elena Bach towards the car after consultation. 'I think we've earned it, don't you?' He refused to accept any protest. Thus it came about that she was sitting in the car, watching him, the 'King' – no, the 'one-time King'.

He drove through the Black Forest, head back, that dreamy yet alert expression on his face that told her he did not miss a single tree, a single new vista, neither a meadow nor a brook nor an old house. This was a relaxed Klaus Brinkmann, contented in the red-gold haze of early evening.

Elena Bach did not speak. She did not want to spoil the magic of these moments: the overlapping of past and present, although the memories gradually took over, memories of other trips in the car, long journeys beneath the lowering skies of Normandy, along the chalky cliffs of the Bernese Jura, or from Geneva to Lugano, Simplon, Centovalli – that unbelievable feeling of flying down into the magic garden which Ticino had become for them.

She shook her head: this was neither Lake Maggiore or Centovalli, but the Kinzigtal. No palm trees; only the pines that people said would not survive much longer. And even that was part of it: the parallel feeling of threat, of an inevitable ending that was approaching. 'We should treat ourselves to something nice,' he'd said. Well, she wasn't fooling herself, she knew that. On the contrary: Elena felt a deep unease about this journey. That was why she had not asked where they were going or why.

They passed through Hornberg and Nussbach before turning west at St Georgen. At Schönwald they had coffee; Brinkmann happily smoking his pipe, she deep in her own thoughts. Now they were approaching Triberg on the B31. The hills were densely built up: hotels, guest houses, small country houses. On their left they passed a sports ground and then a cemetery.

He turned to her. 'What now? A snack? Dinner. A banquet, perhaps? What can I offer you, Frau Doctor?'

'Just a salad and a talk. I really don't want smoked meat and schnapps. Is that all right?'

'Whatever you say.'

But they ended up with the smoked meat, lots of it, which Brinkmann ate with gusto. And when she reminded him that eating too much smoked food increased the danger of cancer, he just grinned, and told her no problem: he'd take his own stomach out with his left hand.

'God, what vanity!' she said, affectionately.

She had trout – unsmoked – with her salad. She sipped the clear, dry wine as Brinkmann made sarcastic remarks about the clientèle of Wehrle's Park Hotel on the opposite side of the small town's market square. He downed a third raspberry liqueur as she toyed with a piece of bread and waited uneasily for what she was sure was coming.

Nothing happened. He chewed on his pipe, drawing patterns on the tablecloth with his knife. She suddenly felt a surge of tenderness that grew stronger as she realised how grey he was becoming. More and more grey hair, still stubbornly dark at the crown, but growing lighter along the parting. The memory of running her hands through that hair, pulling his head towards her, as she used to . . .

'What is it?' she asked, softly.

'What is what?'

'Something's bothering you.'

He was mulling something over. How often she had seen him sit there in front of her just like this, hunched forward, the defenceless face full of doubts. The last time had been in her flat in Zürich. Only when she took him in her arms had that tension disappeared . . .

She put her hand on his. 'Come on, now, Rossi. Spit it out.'

'Wasn't it you who wanted . . . ?'

'Sure. But that isn't important now.'

The corners of his mouth turned upward in a slight grin. 'You know how it is, painting the clouds with sunshine. I think maybe I'm at the end of my physical tether, Elena. Getting the clinic going has taken more out of me than I thought it would.'

'Are you having trouble with the board of administrators?'

'No. Those tiresome nitpickers come with the territory. They're like plant lice: you have to get used to them. No, that's not it.'

'What, then?'

'Same old thing: work. This damned job of ours. The people we work with. That breast operation this morning . . .'

'Mrs Oprecht, you mean. That was really something.'

'Something? You can say that again. All you do is give her the anaesthetic, say a few kind words to a nice old lady, and that's it.'

'Hold on a moment –!'

'Sorry, Elena.' Now it was Brinkmann's turn to stroke her hand. In doing so he accidentally knocked some cutlery off the table with his elbow, followed by half a glass of Schladerer schnapps. He hardly seemed to notice them, or the waiter who hurried across to clear up the mess. He just stared at Elena, his eyes wide and troubled.

'Be glad I've spared you the details, Elena. The case is a nightmare. That poor woman had already been to see me in Karlsruhe. I'd already more or less pieced her case history together from the little I could lay my hands on . . .'

'When was the tumour first noticed?'

'Three years ago. She was living in Hesse then. I won't tell you the names of the people involved: it's not necessary, and besides, you come across cases like hers everywhere. That's what makes me so bitter. There should be a new code of professional conduct in surgery, new laws. We need specialised clinics staffed only by surgeons who do nothing else.'

'Don't start on that again, Klaus. Tell me about Mrs Oprecht.'

'What can I tell you? The usual. The gynaecologist who saw her detected some nodules, and she was admitted to the nearest hospital. Not a provincial clinic like ours, one of the big ones. The poor, trusting soul. If only she'd known . . . But you know what happens: she has a chat with the senior doctor, they find out she's past child-bearing age, she signs the necessary papers, that's it, let's operate. After all, the assistants need experience. But this isn't minor surgery. Oh, sure, the biopsy had shown a tumour. But at her age, with the slow growth rate? It was only the size of a plum, Elena. In the medial quadrant. Just a few mastopathic changes. You know the way it is with test biopsies: if you're not a really experienced cancer surgeon, you can get into deep water very quickly. The whole thing isn't anything like safe enough, to my way of thinking. So what do they do, these Hessian doctors? A Halstead! Everything out! They did it by the book: opened the breast muscles up, right down to the ribs. Cleared out the armpits in case there were any cancerous lymph nodes. Imagine it! The Halstead, one of the most difficult of all operations. And to let any old 0815 team have a go at it instead of a hundred per cent expert is criminal. Well, you saw the results.'

'Her problem breathing, you mean?'

'What else? The whole thorax is affected. And to add insult to injury, the poor woman was subjected to radiation therapy afterwards, resulting in radiation burns. Is it any wonder she has trouble with her breathing and her heart? I tell you, it makes me so angry when I see the way they turn women into cripples!'

She said nothing. At the next table, someone laughed. Brinkmann puffed furiously on his pipe.

'Shooting sparrows with cannons . . . well, it happens once in a while, I suppose.'

'With cannons, you say? Atomic bombs would be nearer to it! I tell you, it can't go on. It's got to be changed!'

'You're a fine one to talk. You have to treat all kinds of problems in your clinic, too.'

'You think I enjoy it?'

'In spite of everything, yes, I think you do. It's a good thing there are surgeons like you, Klaus. I mean it.'

'Me? Are you making the mistake of thinking I'm a talented

187

surgeon? I'm an old firehorse, nothing more. But at least I know what to do. And more important, what to leave alone.'

He reached for his glass. It was empty. Well, he'd probably had enough. He rotated the glass between his fingers, watching the slow movement of the remaining drops of liquid.

A faint thread of worry touched Elena's mind: was he operating tomorrow?

'The illustrious standing of the medical profession!' he said, returning to his theme. 'The gentlemen who enjoy God's grace. We know everything, no one knows more than us. If you were to take a car out on the road without driving instruction, even if you knew how to drive but drove carelessly, you'd be in for trouble. But us? Specialists have to be content with whatever crumbs they're thrown after ten years of training, but our dear colleagues, those ingenious improvisers of general surgery, they take on everything, anything, right down to the toenails! When will someone finally stop it? When will those idiots wake up?'

'What is all this? One of your lectures?'

'No, it's a discussion with someone I hope understands how I feel. I don't have anyone else to talk to.'

She felt warmth rise to her cheeks. Did this mean he was finally coming to his senses, finally beginning to realise what he needed most? A partner, not only for bed, which little Christa had probably already become, but someone who had enough experience to understand his thinking. And the way he ticked, all his thoughts centring on one thing and one thing only – surgery.

'A place like ours is like a military hospital at the front during a war. We're coping with a population of twenty thousand, say the equivalent of two army divisions. When the chips are down, whatever happens, when people are dying we have to cope. And that means me. I have to do everything here. Well, I expect at least that of myself. Udo is shaping up, too, he has what it takes. The only thing is, he's not cautious enough. But you know, when I think about it all, I think in many ways my friend Ignaz is right.'

'Ignaz Marker? The country doctor?'

Brinkmann nodded. 'He told me I was blinkered. He called it my torture clinic. And I've dropped him in the shit.'

The accusation, his cynicism hiding anger, and now his sadness:

the typical Brinkmann mixture. He had always been a loner, but never before had he so clearly formulated what bothered him.

'How is the inquiry going? Weren't you supposed to appear as an expert witness?'

'I've already done so. The case came up yesterday.'

So that was what it was, Elena thought. He had not mentioned this before.

'You were at medical school together, weren't you?'

Brinkmann's smile was sour. 'One school friend helps another, right? Well, I did just that. I got him off. His lawyer shook my hand – damned nearly kissed me. But Ignaz didn't even look my way. Just left me standing there. Got into his car and drove away. Never once looked back.'

They were silent.

'Get it all out of your system,' Elena said, abruptly, 'before it chokes you.'

'How?'

'Go and talk to Marker.'

'And how do you think I should go about it?'

'Try calling him.'

Brinkmann stared at nothing. He got up without a word, smiling, and went across the room to the glass door and into the hall. He opened one of the telephone booths and picked up the directory.

Mahler, Malzer, *Marker, Dr Ignaz.*

He hesitated. The door of the booth was open. He could see the wood panelling, the wall lights, the carpets and a wooden statue of the Madonna. She looked him straight in the eyes. The blue cloak, the crown, that Madonna smile: Bodensee baroque, and rather splendid. All the same, there was something about the pink face of the Virgin that Brinkmann found disturbing: understanding, yes, but also aloofness. Ironic, to understand everything and yet want nothing to do with any of it – particularly when it was a dope like Klaus Brinkmann!

He closed the door and dialled. Even as he dialled and listened to the dialling tone, he recalled the scene in the county courtroom.

The official noticeboard with the announcement of the charges: *Vs. Dr Ignaz Marker in the matter of bringing about death on request by failing to render assistance.*

Brinkmann had sat on a bench next to the noticeboard and smoked a cigarette until he was called. *Failing to render assistance?*

Ignaz sat on the defendant's bench, his grey head bent. He had not moved nor looked at anyone while the trial machinery was warmed up by the defence counsel, who claimed Professor Brinkmann's testimony was prejudiced and that it should be replaced by testimony from an independent scientific expert. The request was denied, eliciting loud interjections by that unspeakable saphead Lutz, the co-plaintiff, who was simply unable to keep his mouth shut. Then the usual questions: case history, illness, cause of death. It didn't take them long to get to the nitty-gritty; poisoning due to an overdose of sleeping pills.

Was it difficult for a doctor to diagnose such an overdose? he was asked. He had to answer 'no', of course. And anyway, when it came to diagnosis, Ignaz was one of the best, and not only when compared to other village doctors.

And then they reached the heart of the matter. 'To put it another way, Professor,' the judge had asked. 'Was it inevitable that Mr Lutz would have died that day?'

'No. One can never say something like that with absolute certainty. He could have died. His condition was serious enough as it was, without sleeping pill poisoning.'

'Please be more specific.'

'If a stomach pump had been used the effect of the poison would have been ameliorated, but, by the same token using a stomach pump might well have killed the patient anyway. In his condition, with renal failure, constant heart weakness and severe diabetes, he could have died at any time. Anything else I might say would have to be in the realm of vague supposition.'

'But if Dr Marker had admitted Mr Lutz to a clinic immediately, what would his chances have been then? How long could Mr Lutz have been kept alive in that event? What would his life expectancy have been?'

'Life expectancy? I think perhaps death expectancy would be better.'

'Professor, you are causing a certain amount of confusion with this line. The ethical-moral aspects of the case are not under discussion here.'

But they were! Brinkmann had given a lot of thought to that.

And to what had gone before, not just in Marker's garden, but in everything he had seen and experienced in the preceding decades. He looked at Ignaz, sitting there isolated from everyone and everything. Looking at him, Brinkmann found it unbelievable that he had not been able to understand Marker's position that afternoon. This would be the moment to put that right. As far as the ethical-moral aspects of the case, as the judge called them, were concerned, there was only one position to take, and that was the one Ignaz had taken. Now he, Brinkmann, would support him.

'It would have been possible to extend the dying patient's suffering for days, perhaps even weeks. On the basis of my experience and criteria, I must say I believe that would have resulted in an inhuman death. It is not only the moral norms which influence a doctor's course of action. There are also the wishes of the patient who has been entrusted to him, and who trusts him. The doctor's duty is to prolong life, not to prolong dying! This is even more true when he is supported in his actions by a patient who rejects an inhuman, slow death.'

He could still see himself standing there in the courtroom, and Marker who had not once looked up. And then he heard his voice on the phone, first as he cleared his throat, then as he said hello.

'It's me. Klaus.'

Again the clearing of the throat. Brinkmann waited. Then he heard Marker's voice, a little hoarse but calm.

'Funny, I would have bet it would be you.'

'Really?'

'Perhaps there is such a thing as telepathy after all, eh? I'd already called you, but you were out. Where are you, anyway?'

'In Triberg.'

'Ah, I see.'

'Why did you call me?'

'Why? I thought you were rather good. Really, Klaus, I thought what you said in court was splendid. Why are you asking, anyway? You're just a vain old rooster!'

Brinkmann laughed. 'At least I don't go digging around in the same old manure heap the way you do!'

'True, you're pretty good at changing sides. I've got to hand it to you, you're flexible. All right, let's not talk it to death. Come over

191

and see me soon. I've got a rather good bottle of Ruländer in the cellar. What do you say?'

'I'd like to. Very much.'

'Good,' Marker said. 'I'll be seeing you. And . . . thanks, Klaus.'

THIRTY-ONE

Brinkmann grinned at the Virgin Mary. He was still grinning as he crossed the hall to the entrance. Then the door opened.

'Hello, Klaus.'

The man wore national dress: leather shorts and black velvet jacket with a crimson tie. The man knew Brinkmann. His name was Friedrich Schachner, if Brinkmann remembered correctly. Another school friend. There were altogether too many of them around here.

'Please forgive me, Klaus. I saw you earlier, but I didn't like to disturb you and your friend during dinner.'

They shook hands. 'No problem.' But it was politeness, nothing more. Schachner blinked red-rimmed eyes. He was tall and thin, the colourful folklore package contrasting comically with the pale, strained face. What could he want?, Brinkmann wondered, and then remembered that Schachner was the mayor of Kirchstett. Of course, Finingen's 'miracle spring' was in his bailiwick.

'It's about that interview in the Kinzigtal *Advertiser*.'

'What about it?'

'What about it? What about it?' Schachner said, vehemently. 'Did you have to do it?'

'A reporter asked me a question. I answered it. You know how it is. You know that better than anyone.'

'You answered, fine. But what you said hasn't been at all helpful to my parish. Or the spring.'

The spring? Brinkmann thought of the case of diarrhoea Kate had suffered: that hadn't been at all helpful, either. Then he thought about the report he had asked the government laboratory to undertake. The analysis had been damning: the stuff from Schachner's spring was crawling with bacteria.

'Come on, Klaus, try to see it from my point of view. It's not that difficult, is it? It's not just Finingen – the whole area's become popular with the tourists. Everyone's making more money; there's even talk of a spa hotel being planned. That takes a lot of investment capital, and all it needs is a few shots across the bows such as yours, and our investors will naturally . . .'

'Poor darlings.'

'What do you mean?'

'You know perfectly well what I mean. The water is worthless, Friedrich.'

'We think otherwise. And the irrefutable cures we've had can't be dismissed out of hand.'

'Cures? Up to now all I've heard of is an ankle somebody broke, and it was our orthopaedic unit that cured that, not your miracle water. Apart from some old man who had a heart attack as a result of queuing all night, and even we couldn't help him.'

'People are unreasonable. I don't have to tell you that. There's nothing else we can do. Although, believe me Klaus, we're getting much better organised. I have been made responsible for planning and we have organised the whole project with military precision.'

'With military precision? Really?' Brinkmann murmured.

'So, please, in future no more stabs in the back, okay?'

'Listen, people are even bringing that witch's brew into the clinic with them.'

'And what harm does that do?'

'My housekeeper got diarrhoea.'

'Oh, come on, Klaus, what's that got to do with what we're talking about? Look, we're old friends. Besides, doesn't the clinic profit, too, perhaps? Think of the hordes who'd flock down here. And well, you know . . .'

Brinkmann rubbed his nose. It was itching, and that wasn't a good sign. What should he tell the man? What could anyone say to the likes of Freidrich Schachner? The Department of Health already had the report. If necessary he would reinforce it with a second opinion.

'You know how it is . . .' Schachner's voice was almost pleading. Brinkmann nodded and turned away.

'Yes, I know exactly how it is. Be seeing you.'

He went back into the restaurant. The lights were on now, and a candle was burning at his table. Elena looked small and pensive and somehow lost. As he crossed the room he felt a twinge of conscience. He was such a damned egotist. With the exception of two or three evening meals, when Kate had also come along, he had avoided meeting Elena. Yet he still expected her automatic support, although all under the guise of 'old friends' and 'business'. As if there were any such things. She barely glanced at him as he sat down and called the waiter across.

'Two more.'

'Not for me, Klaus.'

'I'm off tomorrow.'

'I know. But it's still a long way home.'

Brinkmann pulled a face. 'All right then, a bottle of mineral water,' he said. 'Dammit, Elena, it's bad enough I get nothing but aggravation, but then you begrudge me the wine as well.'

'Marker?' she smiled.

'Oh, no, that's all been taken care of. I ran into someone else outside. A schoolfriend, the mayor of Kirchstett. He's upset because he thinks that if only I'd stop putting obstacles in his way, his miracle well would make him a millionaire.'

'How come?'

'Ask him. Maybe he's right. But that damned stuff is just generally dangerous. Best to keep well away from it. You know, sometimes I wouldn't mind giving the whole thing up. I should have become a pediatrician. No, psychology, that would have been the right choice.'

'You're a bloody awful psychologist.'

'I know. See, I'm talking about myself again.'

'You don't have to apologise,' she said. 'It doesn't matter. I like being with you. But you shouldn't feel under any obligation.'

'Under any obligation?'

'That was why you invited me, wasn't it? Or was it a kind of farewell outing?'

'I don't understand anything any more.' Brinkmann sipped the water; it tickled his tongue. 'If only we could spend one evening without agonising over our problems.'

'In my case not so much agonising over them as calling them by their correct names.'

'Really? Then go ahead and name them.'

Elena sat back and looked around. 'It's a pretty place. The journey was lovely. The hotel, too . . .' She broke off, looking into his eyes. 'Be honest with me Klaus, just this once. It was duty, wasn't it? You'd prefer to be here with Christa, wouldn't you?'

His mouth suddenly felt dry. 'Elena, we agreed in Karlsruhe . . .'

'To part and go on as friends. We've agreed on that a hundred times and never done it once. Please don't talk as if what we said was serious. This time it's something else: you're involved with that nurse.'

'How did you work all this out?'

'Klaus, we've always been honest with each other. But if you really want to know . . .' Her voice rose slightly, and its harshness irritated him. 'All right, you asked and I'll tell you. You know I'm not the type that goes through a man's pockets looking for proof. I don't need to. The others bring it to me with their sympathy. They're the ones who tell me. Even your own son tells me.'

'What in the name of God has Udo got to do with this?'

'Yes, indeed, what in the name of God? He has a lot to do with this. For years I couldn't talk to him. For years his dislike, or should I call it hatred, haunted me. Yes, you could almost say hatred.'

'Elena, look, you know very well that he's always considered you partly to blame for my wife's death. But to assume from something that happened a long time ago . . .'

She was sitting bolt upright, rigid. Her demeanour was familiar: the discussion was ended, he knew that. He signalled the waiter to bring the bill. Elena's face was as red as if she had been slapped. In stark contrast to her usual cool, aware manner, she ignored the dark-suited young man who was preparing their bill.

'The whole clinic is talking about it!'

'Elena, please!'

'Why don't you say it? Why don't you just tell me that this time we're really through?'

He just looked at her, so much entreaty in his gaze that she fell silent.

'Sixty-six Deutschmarks twenty, Professor. Do you want a receipt?'

Brinkmann looked up. 'What's that? Oh. No, thank you.'

The silence was worse than any noise.

The car glided down the dark wooded slopes towards the valley. Brinkmann concentrated on his driving, taking the curves as if each was the most important task he would ever perform. Elena sat wrapped in a cocoon of silent accusation and memory until he could stand it no longer.

'Do you have the slightest idea how much I value you and your friendship?'

She did not reply. The red tip of her cigarette glowed in the dark and he heard her exhale. 'Oh, yes,' she said. Nothing else.

'Listen to me, Elena. If I behaved the way people say I do, you know where I'd end up. The same goes for you . . . There's nothing going on between Nurse Christa and myself, no relationship, no affair or whatever you call it. Although it's perfectly true that I like her very much.'

'You don't owe me any explanation.'

'Oh, what a sentence! But I want to explain, damn it! If only I could. I'm not even sure how I feel myself. At my age things don't happen just like that. Think about it: she is young, she's a nurse. I'm a doctor. The old story, but it's not that simple. God, don't you understand that?'

'What are you shouting for?'

'I'm shouting because I feel like shouting. What do you expect? Do I have to go to the guillotine because I like her? Things like that need time to develop, right?'

'Then let it develop.' Elena Bach stubbed out the cigarette in the ashtray. 'Did you say you wanted to be a psychologist? Poor Klaus! Be grateful that you're a surgeon. Can't you see what's wrong with the girl?'

'Be kind enough to let me find out for myself.'

'Then why do you insist on lying to yourself?'

He turned to glance at her. The faint light from the dashboard lit his thin, plaintive smile. 'Because I'm a man, Elena. And man alone among all living things is capable of self-delusion. But he is also capable of thinking things out for himself.'

'Then do just that, Klaus.' She leaned back against the head support. 'You said you valued my friendship. I value yours, too. If there's anything I hate it's jealousy, half-truths, pretence.'

'Fine. Then we've got things straightened out?'

'Yes, Klaus. We have.'

'When will it end?' the girl asked, querulously.

'What?'

'What? This coach tour! I've had enough!'

So what, that was *her* problem. Udo was already doing 140 kilometres per hour on the damned autobahn. The Salzkammergut was behind them, they had crossed southern Bavaria and the Allgäu. There up ahead on the horizon were the dark hills which were the forerunners of the Black Forest. It had been half-past nine when Udo Brinkmann left the hotel garage in Bozen in his Alfa. He was making record time and all she could do was complain!

'Have you got something to eat, Susi?'

'You want some Chewy?'

'What?'

'Gum, you idiot!'

Correct: you idiot. But that didn't begin to cover it. It was not the first time in the last two weeks that he had wondered during the ridiculous journey what made him such an idiot, why everything had gone wrong yet again, and why he was once more coming home with empty hands, albeit richer by another experience. All right, he'd tried. But even if he hadn't it would have made no difference. It was his own fault things had gone wrong. Any sane human being looking for a job would have written letters, organised connections, phoned. Instead, he had taken his holiday, just got into the car and driven off. He could still see their faces, surprised, ironical, one or two giving him a compassionate smile.

'I see, you're from the Black Forest Clinic. Yes, of course we've heard of it . . .' Worse still was the cutting 'Oh, really?' He could take irony, but not cold, blunt indifference, not the 'sorry' that wasn't sorry at all, or the 'we don't need anyone' that silently added the humiliating 'especially you'.

He had forgotten all the names and all the places he had been to, all except the musty hall of that hospital in Feldkirch and the expression on the face of the administrative assistant, who said 'Good Heavens, man, what are you thinking of? What do you think would happen if everyone just came marching in here . . . ?'

What if everybody came? As for you, you're even less than everybody, anybody, nobody. That was what it came down to.

Udo had given up and driven south, over mountain passes he did not know, through places he had never heard of, first Austria, then Italy, finally winding up on a beach south of Cesenatico. The leftovers of the tourist season were spread all over the place like a rubbish dump. He got undressed, jumped into the water, and swam until he felt tired. There were cold currents in the sea, but if you floated on your back and spread your arms it was bearable.

So there he was, floating beneath a strange sky, not moving, not thinking. Not even thinking of when he had come here as a child with his mother, floating past on a white steamer en route from Venice to Ancona. They had been on deck, sitting in a deckchair. Her hand, her face, her voice: 'You know, little one, perhaps one day we shall come to live in Italy. To Venice, or up there in the mountains. Would you like that?'

He had a bag of potato chips in his hand, he could remember that, remember the salty taste, the sound of the waves, the gulls that circled overhead and swooped down for the chips. And her soft voice: 'Would you like that?'

He would have liked anything that she suggested. But she was gone. And so were her voice, and the dream about Italy.

That evening he ordered wine, too much wine, in a gaudy neon-lit bar on the beach. He invited a yawning waiter to join him, stroked the cat and, because he was running out of money, had slept in the car. Correction: tried to sleep in the car.

Next morning he ran into Susi.

She was standing by the Espresso bar at the gas station, her short, red hair shining. She smiled and asked him if he was driving back to Germany. At first he hesitated, but while he was shaving in the toilet of the gas station he thought, why not? Hair like a squirrel. A funny, short upper lip. Snub nose. A backside in jeans that was something to look at. Why not?

Yet it was none of those things, not even that he needed a woman. He just didn't want to be alone any more, that was really what it was.

Later, when she opened her mouth, Udo realised that he would be lonely anyway. The night in Bozen didn't improve things. Susi with her 'well, if I must' face and cool eyes, his sweaty and, worse still, grim efforts to make love to her . . . Eventually he held her in his arms until she fell asleep: two casualties on the road back to Germany.

'What kind of a dump is Offingen, then?'

'You'll see.'

'Black Forest?' she mused. 'Lots of trees, I suppose? Are there still trees or have they all died off? And clean air?'

They drove along a poplar-lined road. Udo turned off to the right. To one side loomed the dark bulk of Donaueschingen castle. Clean air: Jesus!

Udo felt the pressure in the pit of his stomach again. Crushed! Beaten. A failure. What else? It was as if his thoughts were hanging in front of his eyes, dangling from threads. Nothing was any use. All that remained was the thought of the old man. His smile. Renz's pointed questions.

He put his arm around Susi's shoulders. He didn't even know her surname, and yet he felt a kinship with her: she was running away, too, equally childlike and determined in her search for a 'better life'. Waitressing in Rimini: she could not think of anything better. And what about him? Assistant something in Southern Bavaria, or the Vorarlberg? What was the difference between them?

'Can't you bloody well stop somewhere, for God's sake?' she said. 'Me belly thinks me throat's been cut. You really in that much of a hurry?'

Yes, he was! He wanted to put it all behind him. The road unwound beneath them: Rohrhardsberg, Schönenbach. She seemed to be enjoying it. The Alfa ate up the main road, roaring along the high ridges between Elz and Kinzig. Then suddenly Udo slammed on the brakes so hard that Susi had to brace both hands against the dashboard.

200

'Holy God, can't you be more careful?' she gasped. 'Got no eyes in your head or something?'

He said nothing.

'What's going on. Who are all these people?'

The road was half blocked off by a barrier. Behind it were two parked police cars. A policeman bearing a STOP sign waved them down. At first Udo thought it must be an accident. Then he saw the coaches, half a dozen of them in the car park further down. Private cars took up the whole side of the road.

Udo put the car into neutral and let it roll forward. It was an incredible sight: a long column of people winding up the hill like a caterpillar between the trees, new ones hurrying to join it. Most of them carried small plastic bottles or containers that shone in the sun. Parking attendants herded them off the road like lost sheep.

Udo came to a stop next to the policeman who was about to wave them through. 'Tell me, what's going on? Are they looking for buried treasure? Or Easter eggs?'

'That's a good one. They're looking for good health.' The man's expression didn't even change.

'In the forest? Well, that's a new twist.'

'At the spring. Can't you read? It's written on the sign.'

'*Heilquelle*,' it said. 'Curative Spring.' It was daubed in bold blue capitals on grey card which had been cut into the shape of a dart pointing to the hill where panting old women and puffing white-haired pensioners laboured up towards the woods.

'Haven't you heard about the miracle spring?'

'It says curative spring.'

'Miracle spring! Even the newspapers called it that. They say someone from Rastatt had their sight restored.' The policeman grinned. 'That started the whole business. Now we've got to stand here till our feet fall off. I'm surprised you haven't heard about it.'

'I've been on leave,' Udo said, and put the car into gear. Susi turned around as they moved off, unable to take her eyes off the horde of people going up the hill between the trees.

'Well, I never . . . Did he say someone had their eyesight restored?'

'That's the language of miracles,' Udo replied sagely.

THIRTY-TWO

You might as well bring some fresh country eggs, Kate had said as he left. Brinkmann had his doubts: the management meetings were like marathons, seventy per cent wasted energy. He had to find some way to reduce this wastage: perhaps he could get Schaefer to take his place. After the meeting, he had a 'consultation' on his schedule, although it was not listed in his diary. It might at least have been a good idea to look at Christa's roster, he thought. Well, where there's a will, where the emotions are involved, there is always a way . . .

He shooed Mollie into the hall and started upstairs, then stopped as a car drove up and came to a halt outside. He knew that dashing style: Udo!

There was a girl with him, of course. Reddish-brown hair, cut short. Sexy, but a type he had not – in spite of everything – expected Udo to turn up with. The girl stayed in the car as Udo opened the boot and took out luggage.

Kate was right, Brinkmann reflected. What business was it of his, anyway? When would he finally accept Udo for what he was, a freak of nature creating unanticipated after-effects. There seemed to be a quarrel going on.

'What's the matter, Susi? Get your stuff out, the car's had it. It won't go another yard. It'll have to go in for repair.'

The girl remained stubbornly seated. Udo had seen his father approaching. He put down the overnight bag. 'Hi!'

'Hello, Udo.'

Udo tried to summon up a smile, but didn't quite make it. Brinkmann felt sorry for him, although he had long since become used to that strange twisting of the lips that was his son's failed grin. The least he could do was direct his gaze instead at Madame in the car.

'How did it go?'

'Do you know, I don't really know myself. I stuck on a few days holiday and went down as far as Cesenatico.'

'Good for you. And the new job?'

'Nothing. There's nothing going in the smaller places, and I don't stand a chance in the bigger ones.'

Brinkmann nodded. 'Hardly surprising.' He saw the unspoken question in Udo's eyes, and added quickly. 'Your job here is always safe.'

'Thanks,' Udo said. 'And if you don't mind, Father, I'll move back into the house. Of course, I'll keep on looking for a place of my own.'

'Sure . . . of course.'

Udo stooped to pick up the suitcase, concealing his flushed face. Lucky it was there, Brinkmann thought as he also grabbed a bag and carried it to the front door. He grinned at the unexpected picture of little Udo who never quite knew how to get out of the messes he got himself into.

'You know,' Udo motioned towards the car, 'that one out there gives me a pain.'

'That so?'

'Look at her! I honestly don't know why I have such bad luck with women.'

As if in confirmation, her voice echoed across the courtyard. 'What's wrong now, you bleedin' berk?'

Udo took a deep breath and went down the steps. 'I told you, the car's clapped out. I haven't got any petrol, either. You'll have to hitch the rest of the way, Susi.'

'You miserable sod! In that case, give me back the money I loaned you for petrol in Bozen. What a bloody nerve!'

'Look, I haven't got any . . .'

Seeing Udo's look of desperation, Brinkmann abandoned his role of disinterested observer and took a hundred-Deutschmark note out of his wallet, handing it to his floundering son. He waited until the garden gate closed behind the aggressive, red-haired oddball called Susi, and for the first time in a long while he felt really sorry for his son.

'Thanks,' Udo said, gratefully. 'I appreciate that, Father.'

'You're welcome. When the chips are down, we men have to stick together.' They grinned at each other.

'Where's Kate?'

'Kate? On a bed of suffering.'

'She's ill?'

'As a matter of fact, yes. She's had a bad case of diarrhoea brought on by equal amounts of coli bacteria and her own stupidity. There's been a big kerfuffle about a new spring, you know. Apparently it . . .'

'At Finingen? The miracle spring? I saw it. People must be barmy. You can't get through the place for buses and old ladies.'

'I know. And Kate, being Kate, couldn't wait to try the stuff. She asked someone to bring her some: they're even selling it in the kiosks and pubs over there.'

Udo leaned against the handrail, looking up across the facade of the house towards Kate's room. 'Poor Kate! Why didn't you just pour the stuff over her head?'

'Me? Are you joking? You know what she's like. You know what she said? "All these years, and have you ever been able to give me anything for my migraine? Yet just one sip of this, and it was gone."'

Udo laughed so heartily he almost choked. His father gave a rueful grin.

'And so?'

'So now we're putting the blocks on these springwater merchants. In fact, it's already half done. But I wouldn't mind betting

204

Kate has got a couple of dozen bottles of the stuff in the cellar. She swears that it wasn't the water that gave her the squitters, it was some unripe plums I brought her.'

Hardt Street was in one of those areas of town where stately old houses with the patina of time about them stood like islands defying the building boom of the Seventies. A lot of brown sandstone, bay windows, white-painted frames, glistening greenhouse domes in gardens where leeks grew and chestnuts blossomed.

Brinkmann left his car in the parking space by the steps and walked, hands in his pockets, enjoying the summer evening. The fatigue brought on by the difficult afternoon meeting fell away. He checked the street numbers: forty-six. It must be further along. Then he saw Christa's green Volkswagen, and felt the quickening of his heartbeat. For the first time he admitted to himself that it wasn't just the talk he'd planned to have with Christa that had brought him here, but also curiosity. What was the area like where she lived? How had she planned her flat? How did she spend her days, and what did she do during those hours when she was not near him?

A metal plate held on to a grey plank on the garden door by rusty screws said *No beggars or hawkers*. Next to it the names of the occupants: among them, C. Meurer.

Brinkmann suppressed an impulse to turn around, get back into the car and forget the whole thing. Good God, he hadn't even brought flowers, or wine, or a book – just turned up. And on top of that with his throat as dry as a schoolboy's. What was it, shyness? No, a feeling he hardly remembered, although he had experienced it often enough: a mixture of fear and hope, mixed with a bit of anxiety over the fact that another human being, this woman, was becoming more important than you cared to admit.

'Hey, mister, can you throw the ball back?'

Only now did he see the boys. They came hurtling out of the garage, faded jeans on their thin legs, hockey sticks in their hands. The grim, determined expressions on their hot, flushed faces reminded him of the days when he had played football with Udo – how long ago it seemed . . .

The entrance was at the side of the house, where the branches of an old elm brushed against the grey-flecked walls. Through one of the kitchen windows he heard a nagging female voice, and then that of a man replying with exasperated patience.

He looked around, saw dustbins bulging with plastic wrappers, a cat sunning itself on a wall. A battered child's tricycle with rusty spokes, a chewed-up ball. On the balconies, washing flapped in the breeze coming up from the valley.

The place wasn't what you'd call clean, and was wretchedly dull. How could she put up with this? The thought stayed with him, as he pushed the door open and looked for her name on the row of letter-boxes. 'Second floor', he muttered, as he deciphered the words in the half-darkness.

He went up the polished stairway, found himself facing two doors, rang the bell and waited for some sound inside the apartment. There was no sound, nothing. Apart from the stupid throb in his throat.

Brinkmann tried again, and again there was no answer. The realisation that she was not here, after he had thought it all over so carefully and arrived in such a state of anxious expectation, depressed him. So perhaps it was some subconscious rebellion, or defiance in defeat, that made him try the door handle: the door opened.

Brinkmann hesitated, coughed, then decided to go in.

'Christa?'

Nothing. The only sound was the ticking of an alarm clock. Brinkmann stood in the tiny hall. Light streamed in through the glass in the kitchen door. A trench coat hung on a hook on the wall: Christa's coat! Her green scarf was there, too. Brinkmann caressed it, as if he could touch her with this subconscious, reflex gesture.

'Christa? Anybody home?'

No reply. He could smell her perfume. Her presence seemed even more real than the bickering voices of the neighbours he could still hear. There was a small red carpet at his feet and he found himself thinking, she walks across this every day. He chided himself for such adolescent nonsense. Or did these feelings contain a kernel of truth?

Brinkmann struggled to put the flood of impressions sweeping over him into some kind of order. It wasn't easy, but he knew he ought to be able to summon up that other, more rational observer in himself. He saw his reflection in a mirror.

Klaus Brinkmann! Going astray, Chief? A little scurf on the lips, eyes which seemed calm enough yet saw nothing. Most of all, wrinkles. And the grey at the temples. Klaus Brinkmann, caressing the shawl of a girl at least twenty years younger than himself. A girl he knew so little about . . .

He did not move. The tiny hall was like a cell, imprisoning not only his thoughts, but time itself. The present was suspended between past and future: point zero.

But there was no such moment as point zero. Strictly speaking, Brinkmann thought, there is no present, only future and past. The present is nothing but an illusion.

Coffee break.

Nurses gossiping, giggling, sitting around the little table in the corner of the day room eating homemade cake or fruit tarts given to them by the patients. Cigarette smoke and open boxes of chocolate. They were in good form, all of them, including some visitors from the other wards. Lydia, the tall, dark nurse from gynaecology, led the conversation.

'One to sleep with, the other to show off with. Useful arrangement, eh?'

'Come on, Lydia – he sleeps with her?'

'You know what they say about still waters – although I have to admit, I can't see Christa . . .'

In the room next door Christa Meurer was taking off the coat which had been soiled while she was changing bandages. She froze as she was reaching for another, resting her hand against the cupboard, feeling the chill of the metal go through her hand and into her heart. The conversation went on, to and fro, malice mixed with boredom, frustration, jealousy: not even intelligent enough to hurt. Or was it?

'Serves her right. She's an arrogant cow, that Bach!'

'Is it true what they say about the old man and Karlsruhe . . . ?'

'Karlsruhe? Have you been living on the moon? Everywhere with her. And for years!'

It hurt, all right. Christa squared her shoulders: maybe she ought to go in there and throw the lot of them out. Her glance fell on a magazine with an advertisement for watches: *Time for action.*

'Then Christa's got problems. What would you do if you were her?'

'She keeps it in the family. First the kid, then the old man.'

Enough! She wanted to stand, but found she couldn't. Then she heard Elke's voice cutting sharp and clear through the giggling.

'You're all so spiteful and cruel! I can't stand any of you!'

'What's wrong, Elke? Don't go on so. After all, this should interest you as well, right?'

'Go on, get out of here! Go!'

They went on laughing, knowing no better, destroying something they could not understand. Christa's eyes burned; she tried to put her thoughts in order, but could not manage even that. She sat in the wicker chair, her head in her hands, wishing she was anywhere but here.

She had no idea how long she sat there. It was only when she heard Elke that she looked up.

'Christa?' Elke was pale, her ears pink with anger. She stared at Christa. 'Oh, damn it all, you must have –'

'Yes. Everything.'

Elke took a deep breath, pulled over a stool, sat down. 'Such rubbish! I can understand how you feel. But you aren't taking all this mud-slinging seriously, are you?'

Christa said nothing.

'Christa, love, you're crying! Listen, they're not worth wasting your tears on. Here, dry your eyes!' She gave her a tissue. Christa took it. It was true: tears were a waste of time.

'Perhaps they're right, at that,' she said. She thought of her apartment. She had never really cared for it, but right now she felt an almost unbearable longing to be there. Seven o'clock. Mischa had repaired the VW and promised to leave it at the gate. She could go for a drive.

'Elke, I want to get out of here. Would you take my shift?'

'Of course I will. Get yourself some fresh air.'

'There isn't enough to blow away what's bothering me.'

Even then, it was not over. A little later, as she was waiting to go down in the lift, Dr Elena Bach emerged, hands thrust into the pockets of her cream-coloured suit, a thin smile on her face. Only

208

women who sense that they are rivals can smile at each other like that, Christa thought. She heard the malicious voice again: 'One to sleep with, the other to show off with.'

'Oh, Nurse Christa, before I forget. I've put your name down for duty in surgery tomorrow.'

'I thought that was Sister's job?'

Elena Bach's large eyes studied her face, still smiling. 'You're right, it is Sister's job. But Sister has accepted my suggestion.'

Christa searched for a suitable reply, but Elena Bach beat her to it. 'If you're asking me for my reasons, Nurse, I can only draw your attention to the professor's instructions. And you ought to know those better than I do.'

It would have been better had she just walked past, accepting the situation as it was. Yes, Frau Doctor, but of course, Frau Doctor, anything you say. So why didn't she say it? Why didn't she just walk away?

'I believe the idea is to familiarise young nurses with operating-theatre procedure, but perhaps I ought to tell you I have been in charge of a ward for three years.'

'And you mean because of that you think you have nothing more to learn?'

'Learn, Frau Doctor. How do you mean?'

It was not her condescension, nor that pale, aloof face. No, all that mattered now was herself, to maintain her own self-confidence.

'Perhaps it is of no interest to you that I have studied medicine and passed my preliminary exam, Frau Doctor Bach. And I assure you I love my work and take great interest in it. But I'm not qualified to be a theatre nurse.'

She managed to say it in a matter-of-fact way, but her voice trembled so that Dr Bach noticed her distress. She was surprised by the effect her words had. Elena's expression changed from feigned control to astonishment, and something like understanding showed in her eyes.

'I see. I didn't know.'

There are a lot of things you don't know, Christa wanted to say. Instead, she said: 'If I have already been assigned, then I shall be in theatre tomorrow, Frau Doctor.'

When she got outside, Christa drew the fresh air into her lungs until she thought she would burst. Ten-past seven. She decided to walk home: it would do her good.

She found herself longing to hear Klaus' voice and see his smile. However much his searching and artless but always precise way of looking at things sometimes annoyed her, she could have done with it now. She needed him . . .

Cutting the cord, the process was called. Hard as it might be to extricate herself from the embrace of her dreams, the time had come. She would have to tell him, if not today, then tomorrow.

She walked slowly over the ramp, past the emergency entrance and out of the grounds, leaving behind the kitchen noise, girlish laughter, the gurgle of water pipes somewhere, the squeak of stretcher trolleys being pushed down a corridor, people talking. All the myriad tiny sounds which, woven together, had become as familiar as a second skin.

The clinic.

Her clinic? Wasn't that how she thought of it sometimes? Well, that was all over now. The next clinic would feel just the same. What other choice did she have?

THIRTY-THREE

The little travelling clock by the bed ticked on. Klaus Brinkmann looked at it: seven-twenty. Where was Christa?

He looked around the room. It was a surprise: he was not quite sure what he had expected, but it was not this straightforward and convincing simplicity. The slanting, golden rays of the evening sun fell on the bookshelves. A ball of wool with two needles stuck through it. A bunch of flowers, just a few stems but arranged in such a way that their shadow completed the picture. A wide sofa, books. His feeling of intruding on someone's privacy was heightened by the ticking of the clock.

What are you doing here? What do you want?

All right: you are looking for her. Admit it: maybe you are looking for something which has eluded you up to now, a girl – no, a woman – whom you love but know almost nothing about.

The bookcase was so low that Brinkmann had to bend down to read the titles. A few books by Tucholsky, South Americans like Marques and Llosa, then Carl Gustav Jung. Many of the titles were familiar; there were others he would have liked to have read. Many medical books, of course: text books, holistic medicine, psychology, even a book on surgery: *Organ-Bereich-Spezialisierung: Eine Neudefinierung der Chirurgie*. Its author: Klaus Brinkmann. Where on earth had she found that?

As he straightened up his head spun, and he had to breathe deeply to steady his heart. Diagnosis? Pure dizziness, what else? The sun had disappeared behind the top of the trees, and violet shadows were creeping across the floor of Christa's room. Down below the argument had stopped. A radio was playing somewhere. It was time to go!

Yet still somehow Brinkmann could not tear himself away: it was as if something was holding him back. He ran a hand over the writing desk and sat down on the attractive antique chair. On the desk lay a drawing pad. He lifted the green cover: watercolours of rocks and trees. The pictures had that same quality of uncluttered simplicity that the room itself exuded. The little things that tell you so much about the whole, he thought. Somehow very austere. Oh, for God's sake, man!

As he put the pad back on the desk a slip of paper fell out. On it were scribblings in pencil, all crossed out. He bent over it, putting on his glasses and holding the paper up to the light.

'Dear Chief of my Dreams' The first words he managed to decipher pleased him. Then his smile disappeared. 'I wish I could call you that. I can't. It would only reinforce what has been bothering me since that evening outside my house, a feeling of deliverance . . .'

He nodded. Now he knew.

He carefully replaced the piece of paper. He found himself wishing he was wearing surgical gloves, as if he was afraid he might leave fingerprints . . .

She knew the moment she walked into the operating theatre the next morning that she had been wrong and Elena Bach had been right. This was what her profession was all about: a reality apart from all else. Even the clock on the wall had laws of its own. Each minute had a weight, a yardstick of craftsmanship, failure or botch-up. Each second, fragmented into the thousandths of seconds to which the electronic impulses of the instruments were

212

geared, could sometimes seem endless, as the fate of patients and sometimes even their deaths were decided.

In this world, tiled, mercilessly lit, controlled by instruments, you felt as though you were in a space capsule. Here neither lies nor fraud would work. The only thing that counted here was the scalpel. Any minute in the operating theatre was infinitely more important than hours of making beds, changing bandages, dressing wounds.

Two other nurses were detailed to work with Christa. They were the smallest cogs in the machinery of the operating theatre, ready to turn their hands to anything that was necessary. The other trainee nurses were from gynaecology; Christa did not even know their names. Their nervous, jerky movements betrayed how heavily the environment weighed on them.

The doctors were also present in force. Schaefer asked to be excused, and Christa fleetingly recalled the gossip she'd heard about his taking a few days off because he wasn't feeling well. In his place Brinkmann had invited not only Udo and Renz but also Rebhagen, chief of gynaecology, to assist. A complex stomach operation was their first task. This dangerous second operation was being undertaken to correct a botched ruptured hernia repair that had caused deformation and tumours. It would also by its nature take the surgeons into areas usually treated by gynaecologists.

Elena Bach had already administered the anaesthetic. Brinkmann had just finished studying the X-rays. He turned to see Christa. He walked towards her, his hands outstretched. She pulled the surgical gloves over his fingers, and it was as if to her at that moment only these brown strong hands with their wide palms mattered in all the world, the tips of his fingers with their nails cut short, the fine, reddish-blond hairs that shone in the lights of the operating theatre. His hands!

Surgeon's hands, and he was proud of them, otherwise he would not have referred to them so often, not sadly but with a gentle irony, as if they were creatures independent of himself. 'Still working,' he murmured, flexing his fingers. 'And with any luck, they'll keep going a little longer.'

Christa's hands were also protected by gloves, and the thin rubber skin permitted no feeling, not a spark, not even the tiniest contact. But then there was the smile in his eyes, holding hers so

213

long and so intensely that she knew Elena Bach had lied to her. It had not been because Sister needed a new nurse. It was his idea!

She felt her heart beat a little faster. Was he right, after all? This was his world. And if there was any way he could prove he trusted her, then this was it: by making her part of his team, by having her near him . . .

They both smiled behind their masks, a smile which no one could see but which they both felt. Without even looking in her direction, Christa knew Elena Bach would be aware of it too.

'Thank you, Christa.'

Brinkmann turned and walked to the head of the operating table. 'How's it going? Can we get started?'

Elena Bach nodded. 'We can.'

September.

The days had slipped by, fitting into each other like the identical links of a chain. After a period of oppressive heat, nightly thunderstorms and heavy daytime rain, the summer was again trying to muster its full power. Day after day the sun shone in a bright blue sky above the fields where the corn had either been harvested or flattened by the storms, apples ripening on the trees, rotting pears, fruit trees, tomato plants, asters in gardens.

It was not just the weather, however, which was bothering the team at the clinic. Nor was it just the work, although the events of the past few weeks had affected them all. As if impelled by some mysterious, almost ghostly random factor, the death rate had increased: heart attacks, accidents, cancer deaths, motorway pile-ups.

These days both the operating theatres looked like first-aid stations on the front line, working around the clock. Schaefer was back, although he let Renz do the operations and merely took on the role of first assistant. Udo, on the second shift, took on more and more major operations on his own responsibility.

Fortunately, Brinkmann had won his long fight for a new assistant in surgery. The 'new boy' was Manuel Ortega, a tough, thin Chilean who had gained his experience working in Red Cross missions overseas, and who had been able to start right away.

All this affected the outward, the visible routine. Less visible was the feeling of edginess that remained. Meanwhile the team steered through the high breakers of catastrophe as best they could.

Christa Meurer felt exhausted, beaten, and at the end of her tether. She needed a holiday, distance, time to think. Almost as if to confirm her own mental turmoil, she helped out in the theatre at every opportunity. It was as if she was being drawn into a magnetic field whose central source of energy was the Chief. Brinkmann seemed to take her presence more and more for granted.

Why do it?, she asked herself over and over. She could find no answer. Why didn't she at least ask for leave? There was no doubt that Brinkmann's ability to transmit that feeling of belonging, the work they shared, kept the whole thing going. It was like a drug. But in Heaven's name, did she have to share that with everyone else? With everyone? And above all, with Elena Bach?

She finally sat down and applied for leave. It had been another of those mornings and, after she had done it, Christa felt a sense of freedom and release for the first time. She walked down the corridors of the hospital, stopping to comfort old ladies, helped exasperated new admissions or groaning patients who needed their bandages changed, and no longer felt annoyed when the lords of surgery disappeared into their offices for a smoke and some shop talk.

But Brinkmann always had a smile for her, a lift of the hand, a 'Thank you, Christa!' His smile was like a secret caress, an unexpected bonbon whose taste sweetens the rest of the day.

And the nights? Who wanted to talk about them? A depressing vacillation between dreams, hopes and bitterness so intense that it sometimes frightened Christa. She asked herself whether perhaps she wasn't being fair, told herself to try and think of his position, try to see the whole situation objectively.

She knew she could do no such thing. It was useless pretending otherwise. The Christa Meurer who had always been in control, always sceptical and ruled by reason, no longer existed. You are in love! Hopelessly and uncontrollably in love. And worse than that, up to your neck in a tragicomedy – she did not like the script and she could not foretell the ending.

In love! And with whom, of all people? With a mature gentleman who had an even more mature lady to look after him but who could not do without his former lover, a gentleman who nevertheless occasionally makes an effort to show you how much you matter to him – for instance, with truly special invitations.

'Why don't you come over this evening? Really, Kate insists. She wants you to come very much . . .'

Kate wanted her to come?

But when she arrived there it became clearer. 'He's just crazy, Christa,' Kate would say. 'He's driving me completely mad. He has so many problems at the moment. You must be patient with him.'

She could hardly argue or fail to respond to the motherly smile. To Kate they were all prospective brides. Maybe that was her technique for putting you off balance: she treated everyone alike, made no comparisons. If they had Brinkmann's interests at heart, they were all acceptable.

Sometimes in the evening he took her to the villa. Those hands which played such a dominant part in her dreams touched her body, caressed her. A clumsy kiss on her neck, her ear. Although her being near seemed to mean a lot to him, he always held himself back. For God's sake, he was a man and she was a woman, wasn't she? Yet for some reason, he held the man inside him in check. Or was it something else? Was he afraid?

'Tell me, Christa, have you ever thought of resuming your studies? You could go on, couldn't you? I think you really have what it takes.' That, too, was part of their hours together: his persuasive voice, the opportunities that were part of the professional future he described to her.

Have you ever thought of resuming your studies? For years she had thought of nothing else. What could you do with a man like that? He knew . . . What else could you do with a man who adopted this fatherly role yet so clearly enjoyed being treated like a small boy? What could you do with a Brinkmann who won't take off the velvet gloves, and courts you in such an earnest, old-fashioned way, as if he was still living in the preceding century?

And what can you do about the other Brinkmann, the one who storms through the clinic, who wants to save life and who does it, then wears the martyred expression of someone with the weight of the world's woes on his shoulder, never giving a thought to such a thing as a private life? What the devil can you do with a surgeon?! And one who not only seems to have come from another world, but another generation?

216

I love him.

It was so utterly simple that it seemed almost silly. But there was nothing she could do. You love him without deliverance or hope. The smallest wheel in the machinery: Christa. No, she thought, you're not the smallest wheel any more. You've fallen into the machine.

THIRTY-FOUR

'Christa, shall I see you tonight?'

'I don't know.'

'What do you mean?'

'You have to work. And I'm on night duty again.'

Night duty again. Walking the corridors, opening doors, closing them, thermometers, plasters, foaming peroxide on scabbing wounds, faces distorted by pain, some pale, some smiling, looking at her and nodding with relief when she tells them what they want to hear. Some grab her hand. In the men's ward, mischievous, cheeky, obscene remarks. That, too.

We're all playing our parts, she thought. Doctors, nurses, patients. Yet no night was ever the same. The words that seem to you to be trite and hackneyed because they have been spoken a thousand times still possess the magic of a spell. That was what was so gratifying about the job.

The light was still on in the Chief's office. But first one had to cross the dark anteroom to reach his inner sanctum, where he sat, his head bent over books and graphs, working on reports or catching up on work that had been neglected.

Shall I see you tonight?

Sure: if the ward telephone doesn't ring and the coast is clear. Or if he's able to make it into the kitchen for a chat. Or maybe in his office, like last week. Christa felt a sharp stab of anger: how could you let yourself become so dependent on him? Wasn't this just a new version of the old game: to be available whenever he snapped his fingers? Her anger was directed at herself rather than him.

The waiting room. Plastic easy chairs, rubber-tree plants. On the wall was a poster of some Spanish beach resort. There were fishing boats, brown, red, yellow. And the sea.

Holidays! To see something different. To immerse yourself in another world . . .

Twenty metres to the left a brass plaque on the door: Professor Brinkmann. Better forget about fishing boats and Spain. Concentrate on your own problems, accept things as they are, look for a job in the paper . . .

Christa opened the next door along. A woman, her face illuminated by the bedside light, looked up at her. Abundant, beautiful white hair framed a face marked by death. It was painful to see how even the effort of smiling hurt the cancer patient.

Christa put down the syringe near the doorway. She crossed the room and sat down next to the woman, holding her hand. It was hot and dry, like a fire burning under paper.

'Oh, Christa . . . I've been waiting such a long time.'

'I'm sorry, Mrs Scheufele.'

'It doesn't matter. Honestly. I'm happy today, Christa.'

Hedwig Scheufele closed her eyes. 'He came today.' The smile on her face was as gentle as a reflection in the water.

'Really?' Christa said.

'He was here the whole afternoon. Three hours. And he brought me flowers.'

There were no flowers in the room, nor outside the door. 'He' had a name: Ralph. He was tall, capable, successful. An engineer with Dornier. He had a house on the Bodensee, a wife and three children: Ralph Scheufele, her nephew.

'You know, Christa, I've always been lonely. My whole life. I

219

haven't got any family of my own. If it wasn't for Ralph coming to see me all the time . . .'

He had visited her. Just once, four months ago. Christa remembered him, a tall blond type with an embarrassed grin. He had never come back. But to Hedwig Scheufele he appeared every week: Ralph, her phantom companion and guide through the shadow world of her final hours.

Her head lolled to one side. She continued talking, indistinctly and incoherently. Christa tiptoed to the tray and picked up the morphine injection. Hedwig Scheufele did not even feel the needle.

'Christa?'

She ignored him. She was not going to let him distract her while she was disinfecting, and did not look up as Brinkmann crossed the room to the bed. For a while he silently watched the patient. She knew what the expression on his face would be without needing to see it. 'One cannot suffer with each person, or die with each dying patient' – that was the golden rule in every medical establishment. He himself did not observe it. He suffered with them. Maybe that was one of the reasons she loved him.

'Is she holding on?'

Christa nodded. 'Yes: she has her Ralph.'

'Her Ralph?'

'It doesn't matter.' She was too tired to explain.

'Are you coming?'

She would go. There was nothing more she could do here. Are you coming, he'd asked. Where? He was standing beneath the poster with the fishing boats, smoking that damned pipe. He smiled, and when she saw his smile Christa decided to wait no longer.

'I've applied for some leave.'

'I know,' he nodded. 'It was long overdue. Where are you going to go?'

She looked at the fishing boats, deciding on the spur of the moment. 'Sylt,' she said.

'Sylt? Wonderful idea! Sylt in September . . .'

Yes, Sylt in September! Should she tell him she would have preferred to go to Spain but that she couldn't afford it? That she would rather go to Australia or South America or Canada? That she

220

had only said 'Sylt' because there was a house there she had known since she was a child, a house whose brick walls had always been like a fortress to her.

He was still smiling.

'It might be a . . . prolonged leave, Klaus.'

His smile disappeared; he stared at her in puzzlement. 'Prolonged leave? What does that mean?'

His surprise, the almost childlike astonishment in the way he asked the question, gave her the strength to face the truth.

Christa went back to the ticket office, looked through the papers on display there, chose a few women's magazines. She was in no mood to cope with other people's problems; she had enough of her own. As she took out her purse to pay, she saw the dog: a brown and white creature too fat for its size, rushing about with its lead trailing, sniffing trouser legs, suitcases, packages, attracting the attention of everyone in the station. Christa's heart skipped a beat: Mollie?

'Mollie!' someone called at exactly that moment.

He came towards her, the camelhair coat draped casually around his shoulders, his face angry – yes, *him*, the boss, the Chief! Why the hell did Brinkmann have to show up just as she was getting away from him? Or anyway, trying to.

Now he saw her, or rather Mollie did. Dirty paws on Christa's jeans, round eyes appealing, red tongue hanging out. Brinkmann's angry expression disappeared and was replaced by a smile.

'So there you are!' he said.

'Yes, here I am. What are you doing here?'

'Well, now, shouldn't saying goodbye be pleasant?'

'I don't like saying goodbye. Especially on railway stations.'

He did not seem at all impressed. He thanked the paper lady for her effusive 'Good morning, Professor!' with a friendly smile, and looked around at the people who knew him. Christa had not yet paid for her magazines but he was too quick for her. He picked up her pile of papers and, all in all, seemed to be so much in command of the situation that she was unable to suppress her anger.

Yes: goodbye!

Everything she had done that morning meant just that: getting up, packing, the last look around her flat, the sound of the key turning in the lock, the last look out of the taxi window across the market square to the hillside on which the clinic stood, and finally buying the ticket, a single to Sylt. She'd coped with all that, and at the same time with the distressing and simultaneously choking feeling that this was final.

And now he had to turn up and ruin everything!

'I hope the weather's good in this Sylt of yours.' The way he said it made it sound almost malicious. This Sylt of yours!

Christa nodded vehemently. Don't worry, she was going to Sylt, where as a child she had once built sand castles, in those far-off days when the beaches were empty and her parents were still living together and the world was still in order. She would go to List and Kampen, Morsum and Westerland, chat with Erika Harmsen and walk across to the Vogelkoje. And when her stay on Sylt came to an end, she would get a removal van to do the rest . . .

'Is that your case?'

She nodded, unable to do more. All at once she felt exhausted and as mixed-up as ever. What irritated her most was that beneath her anger she detected a sudden childish surge of happiness. After all, wasn't this really rather kind of him? Yes, he really was nice. He went ahead of her up the platform, the delicate surgeon's hands grasping the heavy suitcase handle, while she followed with Mollie on the lead and the papers under her arm. Brinkmann put the case on a trolley while he caught his breath.

'Oh, Klaus!' she said, touched. 'I don't know what to say. This is sweet of you, but it wasn't necessary.'

He nodded earnestly. 'I couldn't just let you leave.'

'Why not?'

He did not avert his eyes, and she felt herself blush. It made things worse. What else was there to say? Thank you very much, Professor. Not just for helping with my case, for everything, although you really didn't have to come. What the hell did he expect?

The sound of the loudspeaker came as a relief. 'Fast train to Offenburg now arriving . . .' Doors flew open. Christa was about to pick up her suitcase but Brinkmann shook his head, heaved it up and lugged it through the carriage, depositing it with a powerful heave into the luggage rack and collapsing with a grateful sigh on the upholstered seat. He scratched Mollie's ears and looked out of the window, nodding when someone gave him a friendly greeting.

Christa pushed Mollie off her seat and sat down. 'Klaus, the train only stops for three minutes. You'll have to . . . ?'

'What? I don't have to anything.'

She patted Mollie's head. 'I liked you a very great deal, little one. Be good, now . . .' She gave him her best smile. 'And you, too.'

He didn't move.

'All aboard, close the doors! Train departs in five seconds!'

'Didn't you hear? The train is leaving! Hurry up!'

He shook his head. 'They never leave on time.'

She felt the tug as the train started to move. Faces glided past, then she saw a man in uniform, then the signboard: Offingen. Christa stared at Brinkmann.

'I'm coming with you as far as Hornberg. Then I'll take a taxi back.'

'Have you gone crazy? Why are you doing this?'

'Another quarter of an hour with you,' he grinned. 'Move over. As you see, Mollie loves trains.'

She closed her eyes for a moment. Overcome, pleased, moved? No, annoyed: once again he had managed to put her off balance, and to add insult to injury he seemed to be whistling, smiling at his reflection in the window.

The world could be so beautiful, she thought. Why in damnation did he have to make things so difficult? Why didn't he say something instead of just looking at her that way, with those eyes . . . ?

A tunnel, houses, the train rattling over points. A station. People with rucksacks walking along the train. Through the open doors of the compartment she could see Loden jackets, T-shirts, Boy Scout uniforms and young, sweat-streaked faces. Brinkmann remained where he was, still smiling that smile.

'Klaus,' Christa said, 'stop being silly!'

'Me, silly?'

'If you don't get out now you'll have to go all the way to Offenburg.'

He leaned back and linked his hands behind his head. 'As far as Westerland, actually.'

She gasped, too surprised to ask the next question. He answered it anyway.

223

'I'm attending the medical congress,' he said. 'For three days. At first it looked as if I wouldn't be able to make it, but I managed to come to an arrangement with a colleague in Villingen . . .'

'But you haven't got any luggage!'

'I sent it ahead.'

She shook her head in bafflement.

'What's the matter? Don't you think I deserved a break, too? And something else, my little one. It's only a few kilometres from Westerland to Kampen. And that congress won't go on from early morning until late at night . . .'

Little one?, she thought, astonished again. 'You're impossible!'

He nodded sagely. 'I agree.'

'And a liar.'

'What else was I to do? It's Mollie's fault really. You know what she wants? To run along the beach, roll in the sand, jump in the water, find dead fish and lovely things like that . . .'

The cognac which rounded off their opulent breakfast arrived while the train was between Baden-Baden and Rastatt. Christa needed it. She wasn't just hungry, she was ravenous. Brinkmann's face wore the beaming smile of a happy schoolboy playing truant.

Christa sneaked another sliver of Swiss cheese to Mollie only to precipitate a calamity: the waiter discerned the wagging tail, with the usual result – can't have that sort of thing here, absolutely not! No dogs allowed in the dining car!

They returned protesting to their compartment, a little vexed to begin with. Then they started to laugh: what did it matter?

Brinkmann looked out of the window. Christa watched him, enjoying a feeling of relaxation she had not felt for a very long time. It was as though she had been taken out of this world. Yesterday she had imagined herself walking along the cliff path alone, her heart in turmoil, trying to distance herself from him and find her own balance. And now? The only thing that matters now is the two of us, she thought, even if it's only for a few days. We have taken off. Distance? To hell with it.

A motorway bridge flashed by. A level crossing, the warning bell clanking. Huge grey blocks of flats. Villas on the hillside. This must be Karlsruhe. His Karlsruhe.

'Whereabouts is your clinic?'

He shrugged. 'Does it matter? Over there somewhere.'

Somewhere . . . perhaps his indifference was an act, or even a lie. No matter. She thought about Elena Bach. Somewhere, under one of those countless roofs, she and Klaus had loved each other, fought with each other, slept together. *Our relationship is not what it once was. It's just business now.*

Perhaps, she thought, stroking Mollie's head. What if – well, does that matter, either?

THIRTY-FIVE

They had the compartment to themselves as far as Hamburg, but now it was full: there were even people standing in the corridor. Outside, bathed in the last pink evening light, Christa could see the marshes, buoys, the violet silhouette of the island, a fishing boat pushing up the channel, herring gulls wheeling in the darkening sky.

She took Mollie's green plastic bowl and filled it from the tap in the toilet, but Mollie wasn't interested. Christa fought her way back to the compartment through the crowded corridor.

'Look, Klaus, we're already on the Hindenburg-Damm!' The other people in the compartment smiled at her excitement: the Hindenburg-Damm was the link connecting Sylt with the mainland. They were almost there. Brinkmann nodded. 'Imagine that!' he grinned.

Half an hour later, as Christa Meurer sat waiting on a bench near the station, a sleepy Mollie in her arms, a taxi drove up and flashed its lights. Brinkmann got out and Christa went across.

'Amazing!' she said, impressed.

'What do you mean, amazing. Did you think I couldn't do it?'

'No,' Christa said. 'After all, you're a professor.'

'But not an absent-minded professor. They belong to the past, and cheap jokes.' He was happy, proud to be with her: it showed in the way he got a kick out of being the hero who had hijacked a taxi from beneath the noses of the hordes of tourists on Sylt, grabbed a porter, stacked her luggage in the boot. Now he held the door of the taxi open for her with an elegant flourish, like a British butler.

They didn't have far to go.

It wasn't long before they were sitting by candlelight at a wooden table beneath suspended cartwheels and carved beams in a room with leaded windows, half Störtebeker museum, and half farm barn. They were hungry. While they waited for the food they made the mistake of ordering wine instead of local down-to-earth beer: it was terrible.

They ate exorbitantly expensive fish followed by a soufflé that had no flavour they could detect. None of it mattered. Looking at each other, smiling, they held hands across a table littered with cutlery, farm bread, uneaten cheese.

Three days, Christa thought.

'What are you thinking?'

'Nothing.'

'But you are. One always has thoughts.'

'Do you think so?'

'Sure. The mind is always working.'

Bathed in a glow of wonderment, she let the stream of feelings his touch released flow over her, feelings which embraced them both: love, as well as wanting to make love, dreams and eroticism combined. She looked at him across the table: blue suit, shirt open at the neck, the pale eyes searching hers. She felt a tingling sensation course down her spine and upwards from her knees.

'I was thinking that if we sit around here much longer, the guest house where I'm staying will be locked up for the night. And you've still got to find your hotel and check in.'

'Where are you staying?'

'I told you, in Kampen.'

'That's not far. We'll take a taxi.'

Christa knew exactly how far it was. She had stayed at the little family guest house called 'Red Sand' for the first time when she was

227

fifteen. How well she remembered the breakfast room, and Erika Harmsen's mellifluous voice calling her guests down for enormous plates of sausages and cheese served with tea or fresh coffee. A good sort, Erika Harmsen, but her rules were iron-clad: don't forget the keys and don't be late. 'Otherwise everything would fall apart. We've got to get our heads down, too. We work till we drop.' Good Lord, she thought, I haven't even called her!

She made the call. The reply – in Plattdeutsch, the local dialect – was friendly, but there was a steely undertone in the words, 'So late?' Why on earth hadn't she phoned earlier? They had waited all evening and given her the nicest room in the house – 'You know, Christa, your old room' – so now it was, 'What? You're still having dinner in Westerland? Oh, for Heaven's sake . . .'

Christa went back to the table. 'I'm sorry, but I've got to leave. Right away.'

'Right away?' He looked at her. 'What do you mean? If need be, I have a perfectly good room at the conference hotel . . . ?'

'A double room?'

He nodded, looking faintly embarrassed. She decided not to mention that her room at Erika Harmsen's house was also a double.

'That's decided, then,' he said. 'Hotels always have night porters. We'll go to Kampen first.'

The asphalt road ended abruptly. Beyond it was a track across the sandy dunes.

'Here we are!' Christa said.

As far as she could see in the luminous night, the house standing behind the green oil-painted stake fence looked much as she remembered from the time she had lived here with her brother Albert and her parents. She thought she could hear the sound of the waves nearby. The sea. Was she imagining it? You could smell it, anyway. The air was soft, as pleasant as a caress.

'Well, then . . .'

'What now?'

Brinkmann took her suitcase out of the car. He asked the quiet pipe-smoking driver who had brought them here whether he would mind waiting a moment.

'Got nothing else to do.'

They crossed the soft ground to the garden gate and he opened it.

She felt a small shiver of apprehension: my God, what would Erika Harmsen say? What she'd said when, during her days in Göttingen, Christa had arrived with Ulli. Those days were a long time ago.

The front door was not locked, and a light had been left on in the little lobby with its key-festooned board.

'Well,' Brinkmann looked around. 'Nice and cosy.'

She put her fingers to her lips and winked, whispering: 'What would you like? Tea, coffee, mineral water?'

He still wore that same uneasy, half-disbelieving look which had so amused her earlier. It was his game, but she was dealing all the cards. Mischief, delight bubbled inside her. It wasn't the wine – she had drunk only two glasses – but a sort of exhilaration that burst out and surprised her, a combination of the air out there, the silent house, Sylt, the holiday mood, curiosity, all of it.

'One moment, Madame, if I may. It would seem appropriate for me to tell the coachman what is happening.'

Three minutes later Christa heard a motor start up, and Brinkmann came back into the house.

'Nice chap. They're all so squeaky clean around here, and they all have such honest faces. So I told him to go over to the hotel in Westerland and check my baggage had arrived.'

'You did?'

'I did indeed. And furthermore, Madame, I recall that you were kind enough to offer me tea. However, I believe I would prefer a beer.'

She brought him a beer from Erika Harmsen's fridge in the kitchen. The steep wooden stairs creaked. Room No. 8 had sloping walls, flowered wallpaper and twin beds. She opened one of the tiny dormer windows. This time she could hear the breakers clearly.

There was a table and two chairs on one side of the room. Brinkmann stood by her suitcase, hands in his pockets, a dreamy look of wonder in his eyes. His face bore the expression of a man who has seen something for which there is no natural explanation.

'You look like that little boy in the film *E. T.* – Elliott.'

'You mean I'm not him?'

'Well,' she said, unable to stifle her laugh, 'I suppose it all comes down to how you look at it.'

He took off his jacket and threw it on the bed, then sat down, hands between his knees, and looked up at her. 'And how do I look now?'

'Like one of your patients.' She poured beer into the glasses. 'Like someone who has experienced something he can't work out.'

'I don't want to work it out. Do you?'

'No,' she said. 'God knows I don't. But that's what makes it so wonderful.'

She looked down at his head, the hands caressing her fingers as he kissed each one of them. Who dealt the cards no longer mattered, nor even the game.

Suddenly he let her go. 'What will people say when I turn up tomorrow morning?'

'What would anyone say? Mrs Harmsen knows me. She knows I'm a responsible person, and that means if I'm accompanied by someone he is a responsible person, too.'

'Accompanied? Have you been here many times, then?'

'Not for ages.'

'Was . . . were there . . . ?'

'Shush, listen: there's something more important. Tell me, do you have a toothbrush?'

He stood up, looking quizzically at the transparent plastic container in her hand. 'You even thought of that!'

'I bought them at the station in Westerland.'

'Christa, you're amazing. Such foresight!'

'Maybe,' she said, almost timidly, as Brinkmann drew her towards him and kissed her on the forehead. 'No more, not now. I mean it . . .'

'What is it?'

'I'm frightened.'

'Truly?'

'No,' she sighed. 'No. I'm not frightened any more.'

Through the window Brinkmann could see a ship: a freighter or a tanker, he didn't know much about ships. He watched as it continued obstinately westward across the deep blue line of the horizon. Now it passed behind the mast bearing the French flag, heading for the next one, which bore the Italian flag. The flags had nothing to do with the medical congress, they were a year-round fixture. Everything else, from the folder on Brinkmann's lap to the

Bordeaux-coloured uniforms of the hostesses, bore the congress logo.

'And therefore, distinguished fellow-delegates, the time has come, especially in the field of involution symptoms in glandular . . .' came through the loudspeaker. Brinkmann nodded grimly. The time had indeed come! He got up, made his way along the row, past now sympathetic, now surprised faces.

What next? Kampen, of course. But first, a bath. As he entered his room he saw that the ship he had watched earlier was still moving along the horizon. It was in no hurry. And neither was he. A bath and a newspaper – normally that would have been something to look forward to. Now it held no attraction at all. No, he didn't want the damned newspaper. He couldn't care less what was happening at the disarmament talks in Geneva, nor whether Neubert's paper *New Ways to Influence the Coagulation System* was published or not. The only thing that mattered was that he was alive – yes! Klaus Brinkmann was alive again! It was a matter for celebration that he had rid himself of the tightrope he normally walked on, even if only for three days.

Christa!

Just the thought of her name stirred a grateful tenderness inside him so deep and complete that it almost frightened him. As the water cascaded over his head and shoulders and down his legs, another, second Brinkmann awoke inside him, the one who was always in control, always watching. That second person watched him now in the green-tiled shower, saw the happy, unselfconscious smile on his face as he soaped his slightly thickened body. Was it possible that one night could have this effect? Was it really so momentous?

Yes, that was what it was: momentous. As silly as the word might be, it was right: the word 'love' was so questionable, so intangible.

So what was this stupendous event that had taken place? Wasn't he over-dramatising everything? No, it was the feeling of liberation, the satisfaction of being able to cock a snook at everyone, the two of them conspiring against a mad, inimical world. Their fortress: a room with sloping walls . . .

It was stupendous!

Had Christa taken control, then? Perhaps. When had it been

any different in all these past years? Elena, even Kate – everyone expected him to lead.

In his mind's eye he saw Christa come into the little room, her shadow on the wall. Her body was so gleaming, so pale, that it seemed to be lit from within. He saw her eyes, her smile. Her hair hung loose, weaving a pattern on her shoulders. He had never really noticed her hair before: it was always hidden by the nurse's cap, or worn in a bun. Now it seemed to be a living curtain through which she looked at him and smiled . . .

There are some moments, he thought, which are as perfect as a work of art. Most people don't realise it. But one never forgets them. They prove there is, after all, such a thing as the present. Whatever life brings our way blows away into memory, pales into obscurity, like a face in a dream. But moments such as this belong to us always . . .

God, you're sentimental sometimes! Brinkmann stepped out of the shower, dried himself, stumbled over a handtowel and almost fell. He sat down on the edge of the bath and looked at his reflection in the mirror. Taken control? How silly! She made you a gift. She was running away, but she came back to give it to you . . .

Sand, sea, wind. Surf rolled up to the dunes, grey-white spray flying. There were fine grains of sand on the edge of the breeze that spattered on her face like shotgun pellets. And little Mollie jumped into the waves and – to Christa's horror – was swept under, came up again, ran through the foam, spat out the sea water and tried to go back.

'All right, that'll do!' Brinkmann pulled Mollie up the beach. She collapsed on the sand, panting and wheezing, her tongue hanging out.

'Look!' Christa held out a shell, tinted in delicate pink and milk white, transparent when she held it up to the light, like the fine, long hair the wind whipped across her face and shoulders.

She stood before him and smiled. He was lost in wonder: the deserted beach, the sea, the girl . . .

'And look at this!' This time it was not a shell but a piece of driftwood, black, filthy.

'Oil.'

232

'Those damned tankers!'

'It's the same everywhere these days. Even in the South Pacific. You just have to get used to it.'

'You don't have to get used to anything you don't want to get used to!'

He smiled. 'Of course not.' It was like her to react this way. It was the way she was. And on top of that, she was right.

She dropped the piece of wood and nodded to him. 'Now I'm going to show you how to build a shelter.'

Brinkmann had been to the tourist shops around the congress centre that morning and bought a shovel and two yellow oilskins. Then, with the determination of someone organising an expedition, he had set off around the rest of the shops and bought bread, butter, a thermos flask, powdered tea, ham, hard-boiled eggs and even two knives. When he was finished, he needed a kitbag to carry his treasures. Now he dragged the heavy, clumsy thing through the sand along the waterline.

'Oh, God!' Christa laughed. 'Don't overdo it, Professor.'

'I overdo it all the time.'

'Give me the shovel.'

'That's a man's job.'

'Not in this case. Leave it to me. You're used to being spoiled.'

With experienced methodicalness, Christa – assisted by a barking Mollie – dug a large, bathtub-shaped hole in the sand.

'There,' she said, with satisfaction. She brushed a few drops of perspiration off her forehead. 'Now the blanket. There we are. That makes it really cosy. Come on, we can lie in it.'

'Like the gentlemen of the nudist movement? You know they're all over the place up here in the summer. Stark naked.'

'You say it as if it was criminal! For Heaven's sake, you're a surgeon!'

He grinned. 'A surgeon, me? What's that? When I think of the faces of those people over at the congress . . .'

She had taken off her yellow jacket, unfastened her white bikini top and stretched out. Still kneeling on the ridge above, he looked down at her delicately curved breasts, the nipples like buds, her smooth, luminous body, and was convinced he had never seen anything more beautiful . . .

My Christa!, he thought again.

'What are you thinking about?' He couldn't help it, he had to keep asking her.

'Spain.' She smiled, keeping her eyes closed. 'Boats. The beach at Alicante or Valencia. Or it could be Ibiza or Majorca. Anyway, somewhere on a beach where you don't have to dig shelters.'

'Have you ever been there?'

'I've been to Spain a few times.'

'And?'

The corners of her mouth lifted in a mischievous grin. 'And? It was beautiful.'

He felt a tiny pang: jealousy? The unspoken question: who had she lain on the beach with, or slept with? No, it wasn't that. Maybe he was a bit jealous of these young people whose lives were filled with such experiences and carefree adventures. How little time you have taken off in these past years, he thought. You've just stayed on the treadmill, jumping off it only once or twice and then with the greatest difficulty.

'And I was thinking,' Christa went on, as if she could read his mind, 'how wonderful it would be to never see a clinic again.'

He did not reply.

'Come on, Klaus, admit it. You dream sometimes, too.'

'Not often.'

It was a lie, Brinkmann admitted to himself. He dreamed: often! Of orchestras he would like to conduct, pictures he wanted to paint, journeys he would like to make. Too late! – But why should it be? What was stopping him from turning at least a few of his fantasies into reality? A clinic? An old lady on whose care he had come to depend? A son who rejected him and couldn't wait for the day he could tell him so? A whole web of things and people who depended on him, a web he had woven himself. Dependence, the six-day race that permitted him a break only when he was totally out of breath. Permitted? No, he had to fight for that, too.

'Shall we have our picnic?' Brinkmann emptied out the kitbag.

'What a man! You even brought wine.'

Yes, even wine: a French rosé. He hoped it would be good.

And it was. They drank some. He sliced bread, Christa added butter and meat. Now everything was behind him: clinic, treadmill, six-day race, everything.

Christa smiled at him and he smiled back. When they kissed, he

234

could taste the wine on her lips. He surrendered to the sweet, complete feeling of security he felt in her embrace.

Yes, with her, he was enchanted. He watched as ecstasy twisted her face, heard her soft breathing, her whispers, and said, 'I love you. I love you more than words can ever say!'

All these things he said were no longer nonsense: they had become reality. No matter what, they would never be apart again. Never again would he let her run away from him!

Later they lay on their backs and watched the moving clouds and the gulls circling over their heads.

'Happy?' She stroked the hair on his chest.

He nodded, took her hand and pressed his lips against it. 'Happy,' he said.

THIRTY-SIX

Nobody ever found out who started the rumour that Elena Bach had committed suicide. But the rumour overshadowed all the gossip and comments which surrounded the accident that caused her death. One reason for the rumour was that on the evening of the disaster she was driving her Golf convertible alone, at dusk, in bad visibility. It had been foggy that day. Another reason was the carelessness of the police officer who filed the report.

From the report which was submitted to the insurance company two weeks after the accident, one thing could be established with certainty: on the serpentine curve where the Golf had smashed into a tree were not only the black skid marks, which showed Elena Bach had tried to use the emergency brake at the last moment, but also another, darker set of marks, unquestionably left there by a motor-cycle which had come towards her from the opposite direction, cutting the corner.

According to the form completed by the officer at the scene of the accident, the skid marks were two metres eighty in length, and the distance to the edge of the kerb three metres twenty. Supplemented by the other details of the report, these measurements would have presented a clear picture of the events which had led to Elena Bach's death. But *Polizeiobermeister* Schimanski forgot to add his other findings to the folder containing the report, because that same evening he had been called to another accident, and subsequently had to take leave for family reasons.

Fourteen days after it happened, the full picture would become clear, but at the time . . .

Among the first people to arrive at the scene of the accident was a doctor: Ignaz Marker. He had been driving down the mountain road towards Elznach, hunched over the wheel and swearing under his breath at the driver of the brown Opel ahead of him who kept braking because of the fog. Marker's spirits were at an all-time low. A farmer in the Oberprecht valley had called him, told him it was urgent. It was urgent, all right. The man's cow was having difficulty giving birth, and they couldn't get hold of a vet.

Marker had the devil's own job groping around inside the cow until he finally managed to deliver the calf. By the time he was finished, his arm felt almost paralysed. He set off for home, just in time to run smack into the fog.

He had intended to stop off in Offingen and visit Brinkmann, but his secretary told him the professor was attending a medical congress in Sylt. The news did nothing to cheer him up.

He cursed again: had the fellow in front gone completely mad? The fog had cleared, yet the man braked so sharply that Marker almost ran into him. Then the door of the Opel flew open, and a blond man in hunting trousers and a windcheater got out, looked back towards Marker, waved his arm, and ran down the road.

Then he saw it. My God! He acted without thinking, sliding clumsily down the steep embankment, branches whipping his face and hands. He reached the smoking, crushed heap of metal that had once been a car as the blond man in the windcheater yanked on the door handle. No good! He straightened up. He had a broad, good-natured face. He looked as if he might cry.

'There's someone in there!' he shouted.

'How many?'

'A woman. Christ, what a mess . . .'

Marker nodded. 'Have you got a torch?'

237

'Up there, in the car.' The man gave him the trusting stare of someone who has found a leader in a time of unexpected peril. And in the same moment, Marker suddenly realised what he himself had done: idiot, you just ran. You left your case in the car!

'Listen. Go up to my car. There's a case on the back seat. I'm a doctor.'

'A doctor?' The blond man was already clambering up the slope. 'A doctor. Christ, that's lucky!'

We'll see, Marker thought grimly. It was hardly likely that the woman in this wreck was still alive. And even if she was, Marker thought smashing the side window with a rock, would she survive?

Now he saw her. The driver's seat had been torn from its mounting. There was blood on the light-coloured upholstery. A leg, the trousers torn. The other leg bent at a grotesque angle, the upper part of her body covered by a leather jacket. Only a small area of her face was visible, ashen under dark, bloodstained hair.

Marker tried with all his strength but the door would not budge. Damned car, he panted. Then the blond man reappeared, carrying a torch. He switched it on and tossed Marker's bag across.

'Can I do anything?' He shone the torch inside the car. 'Oh, how awful! Did you see the blood? I think I'm going to be sick . . . You've got to get her out of there, Doctor!'

Of course, but how? Marker opened his bag with deft hands. His fingers touched syringes, pills, bandages, instruments. Then he had it: his trusty old scalpel!

'Great!' said the blond man as the keen blade sliced through the heavy material of the cabriolet's roof. The two of them ripped the stuff until the gap was large enough to permit Marker to get to the twisted, bleeding body. He touched the arm. The skin was perspiring, cool. Beneath it, barely discernible, a tiny, racing plea for help: the faint beating of a pulse.

'Is she still alive?'

Marker stood up. 'Just about . . .'

'What do we do now?'

Good question. 'Listen to me. I want you to get into your car. At the bottom of the hill, where the road straightens out, there is an emergency phone.'

The blond man nodded. He looked at Marker and then back inside the car.

238

'Come on, man, shift yourself!' Marker roared.

They wanted to have everything: everything, anyway, that could be squeezed into three days. Walking on the dunes, making love on the springy beach grass, throwing sticks for Mollie to chase along the beach. And swimming, of course, although the water was damned cold, leaving them bright red. Talking – endlessly – hiring a boat, eating some fish or, better still, crab taken straight from the net and still dripping with seawater, red as an apple on the outside, white as an apple on the inside.

'Well, if that's what you're after . . .'

The fisherman on the iron jetty where they hired boats took his pipe from between his teeth, and Brinkmann hastily took out his tobacco pouch, insisting the man try some of his brand. The fellow was as tall as a tree, with a wrinkled face and sunbleached hair.

'Well, if it's crabs you're after, I'm just taking a basketful home to the wife.'

'Oh, she cooks, then? Is that it?'

He gave them a reproachful look. 'Cook? Believe me, she'll cook you a whole pot full. You can eat them over at my place. In the front room.'

It was nine in the morning. The weathervane on the church steeple glowed like the sun, the windows of the houses reflected the lovely weather, and the early light was like lacquer on the roofs of the houses in the harbour. The sea stretched calmly into the distance.

Brinkmann reached up to help Christa into the sturdy little boat, but she laughed in his face and jumped in like a cat. He sat down a little unsteadily. The crab man up on the jetty signalled with his hand: cast off!

Brinkmann pulled the starter. The outboard motor gave an asthmatic cough and subsided. The fisherman grinned at them. Then Christa came to the rescue. 'Hold on a moment!' She took hold of the damned plastic handle, bent back – amazing! The Johnson began to purr and the boat moved in a wide curve towards the open sea.

'You're really something!' Brinkmann muttered, impressed.

'Really? What, for instance?'

'How would I know? A bundle of miracles, a box full of surprises. The woman of a thousand possibilities.'

He winked. And Christa grinned at the faint sourness she detected in his tone.

Later she opened her jeans shirt and let the sun on to her skin. With the same analytical seriousness as always, Brinkmann thought, as he had thought so many times these last couple of days: what a lucky fellow he was. Today, the vascular surgeons would be making their speeches at the Westerland congress centre. It would be interesting, of course, but he was getting too old for working with the microscope. Moreover, the word 'surgery' had been banished from his vocabulary: Christa had deleted it. Her shirt fluttered in the wind, and he gazed tenderly at what it revealed.

'Let me have a go!' she said, suddenly.

'You want to steer again?'

'No, I want to look at you. Sitting here I've got the sun in my eyes all the time.'

She reached out her hand to steady him as they changed places. She was really overplaying it. He made it elegantly to the middle of the boat with a sort of sidestep.

'What are you thinking about?'

'You promised not to ask me that any more.'

She throttled back, and the boat rocked gently back and forth, hardly moving. She smiled and looked across towards the light-houses rising above the flat sandy beaches, their red and white rings vivid in the clear light.

What was she thinking about?

They had talked so much, yet always avoided one topic as if they were afraid of it. He had called her a woman of a thousand possibilities. With a thousand faces, that's what he had wanted to say . . .

She leaned forward. 'Klaus, be honest. It was because of Udo you were always so cautious, wasn't it? Perhaps you had scruples because I . . .' She could not bring herself to finish the sentence.

'Well, yes,' he said. 'Scruples. It's too big a word. But I did feel uncomfortable. And when I give it more thought; there are some situations between father and son that are hard to deal with.'

She nodded. 'Klaus, I want to answer a question you never asked.

I never had what could be called an intimate relationship with Udo. Perhaps . . .'

'Perhaps what?'

'It might have become one, if . . .'

'If you hadn't seen a half-naked girl lying in our garden?'

'Something like that. Or if Udo was anyone else but who he is. It was then, I think, that I realised it. Could hardly avoid realising it.'

He smiled. 'In that case, I'm glad that there was a naked girl in my garden.'

'I'm glad too, now.' She let go of the rudder, bent over him and kissed him on the nose. Then she looked away, towards the lighthouses.

'Your relationship with your son is very complicated, isn't it?'

'Yes.' Brinkmann avoided her gaze as he spoke. 'You could put it like that. It started to become complicated when my wife died.'

He paused, sensing her interest and trying to think exactly how it had all happened, and how he could tell her about something that had so many different aspects, important, serious aspects.

'I had gone away,' he began, hesitantly. 'To a symposium in Münster. And there was – there was this young colleague. She had just taken a course in modern methods of anaesthesia in San Francisco. Well, that interested me. So I stayed on a day longer than I had planned. We had dinner together, and talked and talked. And I went back with her to her hotel because she had her notes there, and I wanted to learn more about it.'

'Dr Bach, right?'

'Yes. When my son telephoned to advise me how ill Brigitte – I mean, his mother – was he was unable to reach me.'

'And?'

'No more. That's basically it. At least, it's all I know. The rest is speculation. I – I can only assume he thinks I was cheating on my wife the night she died.'

'What makes you think that?'

'Because from that day on his attitude towards me completely, fundamentally changed.'

'Why didn't you have it out with him?'

'Why not, indeed?' That was exactly the question. Why did she have to start on that? Well, she was right, wasn't she? She wanted simplicity. She had been frank with him, now he owed her as much. And, anyway, this anguish he felt every time the topic came up was only a defence mechanism! Right, then don't put it off any longer: be honest, at least with yourself. Do you still want to run away? Isn't that why you're so impatient with Udo?

But, even now, Brinkmann could not come up with a simple answer. Maybe he didn't have one. 'You know, Christa, when it's never said upfront where you can see it . . .' he began.

'You mean you're not going to try and put matters right?'

'Try to put yourself in my shoes. Pleading my innocence to my own son: what sort of a picture would that be?'

'A picture of a real human being, I'd say.'

True. That was it. Yet he had persisted in his role.

'You're right. But it wasn't like that. You see, it wasn't like that at all. It was only much later, about a year, that I became friendly with Elena Bach. Up to that time I'd been too immersed in my loss, too busy being sorry for myself. I just didn't have the strength to help Udo, although he must have been suffering badly too. I was a coward, I admit. But at the time, I asked myself whether I could accept having my son as my judge. There was no reason for him to condemn me. That's what I told myself . . .' His voice tailed off. Then came the sentence Christa had been waiting for. 'Perhaps I couldn't accept it because I had already condemned myself.'

'You blamed yourself?'

'That's right. You see, Elena Bach, Mrs Bach . . . I liked her immediately. My interest in what she had learned, although she was fascinating to talk to, was just an excuse to get to know her better.'

He brought his gaze back from the lighthouses and met Christa's eyes, trying unsuccessfully for a smile, hoping that would put an end to it. But she was merciless.

'In which case Udo's behaviour and the scenes he creates aren't really all that unreasonable?'

He nodded again. 'Possibly. But I'm a surgeon, Christa, not a psychoanalyst. Quite apart from which, I could have done with one myself around then.'

Christa rose from her seat, crouched down between his knees and took his hands in hers. 'Klaus, does my talking about it depress you?'

242

He pressed his lips against her hair. 'No, Christa. I'm glad you know about it. Now it's out in the open. I'm done with it. I can talk to you about anything. And that's wonderful.'

THIRTY-SEVEN

News of the accident at Elznach reached the clinic shortly after seven o'clock, putting an abrupt end to the emergency service's faint hope that they might be going to have a quiet evening.

Anneliese Happel, the second operating-theatre duty nurse, would not have time to write the letter to her parents that she had been meaning to write for ages. The card game which Renz, Mischa and Udo Brinkmann had planned would have to be abandoned, and Dr Wolters, who had reserved a table for his wife and their insurance agent at the Wälderstüble, a restaurant near the clinic, would have to wait for another evening to sort out his insurance problems.

They had long given up bitching when such calls came in. Nobody was in the mood today for the ironic jokes the team usually swapped to relieve their frustration and self-pity.

At seven-thirty Mischa reported that the ambulance had arrived. They ran out through casualty and onto the ramp as the vehicle ended its race with a squeal of brakes. Renz had the doors open before the ambulance man could get to them. He immediately recognised the man who jumped out.

'Marker? What are you doing here?'

'I was in the vicinity of the accident. A woman . . .'

The stretcher slid out of the ambulance. It was a moment none of them would soon forget. They stared at the waxen, bloodless face illuminated by the glare of the porch lights. Marker, unaware of the tension, was explaining what he had seen and what he suspected: 'Shock, of course. Severely contused ribcage. I've given heart massage anyway – had to, or she'd have gone: the heart stopped twice. Suspected tamponade due to the accumulation of peri-cardiac fluid. And, most of all, take great care in the pelvic region!'

Renz did not move. Marker stared at him. 'What's wrong?'

'You don't know? That's our anaesthetist!'

Udo was the first to break the spell. 'Come on, move! Get her inside! Oxygen. We'll take care of the plasma later. Does anyone know her blood group? Anneliese, look in her personnel file! Now, fast! While you're at it, call Dr Brösinger at Villingen. Tell him what's happened and tell him we need him here, immediately. Immediately, do you hear?'

Marker thought: the young man is apprehensive. The others, too. By God, they had reason to be! He didn't give the young woman much chance. And Klaus? At some idiotic medical congress. Well, there wasn't much more he could do here.

'I don't suppose you'll need me any more?' All at once he felt exhausted.

Udo stared at him, surprised. 'But we do, Dr Marker! Please, if it's at all possible, stay. We need every bit of help we can get.'

'Where's Dr Schaefer?'

'We have to count Schaefer out. Sciatica or neuritis, they're not sure which. He can't even put his foot on the floor.'

The despair on Udo Brinkmann's face struck Marker. He could understand the young man's distress: it was a colleague, after all. One who, if he remembered correctly, Klaus had worked with at Karlsruhe. What was there to say? A prayer, maybe. Pray the senior surgeon from Villingen would get here fast. He shook his head: it would take him at least forty minutes.

'Come on, hurry up!'

For the first time Marker felt something like admiration.

Whatever else you might say about the clinic, Brinkmann certainly had his people well-trained. The fellows all seemed to know their stuff; and at least they were fast.

'Udo! The heart! Adrenaline?'

The circulation was their top priority. If the heart filled with fluid from the damaged tissues, they were done for. What to do? In his hand Udo had the long injection needle with which he would drain the pericardium. A catheter delivered oxygen to Elena Bach's lungs. Udo hesitated and Marker knew why: what he did next might save the woman's life or prove to be the deciding error which would cancel out everything else.

They listened to the weak racing of the heart beneath the ribcage, distorted by swelling and bruising. The blood transfusion was ready: she was still on the neutral plasma.

'Oxygen, Walter!'

Renz nodded. They worked fast. Lack of vital oxygen to carry away the poisonous products of this catastrophe was also a danger. The woman's pupils hardly reacted to the light beam, but at least they did react: the brain was still working.

Udo looked at the closed blueish eyelids. So many associations connected with the name and face of Elena Bach! Nights spent brooding, the torment of his imagination, all these years . . . And the old man not here. Missing again. Like last time.

He had long since noticed what the others now realised with panic: the swelling beneath the ribcage. Abdominal swelling meant that Marker had been right: there was severe internal bleeding, and that with a woman in a coma!

'Anneliese! Any luck with Villingen?'

Anneliese Happel shook her head. She was the only one in the room whose face was still calm. 'Dr Brösinger isn't available. There has been a plane crash. A private aircraft. They can't spare anyone at the moment.'

It was a blow, but there was nothing he could do about it. You've just got to handle it, Udo told himself. But handle what? What avenues were open to him? Just putting her under the X-ray machine could kill her. To operate . . . Hopeless.

What would the old man do in this situation?

'First stabilise, then operate.' Yes, of course, Professor. But where to begin with the stabilisation? To hell with it!

'Anneliese!' Udo put both hands on the nurse's shoulders. 'Anneliese, it all depends on you now. You've got to find the Chief. I simply don't know where to begin. Call Westerland. Tell him it's Elena, tell him how serious it is, life or death. He'll have to hire a plane, whatever, it doesn't matter. Just tell him!'

The others heard what he told the girl and nodded their agreement. He looked at each of them, one by one.

'And now . . . us.'

The amazing thing about the hours that followed was that later Udo Brinkmann could remember every detail, as if the magnetic tape of his consciousness had not only registered what his eyes saw – the helpless expressions on the faces around him, the feverish activity held in check only by their professionalism – but also everything that was said. Everything seemed to be fused into one memory: the events as well as the time-frame in which they happened.

The business with Dr Klein, the radiologist, for instance. They could not find him at first, but then he called in from a friend's flat. When he finally rushed into the operating theatre, he took over immediately, assuming all responsibility for whatever consequences followed his intervention.

'Let's have a look. I've seen cases like this before. She'll make it. She'll survive. I'll stake my reputation on it.'

They checked the monitors again: the oxygen content of the blood had sunk even lower.

'The heart is working. One thing for sure: we can't give her any more adrenaline.'

The X-rays arrived. Udo saw himself standing in front of the glowing screen, saw Klein's poker face staring at the grey-white outlines of the X-ray picture. 'There: the fracture of the wing of the ilium. We'll have to watch that carefully because of the danger of haemorrhaging. The internal bleeding itself? Probably the spleen . . . or possibly a damaged intestine. We can't exclude the possibility. All in all: very serious.'

'What about her breathing problems?' Renz asked.

'Atalectasis,' Klein replied. 'Something in the lung. A foreign body . . . we can't tell without operating. By the same token, to operate without findings would be pointless.'

Pointless! That was the operative word. The whole time . . .

At that moment Anneliese appeared. She had got Elke out of bed. 'Dr Brösinger won't be able to be here for at least two hours.'

That was the final verdict. And lest there be any doubt of that, Anneliese put an end to it: 'Her temperature is at 41.5°. Should we lower it artificially?'

'Her heart wouldn't be able to take it.'

In that moment, Udo felt a surge of admiration for the small body fighting death so hard. So much energy, so much strength in each small cell . . . and all of it wasted.

'If we don't get the temperature down, there'll be hyperpyrexia.'

'And if we do, what then? Why go on torturing her?'

The fact that it was the quiet, cautious Wolters who spoke, Wolters who, for all his quiet caution was passionate about fighting to the bitter end, gave the words extra weight.

Why go on torturing her?

And why, thought Udo, once the words were spoken, did everyone turn to look at him? Because his name was Brinkmann? Because Elena was not just a colleague, she was also his father's friend? What had it got to do with him? Why didn't he just get out of the operating theatre, slam the doors behind him, take off his sterile garb and disappear into the night, away from their waiting faces and most of all their expectations?

He leaned against the wall of the theatre. 'Does anyone think that we should wait till Dr Brösinger gets here?' His voice was unemotional.

Nobody spoke. What was there to say? Their silence was their answer.

'Fine,' Udo said. 'I concur with your opinions.'

Downstairs at the switchboard, they were still trying to reach the old man.

No crabs, no fish: not cod, nor turbot, nor plaice. They were not going to any restaurants, nor even any of the nightclubs in Kampen which Christa had planned to visit.

No, they were going to stay at home. They would sit at Erika Harmsen's corner table in her lounge, next to the TV and the newspaper stand with its collection of old magazines and books left behind by earlier guests. On the checkered tablecloth sat a large cheese plate, and a pot of steaming, dark-brown tea. The wonderful feeling of the sun's heat on the skin, and that relaxed all-over tiredness that a day on the beach – no, a day of happiness – brings. They enjoyed Erika Harmsen's benevolence. Blue eyes, hair parted in the middle, the face of a Madonna above a body built like a Friesian cupboard. Erika Harmsen put him in mind of Kate now, as she announced, hands on massive hips: 'Let's have another bottle! And on the house, this time!' It was the third bottle; the other two had been on the house as well.

Yes, Kate: twenty years younger, and Nordic!

Erika went into her kitchen where she had a very special bottle of wine. She returned almost immediately, without the bottle. Her smile had disappeared. 'Someone wants you on the phone, Professor.'

They looked at each other: who the devil knew that they were hidden away in a house on the dunes?

'They're calling from the clinic, at Offingen. The man sounds very agitated. He says it's urgent.'

Brinkmann felt as if the room had become ten degrees cooler. He stood up. 'Miss Meis had my holiday address,' he told Christa. 'Perhaps they tried the hotel first, and then put two and two together.'

He went out into the lobby: the telephone was on the glass-topped counter with its map of the island. His arm felt leaden as he picked up the receiver.

'Brinkmann.'

'At last!' It was his son's voice.

'What's wrong?'

'Elena was in a car crash.'

Brinkmann's heart thumped inside his chest. 'How bad is it?' It wasn't easy to ask the question.

'Almost hopeless. We've been trying to get hold of you. At the hotel. They said you'd left.'

'Yes. Give me a brief diagnosis.'

'Unspecified internal injuries, the most severe in the abdominal region. Atelectasis in the lungs. Fracture of the wing of the ilium.'

Brinkmann tried to visualise it, but could not. 'Can't you get hold of Brösinger?'

'He's got three emergency operations of his own.'

'And Schaefer?'

'In bed with sciatica.'

Klaus Brinkmann closed his eyes and tried to marshall his thoughts. Think of something! Concentrate! 'Almost hopeless', Udo had said . . . He opened his eyes and saw the rail timetable next to the keyboard. That was no use, either. 'I can't get a train out of here tonight, Udo,' he heard himself say. 'I can only try to get hold of a plane in the morning.'

'In the morning?' Udo's voice sounded exhausted and bitter.

'Are you going to operate?'

'No. If you were here . . .' He paused. In the background Brinkmann heard raised voices. Then Udo was back. 'I've just been told Brösinger is here.'

'Is she conscious?'

'No. She's in shock. We suspect there's concussion as well. She would have died if Marker hadn't given her heart massage. He was at the scene of accident: pure chance.'

'Marker!' Brinkmann exclaimed.

'Do you want me to call you if there are any developments? Or do you just want to enjoy your holiday?'

Udo's bitter words burned like hot iron.

'You could have saved yourself that one, Udo,' Brinkmann said, slowly. 'Give me a call, okay? I'll get back as fast as I can.'

He put down the phone and stared at the oak door with its heavy, beautifully carved panels. It seemed as if it was a million miles away. Klaus Brinkmann put both his hands on the glass plate covering the map of Sylt. When he took them away there were damp patches. He went back into the lounge.

Christa's look told him she already knew it was something bad. Her eyes were full of apprehension. 'What's happened?'

'Elena Bach, car crash.'

'Do you have to go back?'

He nodded. He hadn't the strength to speak.

THIRTY-EIGHT

Pale-green cupboards containing records. The large desk with the shiny vinyl top. His chair. The visitor's chair. The paintings on the wall and the aerial photograph of the clinic, the view of the town through the window, the three tall birches, the valley . . . everything in its place as before. Yet in some inexplicable way they all seemed different, strange. As strange as Udo's face as he leaned against the door and stared at him.

Brinkmann pressed both hands against his temples. Before him on the table were all the papers concerning the Bach case. Envelopes containing X-rays, charts, the columns and curves of the instrument evaluations made while Elena was still breathing, still fighting.

Brinkmann tried hard to decipher them, to make some kind of sense of the dreadful dynamics of the catastrophe, but it was no good. He picked up the X-rays, then put them down again. The young doctor over there, watching him with tired, dark-ringed eyes, had done his very best. However limited that best was.

'The X-rays you have aren't too clear. But in those circumstances!... Klein is going through them to sort out the best. You'll get them later.'

'Fine,' Brinkmann said.

'Do you want to see them?'

'No. It won't change anything. How did Brösinger do?'

'By the time he got here, it was too late.'

Another pause. There is a frontier beyond which a man surrenders control of his feelings: everything is still, nothing moves, a vacuum which lets in no force. Brinkmann had reached that frontier.

Udo was at the door. 'Would you have operated?'

He looked up. 'No.'

Udo nodded. 'No recriminations, then?'

Recriminations. The word remained in the room like a ghostly echo long after Brinkmann's son closed the door.

There was an old pensioner in Lüneberg, a former director of the county court. He remembered the thin face very well. He had seen this photograph of Elena's father several times: she kept it in her passport. For some reason her brother lived in Leipzig. And, if he remembered correctly, there was a married sister in France. My God, she had known so much about him, yet he hadn't even been aware of her loneliness.

Somewhere in the house he could hear Kate's vacuum cleaner. The sound ebbed and flowed, testimony to the fact that death cannot stop the machinery of life from turning. A picture came into his mind: Christa, the North Sea, surf, her laughter.

Brinkmann checked his watch: midday. No, he didn't feel up to going back to work at the clinic. He had not called a single meeting. He had even less desire to answer questions, offer comment, or have to face those looks. Miss Meis, his secretary, could take care of the funeral arrangements. Then his colleagues would arrive from Karlsruhe. They would shake hands. Then they would sit down and talk about Elena.

Not a chance!, he thought. He couldn't bear it! Never!

He was downstairs, wondering whether to go and sit on the terrace or walk in the garden, or ramble up the mountain where he could hide away and think everything through again.

He found Udo standing in the hall, his face, in the shadow thrown by the upstairs window frame, looking even paler and thinner than it had yesterday. Klaus Brinkmann walked past his son – or was it just an apparition? – and went out into the garden.

'He never even looked at me, Kate,' Udo said. Kate Marek switched off the vacuum cleaner and nodded.

'Nor me. He sat alone in the dark all day yesterday.'

'Taking it badly, is he?'

She turned to face him. 'Why do you say it in that tone of voice? Come to that, why say it at all?'

'Do you need to ask, Kate? Haven't you ever thought about it? It's a tragedy, right? So enormous, everyone has to be silent. First you turn everything to shit and then you invoke silence. The great silent one.'

'I don't like this, Udo.'

'Neither do I.'

'I mean your tone.'

He bent down, switched on the vacuum cleaner, listened to its whine, then switched it off again. Without looking at her, he continued speaking.

'You still don't get it, do you? Tell me, Kate, do you know what the word "duplicate" means? I'll tell you. What just happened with Elena exactly matches what happened with my mother twelve years ago. Same features, same everything! A – a new woman; B – he can't be reached, he's in a different hotel; C – the big grief act.'

'Udo, what do you know about it? How is it, where women are concerned, that you –'

'Where women are concerned? I have my women one after another, however many it may be. I don't have them all at the same time, the way he does!'

'You don't even know what happened back then.'

'Oh yes I do. He was with Elena Bach at her hotel. Exactly as he was with Christa this time. In a different hotel.'

Brinkmann made no attempt to be quiet. He had not even been consciously listening to what they were saying. But when he heard Christa's name he slammed the door behind him. It sounded like a shot. The voices stopped.

He walked slowly up the stairs, full of heartache. He looked at

Kate, then at his son. 'It was a guesthouse, Udo, not a hotel. What's wrong, why don't you continue? I didn't quite catch what you said about "duplicates".'

Udo straightened up. 'As you wish. Elena got to know about three items of information one after the other. The first was that you were on the island of Sylt. The second was that Christa was there, too. The third was that she could not get back her old job at the clinic in Karlsruhe. I talked to her about it, just before she set off on that fatal journey. Shortly before she hit that tree at full speed, and with no safety belt on!'

It was very quiet. A bird sang somewhere: it seemed unreal. Everything is unreal, Brinkmann thought. His anger was gone, his heartbeat normal.

'I don't owe you any explanation, Udo. But if you insist upon playing prosecutor, if you insist upon trying to make me feel guilty, then let me inform you that Elena knew about me and Christa. And she had come to terms with it.'

Udo leaned against the banister, shaking his head so angrily that his hair fell across his forehead and eyes. Brinkmann realised he had seen him do it before: in certain situations, Udo reacted like a shying horse. His voice too had changed, become higher, angry and tense.

'That's just an excuse! Nothing else. Just an excuse, I'd say! And do you know what you'd say if I argued my case the same way? You'd say it was self-protection! Elena isn't here to say how it really was!'

'Can you say how it really was?'

'Me? I'll tell you what I can do: I can use my judgement.'

'Don't you mean "pass judgement"?'

Kate did something Udo had not expected: she pushed them apart, standing between them so that Brinkmann could not see his son's face distorted by passion. By hate.

It was Kate who bade Udo say not one more word, Kate who asked, her voice trembling, if things were not bad enough as it was. But he pushed her aside. 'Go away, Kate!' he said, facing his father. His voice was uneven, but cruel. 'There's something else I want to tell him.'

'You would,' Brinkmann said, his voice bitter. 'My supreme court judge!'

'You don't have to be a supreme court judge to understand

254

something. And do you know what I've just realised? At first I thought, how magnanimous of you not to reproach me for failing to operate. And the whole time we were in the operating theatre, while I was staring at her face and worrying whether she was getting enough air into her lungs, whether her heart would beat a little longer, all that time I kept thinking that if you'd been there you could have prevented her death. Or at least given her a chance.'

Brinkmann found it difficult to breathe. He could picture the scene clearly, and could sympathise with his son. Udo was right. He had thought only of his own pain. He had not given so much as a thought to what the team had gone through.

'I understand that, Udo. I can imagine how . . .'

'Imagine? You can't imagine a damned thing! You have been so magnanimous. You have absolved me of all guilt and professional misconduct. Isn't that so? And why? Why? Because it suits you, that's why! Because now you have Christa, don't you? Just like twelve years ago. My mother died, and you got Elena!'

My mother, he said . . . You got Elena . . . Why didn't he stop now? Why didn't he listen to Kate, who was yelling at him to shut his mouth?

'Be quiet, Kate! Let me go!'

He pushed her aside and came close to Brinkmann, so close that the older man could feel his breath. He looked into his son's wide, burning eyes, heard the cold, quiet voice that hurt much more than all the yelling.

'You always take what you want! You destroy what you no longer need! And everyone else has to keep their mouth shut. That's how it is, isn't it?'

All right, that was enough!

Brinkmann turned away. His steps felt uncertain, and he had difficulty maintaining his balance. He saw the door. Go through it, slam it, lock it! But was that the answer? What was the answer? To stay, to lift his hand and strike him across the face? He wasn't too weak for that. But Udo had spoken of justice, and there was no justice in that. What was just?

He turned back and looked at his son, his set face, the angry eyes. 'And what now? Will you put Elena's photograph on the piano, next to my mother's?'

Finally, it was Kate who slapped him, old Kate whose one aim in life had been to avoid exactly what had happened here today.

At first all she could hear was the dull rattle of the engine. Then the thing appeared on the dune: a bathtub with four huge wheels! A crazy, droning, jumping insect. The sun glanced off the golden strip along the raspberry-red lacquered bodywork as the dune buggy swung to the right, spraying sand mixed with dense black smoke. The boys in the buggy shouted something. One of them, wearing a little cotton hat on his fat head, stood up and waved. The driver, a youngster with sunglasses, hung on to the steering wheel. They raced towards her.

What hair Mollie had left stood up like a brush, bristling. Growling with rage, teeth bared, she looked quite menacing.

'Hey, Blondie! Want a ride to Kampen?'

Christa turned her back and pulled Mollie after her. The dune buggy roared away, spraying her neck with sand.

'Come on, let's go. What good's some woman with a mongrel? Can't get anywhere with her!'

The noise had frightened away all the birds. Even after peace had returned to the dunes they still circled high up in the sky, screaming over their nesting places, the surf and the sea. Christa crouched on the sand. She felt cold. Can't get anywhere with her: it was an apt observation.

The dog pushed its head against her knee. Christa put her hand on Mollie's head, scratched her between the eyes. 'Can we get anywhere, Mollie? What would you like? Shall we go home? – Don't you get it: he should have phoned long ago. Oh, he's having a bad time, I know that. But you see, Mollie, if we meant anything to him he would have phoned. Three days, Mollie! Three whole days!'

It wasn't the days: it was the nights. In the daytime she could walk and walk, until her feet ached and her eyes burned. But at night?

No, she wouldn't call him. She would go on lying to Erika Harmsen: everything fine, Erika, of course, everything absolutely fine. The professor? Called away on an urgent case. That's how it is in his line of work. Was he coming back? Perhaps. Yes, she was going to stay on. The dog liked it here.

256

The dog!

So Erika Harmsen made tea and brought over the aquavit bottle. 'You look really awful, my dear!' Then added: 'Such a nice man, your professor.' Erika Harmsen was quite sure the professor would have got along very well with Christian. Christian Meurer, Christa's father. Erika spoke of him often, but never mentioned Christa's mother. Christian and Christa, that was a pair! She had liked Christian.

Christa remembered thinking the same thought on the train coming to Sylt. They had been thundering through the Ruhr valley, and Klaus had been trying to find out the reason for her mental anguish.

'I think you would have got along well with my father, Klaus,' she said. 'He threw his career away, everything. But he believed in me. He runs a pub somewhere now. His own best customer. But he always wanted me to go on with my studies.'

That was what Klaus wanted, too. How similar his words had been, how one feeling led to another. Clever Christa, the you-can-do-it girl who was never allowed to give up. Now Klaus Brinkmann would not let her bury her dreams, either.

'You must begin studying again.'

'Isn't a nurse good enough for you?'

'Don't talk such nonsense! The question is . . .'

'Go on.'

'Whether you want to become my wife, or a doctor. Or both.'

My wife, or a doctor. Or both!

And now? As she pulled the dog along the dunes, the sea thundered at her feet and the wind buffeted her face as if it had a personal score to settle with her. She kept coming back to the same question: are you to blame because he followed you to Sylt? Are you responsible if a white Golf cabriolet missed a curve and smashed into a tree? What does one call it, then? Fate? Tragedy? The interplay of random factors? It was none of these: just one of those lousy jokes life plays on you just as you are beginning to enjoy yourself and hope again.

She stood there on the crest of the dune, unable to fight back the tears or the weakness that made her sink to the ground, surrendering to the emotion until the sobbing and shaking were done.

Then she went back to the village, called him from a booth in the supermarket: she did not want to use Erika Harmsen's telephone.

'Professor Brinkmann's residence.'

'It's me, Kate.'

Not a sound; just the crackle of the connection.

'Kate! I'm still here in Kampen.'

'Yes?'

'I just wanted to ask – I mean, I expected he would call me.'

Again that silence.

'Dr Bach is dead, Christa. The funeral is over.'

It took Christa a long time to pull herself together. She was relieved to find Kate was still on the line. It would have been no surprise if she had rung off after that last sentence.

'Do you think he doesn't want to talk to me?'

'How should I know? Christa, you have to understand . . . He had a very bad scene with Udo, too. He hasn't talked to anyone since it happened.'

'You know what I'm trying to say . . . I keep wondering whether I ought to cut my holiday short. I – I mean, perhaps he needs me?'

Once again there was a silence. Then: 'Just a moment. Christa, yes?' Then she heard Kate call out. 'Klaus! Klaus! It's Christa!'

She heard steps, and then his voice. 'Christa! Is it you?'

The tired, unemotional manner in which he asked the question was worse than anything she had expected.

'Christa? I'm sorry I didn't call.'

'You don't have to apologise. You must be exhausted.'

'I am. Is the dog giving you any trouble?'

'The dog? Oh, Klaus, what are we doing talking about the dog? The only thing that's giving me any trouble is deciding whether I should come back.'

'No, no.'

'You mean it? You're sure?'

'Of course. You've earned your holiday, Christa. And believe me, I'm not fit to be with anyone at the moment.'

'That's not the problem. I just want to know if I can be of any help to you. Whether you'd like it if I was nearby. That's all I want to know.'

She could hear his breathing. 'Christa?'

'Yes?'

258

'What I prefer to do most right now is just to sit in the garden alone. I can think there. And come to the conclusion that there isn't anything to think about.'

'And what does that mean?'

'It means I still haven't come to terms with it. Try to understand, Christa . . .'

'Of course. Of course, Klaus. I'll try . . .'

THIRTY-NINE

Twice a week, on Tuesdays and Fridays, Dr Brösinger came over from Villingen. Those were the days on which the most difficult cases were scheduled. Brösinger worked with a cool brilliance and determination that won the admiration of the team, especially since they could still not count on Schaefer. Everything ran smoothly.

The tall, heavy, taciturn Brösinger did not say any more than was absolutely necessary, but no one had the slightest doubt that his willingness to deputise for Brinkmann was prompted by his feeling of gratitude towards his one-time teacher, and also by a kind of guilt that he had not arrived early enough to help Elena Bach on the day she died.

'Lucky for us that clinic in Villingen runs itself,' Renz said. 'He has three senior surgeons over there, every one of them an ace. Even so . . .'

'How long is this going to go on, Udo? When is the old man coming back?'

They asked the same question every day. How long? How long

was the old man going to let the clinic go on like this? Udo's reply was to look at Walter Renz, who shrugged and left. The captain was no longer on the bridge, and the helmsman was not qualified to take his place.

The window of the study looked out on the garden, already beginning to take on the red and yellow tones of autumn. Somewhere beneath this roof sat his father, book in hand. He had ensured that the clinic could run itself in his absence. But did he have any idea where he was running to himself?

Over the last few nights, even without Kate's worried voice in his ear, Udo had come to realise how much he had had to do not only with Elena Bach's death but with the strange change in his father's behaviour.

Why hadn't the old man defended himself? My God, if only he'd hit me instead of saying 'I understand'! How did you interpret that? Self-deception? That's your speciality, Udo told himself bitterly. Fine. And you know, too, that this is a slow but certain way of going crazy, and also of losing everything. As certainly as if you had been in a fatal accident!

It's over with. He even helped you when you threw your accusations into his face. What are you waiting for?

Udo cancelled his appointments, left the clinic, and headed home. Kate confirmed what he had anyway expected. 'Your father? Up there, as usual.'

As usual. The sandstone steps, the rose bushes, then the lawn and the birch trees. The same birches under which he had lain that day with Yvonne. Funny how everything, every event is connected to every other. Udo walked very slowly. He saw the deckchair, the books lying on the grass, his father's hand holding the pipe. The last few steps were difficult, but he managed it. His father sat up. The bronzed face remained impassive, but his eyes were alert and there was a fixed smile on his face.

Udo squatted down beside the chair. 'I should have come a long time ago.' His embarrassment had disappeared so totally and unexpectedly that it astonished him. He pulled a blade of grass from the lawn and stuck it between his teeth. He managed a smile as he looked at his father. Even managed to say: 'I'm glad I finally came up here.'

'Why is that?'

261

'There are a couple of things I wanted to say . . .'

He was answered only with a glance, perhaps the hint of a smile. But not a word did his father speak.

'I want to apologise. That is – I *need* to apologise.'

Brinkmann raised his hand as if to wave something aside. Udo shook his head.

'No, please let me say this. I want to say it loud and clear. I'm sorry.'

'I've known that for a long time.'

'I don't know if you quite understand me . . . all that nonsense, the rumours that were going around that I thought were true. Even the ones I put round myself.'

'Do we have to do this. . . ?'

'Yes! I wanted to tell you. There's a further report. It just came in. The accident report was incomplete. It has been established that Elena swerved to avoid a motorcyclist. That was what caused the accident. Not . . . nothing else.'

He had wondered how to break the news to his father. Above all, he hoped that this news would relieve him of the awful burden of anguish he must be suffering over the talk of suicide. At least now he would know that Elena Bach had not killed herself but died trying to save another life.

Still no answer came from the deckchair. Brinkmann's eyes were shut. He seemed so damned remote.

'May I say something else to you?'

'You know you can.'

'I wanted to thank you for making it possible for me to tell you everything. At least you know what was going on inside me. Now it's out in the open.'

'And how do you feel? Relieved?'

'Yes. I believe you can find the reasons in psychoanalytical works. Whole libraries have been written on the subject.'

This time his father was really smiling.

The face of the clock stared at him. It was mounted in the centre of the operating-theatre light, surrounded by a battery of powerful directional beams, a chromium-clad, triangular dial that looked like the green eye of a Cyclops. That was not its only strange feature, however: the clock also rotated, and every time the green shimmering eye turned towards him his whole body stiffened, and he could move neither his fingers, arms, or legs. The moving fingers of the clock paralysed his brain, and a leaden weight flowed through his body, crushing everything.

Even some time after he had awakened from the dream, Brinkmann felt as if he was still paralysed. He realised at once where he was, of course: the bedroom of Jäger's hunting lodge. Or to be more precise, Jäger's wife's hunting lodge. She was one of the Grossmann heirs. The room was appropriately furnished: wood-panelled walls, leather chairs, carpets, engravings of hunting scenes in gold frames. A telephone. Next door, the huge room with the stone fireplace, then the kitchen, the guest room, bathrooms, a terrace, the garage for the Land Rover. Outside, the forest, and on the hillside the autumn meadow.

Brinkmann breathed deeply, lacing his hands behind his head and looking at the Black Forest clock on the opposite wall. Ten. So late! The sun had already wandered across the terrace.

In the preceding six days he had twice had the terrible dream about the eye trying to paralyse him. He knew that dream well: he had dreamed it a long time ago, after his big row with the old man when he had decided to take the job as an assistant in Göttingen and never come back to Offingen . . . He had broken that vow and stopped dreaming that dream. Until now. However depressing, the dream had made him realise how his own and Udo's development had run along the same lines.

Brinkmann sighed, got up and dressed. He felt empty and limp. He went into the kitchen, made coffee and took some eggs from the fridge. But the smell of the hot fat and the burned egg white in the pan turned his stomach and he had to run to the bathroom to vomit. He scraped the eggs into the bin and drank some orange juice. Then he went into the big room with the stone fireplace.

His typewriter stood on an oak table next to the window, the pile of papers and the dictating machine next to it untouched. He had thought he might use his stay in the lodge to write a long-promised article on the complications encountered in hip operations, but even that resolve had disappeared. Later, perhaps; not right now. He did as he had done the preceding day: carried the wicker chair out on to the terrace and sat there looking over the newly-planted trees down the soft curve of the hill on which the house stood. He watched a pair of hawks fly across the sky, then closed his eyes again.

Even though he could see nothing he was part of it all: he listened to the wind moving through the forest, the cracking of dry wood, a bird taking flight. Elena, too, was near – as usual.

He thought of her a lot. And about death, too. He had always looked at death from the viewpoint of his job: a challenge. But these last few days had totally changed his perspective. He plucked a leaf from a hazelnut bush, looked at a flower, examining its structure, impressed by the fine detail of the veins, enchanted by a form and harmony above any functional need, and thought of the inexorable circle of destruction and renewal which existed in the forest – and sought some meaning in all of it. During his walks he tried to find a path of his own – and got lost. If only Mollie were here. He wondered where she was right at this moment.

He forbade himself to pursue the thought. He also suppressed the name 'Christa' because he knew he couldn't change the way things were; only the longing remained, and the feeling that he had made another mistake.

Once in a while he called Udo. His business reports were always short and precise. But at the end of each call, there was always that slightly childish apprehension in his voice. 'Is that all right with you? Or do you disagree?'

He did not disagree. It was all right with him. 'But of course, Udo. You'll manage fine! And if you think the programme should be changed, change it. Give it some thought, then change it.'

Do it! Udo trying to find his own way, his own direction. Handing over the baton. Was the time really ripe? Not quite yet.

Brinkmann was just getting up to fetch the binoculars when he heard the car approaching. Sometimes one of the foresters came by, but they usually drove a diesel. The sound coming through the forest was that of a Volkswagen engine.

Brinkmann stood where he was. The house was built on a hill supported by a heavy sandstone wall which the Grossmanns had built so high that you could only see the roofs of cars driving up on the path below. The roof he saw now was green and rounded. Christa's car! It was Christa!

He eased back into the shadow of one of the pillars which supported the roof. He could not see her getting out of the car, but then she appeared at the gate, looking up. For some reason, only the Devil knew why, he remained hidden, not having the strength to step forward and show himself.

The green band in her hair shone. It was the scarf. He remembered how he had stood in the hallway and stroked it.

Then he started running, down the stairs, through the little winding path between the saplings, down another flight of steps. He did not notice the roots that he'd so often cursed until he felt himself falling, hitting the ground, pain lancing up his ankle.

He got to his knees, shook his head, tried to stand, and then doubled up. She was standing by the trellised gate ten metres away, her hands on the railings, looking up at him in alarm.

'Klaus, what is it?'

'Damn it, what do you think it is? I've dislocated my ankle!'

'Were you in such a hurry?'

'Hurry? Yes, of course I was.'

'But why?'

He didn't know, truly he didn't. He got to his feet, groaning. 'You're right,' he said. 'Why the hurry?'

She shook her head as he hopped the last few metres on one foot. When the usual Brinkmann curses rumbled from him, she started to laugh. They stood facing each other, the gate between them. Mollie gave out her most beautiful and moving welcoming howl.

'Mollie,' Brinkmann said, huskily. 'How are you?'

'Just fine,' Christa said, briskly. 'We'd probably feel even better if you'd let us in.'

'But of course!' He put his hands into his pockets. Suddenly the pleasure fled from his face, and he looked shocked. 'Holy hell!' he swore. 'The keys!'

Christa just watched, saying nothing. It was the same look she wore when she worried about him.

'Where are they, Klaus?'

'Up there in the house. On the terrace. I was . . . I mean . . . it was such a surprise, and I . . .'

She was already up on the railings. She hovered for a heartbeat between heaven on earth, and then landed on the path beside him. Then she ran up the stairs.

He watched her go, saw the shining hair and the green band. He

265

thought how strangely close to each other joy, pain, weakness and strength lay. And how you had to let them all combine, because in spite of all the defeats life was worth living . . .

The boys are back together again!

AUF WIEDERSEHEN Pet.
TWO

by Fred Taylor

Now available: the second novel based on the hugely popular series by Dick Clement and Ian La Frenais, probably the best script-writing team in Britain today.

In response to an SOS from Barry, our heroes reassemble – more than two years since their fond farewell on a building-site in Germany.

This time the scene is Spain's notorious Costa del Crime and Dennis, Neville, Oz, Barry, Wayne, Moxy and Bomber, still chronically short of cash and hungry for travel, adventure and mayhem, rebound from crisis to hilarious crisis.

They and their long-suffering wives and sweethearts find themselves involved in scrapes that make the old days in Dusseldorf seem like a dream cruise on the Rhine . . .

HUMOUR/TV TIE-IN   0 7221 36749   £2.75

A selection of bestsellers from Sphere

FICTION

LADY OF HAY	Barbara Erskine	£3.95 ☐
BIRTHRIGHT	Joseph Amiel	£3.50 ☐
THE SECRETS OF HARRY BRIGHT	Joseph Wambaugh	£2.95 ☐
CYCLOPS	Clive Cussler	£3.50 ☐
THE SEVENTH SECRET	Irving Wallace	£2.95 ☐

FILM AND TV TIE-IN

INTIMATE CONTACT	Jacqueline Osborne	£2.50 ☐
BEST OF BRITISH	Maurice Sellar	£8.95 ☐
SEX WITH PAULA YATES	Paula Yates	£2.95 ☐
RAW DEAL	Walter Wager	£2.50 ☐

NON-FICTION

BOTHAM	Don Mosey	£3.50 ☐
SOLDIERS	John Keegan & Richard Holmes	£5.95 ☐
URI GELLER'S FORTUNE SECRETS	Uri Geller	£2.50 ☐
A TASTE OF LIFE	Julie Stafford	£3.50 ☐
HOLLYWOOD A' GO-GO	Andrew Yule	£3.50 ☐

All Sphere books are available at your local bookshop or newsagent, or can be ordered direct from the publisher. Just tick the titles you want and fill in the form below.

Name _____

Address _____

_____

Write to Sphere Books, Cash Sales Department, P.O. Box 11, Falmouth Cornwall TR10 9EN

Please enclose a cheque or postal order to the value of the cover price plus:

UK: 60p for the first book, 25p for the second book and 15p for each additional book ordered to a maximum charge of £1.90.

OVERSEAS & EIRE: £1.25 for the first book, 75p for the second book and 28p for each subsequent title ordered.

BFPO: 60p for the first book, 25p for the second book plus 15p per copy for the next 7 books, thereafter 9p per book.

Sphere Books reserve the right to show new retail prices on covers which may differ from those previously advertised in the text elsewhere, and to increase postal rates in accordance with the P.O.